*To my very good friend Coleen Carlisle with
many thanks for her help and support.*

CHARACTER LIST

Edward I	King of England
Edward II	King of England, son of the above
Eleanor of Castile	Wife of Edward I, Queen of England
Isabella	Wife of Edward II, Queen of England
Sir Hugh Corbett	The Keeper of the Secret Seal, Edward II's personal envoy
Ranulf-atte-Newgate	Sir Hugh Corbett's henchman, principal clerk in the Chancery of the Green Wax
Lady Maeve	Wife of Sir Hugh Corbett and mother of their two children Edward and Eleanor
Chanson	Clerk of the Stables in the retinue of Sir Hugh Corbett
Ap Ythel	Welshman, master bowman in the retinue of Sir Hugh Corbett
Mistletoe	Former clerk in the English royal chancery, a colleague of Sir Hugh Corbett

Thomas of Lancaster	Great English Earl and opponent of Edward II
Simon de Montfort	Leading baronial opponent of Edward I
William Wallace	Scottish war leader
Robert Bruce	Scottish war leader
Llewelyn	Prince of Wales
Daffyd Ap Gruffyd	Llewelyn's brother, Prince of Wales
Reginald Berkley	Knight of Edward I's household
Walter Dakin	Knight of Edward I's household
Lord Pembroke	English general
Peter Gaveston	Edward II's favourite
Roger Mortimer of Wigmore	Welsh marcher baron
Osiric	Keeper of 'The Glory of the Morning' tavern
Gruffyd	A member of Mortimer's retinue
Owain	Welsh archer
Brancepeth	Welsh archer
Monsieur Amaury de Craon	Envoy of the French King Philip IV to the English court
Nogaret and Marigny	Henchmen of King Philip IV of France, leading lights in Philip's Secret Chancery
Henry Maltravers	Abbot of Holyrood Abbey
Brothers Richard, Crispin, Anselm, Jude and Norbett	Members of the community of Holyrood Abbey
Bertrand de Got	Commonly known as Pope Clement V
Matilda Beaufort	An inhabitant of The Valley of the Shadows
Edmund Fitzroy	Royal claimant

HISTORICAL NOTE

Edward I of England (1272–1307) viewed himself as God's own warrior. Edward had fought on crusade, and when he succeeded to the throne, he soon brought England firmly under his tight grasp by a wide range of domestic reforms. He crushed his enemies within and then turned on the great independent principalities of Wales and Scotland, waging terrible war against both countries. He slaughtered the Welsh princes and cowed Wales with a series of formidable fortifications, castles such as Caernarvon, to dominate the principality and bring it firmly under the power of the English Crown. Once victorious there, he turned and unleashed the dogs of war against Scotland, sharp and cruel, in a series of bloody campaigns waged with fire and sword. The Scots resisted under a succession of war leaders such as William Wallace and Robert Bruce: the latter proved more than an equal for the English king, and when Edward died in 1307, he left a nightmare legacy to his son and heir, Edward II. The new king, however, had troubles of his own. He was not a war leader like his father, whilst he became embroiled in a long-standing and ever bitter feud with his barons, led by his cousin Thomas of Lancaster. Famine and a series of failed harvests did not help matters. The darkness deepened and allowed forces, malignant and malevolent, to emerge and cast their long shadow over the kingdom.

PROLOGUE

John said that he was the king's son and that the kingdom of England was his by right.

Life of Edward II

The cliffs of Caerwent, the Welsh March,
autumn 1300

The attack on the caves, deep, dark, gaping holes that peppered the steep rocky face of the cliffs of Caerwent, was ferocious and bloody. Edward, king of England, had swept into the Valley of Shadows along the Welsh March with fire and sword. He was fighting for himself, his heir and the future of his kingdom. He had personally decided to lead this chevauchée and had summoned up his war host, including his comitatus, his personal bodyguard, the Knights of the Swan. All these warriors were bachelors, single men who had renounced the love of a woman, or so they claimed, in order to support body and soul, day and night, in peace and in war their beloved master the king as long as he lived and after his death.

The war band had poured into the valley to destroy the rebels and their adherents, the minions of the Black Chesters, a coven of witches, warlocks and magicians dedicated to their own dark god of anarchy. This army of wolfsheads and traitors had retreated along the valley floor to the soaring face of Caerwent. The caves there stretched deep, whilst the narrow, twisting goat paths that wound up to them could easily be defended by bowmen and slingers. The rebels had barricaded the mouth of each cavern, creating a collection of small fortresses, making it almost impossible to attack. If the besiegers loosed fire arrows, even scorching bundles hurled by catapults, the defenders simply withdrew deeper into the caves to wait until the fire storm passed. If the king's men-at-arms, hobelars and archers attempted to climb the pathways, they made themselves vulnerable, easy targets for enemy bowmen.

Autumn had come to the valley, and already its greenery was fading in a shock of gold and red, whilst the clouded skies and the threat of snow made the situation of the besiegers even more precarious. Edward was determined to change all this. He and his comitatus, led by its principal knight, Henry Maltravers, swiftly surveyed the situation, then dispatched hunters into the deep forests either side of the valley. They brought back a local man, who openly declared that he was not with the rebels and that he knew of a secret path deep in the trees on the right flank. Edward listened carefully as the man described how this pathway, broad enough for horses and war carts, led to the top of the cliffs.

Marching quietly, boots, hooves and wheels cleverly clogged, the war band reached the summit. There, Edward launched his attack. His engineers, led by

Maltravers, constructed makeshift yet sturdy pulleys, winches, hoists and cranes, using the wheels of the war carts. The carts themselves were protected by rows of sharpened poles, pierced along one side: these had lancets for archers and spearmen as well as a narrow door for men-at-arms to pass through, making them formidable fighting platforms. The carts were crammed with archers and hobelars, the latter armed with long, hooked halberds; each cart was then lowered down the face of the cliff to seal off the cave mouths one by one.

Matilda Beaumont, a woman of the valley, who had stayed clear of the rebels and their retreat to the caves, watched the attack from the shelter of a densely clustered copse. She knew that she had some part to play in the bloody tragedy taking place. Nevertheless, standing amongst the trees in a dark green robe and hood that aided her concealment, she accepted that there was nothing she could do but pray that her beloved Edmund Fitzroy, as he called himself, would escape unscathed from the unfolding horror. She watched, heart in mouth, as the attack grew more ferocious and bloody. All the terrors of hell seemed to have engulfed the cliffs of Caerwent. The rows of war carts closed up against the caves. Arrows and fire shafts were loosed. A sheer blizzard swept through the mouth of each cavern to scorch, wound and kill those sheltering within. Smoke and flame erupted. Spear, arrow and slingshot shattered flesh and smashed bone. Sharp steel gashed and grated, the blood gushing out like rainfall. Matilda could also see the hobelars, their halberds piercing individual rebels as fishermen would lance a pike. They would then drag their victims to the mouth of the cave, and send them hurtling down to the rocks below.

The attack had started just before first light. By noon, it was clear that the battle was over. The remaining cave dwellers surrendered and were forced to descend the steep goat paths. The wounded, the old and the young found this difficult. Matilda watched further bodies fall and bounce against the side of the cliff before being shattered on the jagged stones below. The surviving prisoners, men, women and children, were herded like cattle at the foot of the cliff and made to face a long table. Behind this, in a throne-like chair, sat Edward of England. The king, grey-faced, grey-bearded and resplendent in his half-armour, was intent on delivering judgement. On either side of him ranged the Knights of the Swan in their distinctive royal colours as well as their own personal insignia, a pure white swan with wings extended.

Yet this was no place of beauty. Matilda, who had crept forward as close as she could, felt she had passed through the gates of hell into some chilling nightmare. The stretch of land beneath the cliffs was transformed into a rough, murky prison, full of fear and filth. A court had been set up and the old king was determined on punishment. All able-bodied male prisoners were condemned in rapid succession. Once sentence was passed, they were forced to stand on barrels and carts, anything that could be used. Nooses were fastened around their necks, the other end of the rope looped over the branches of the trees that bordered the rocky escarpment. The footrests of these makeshift gallows were then callously kicked away so the victims dangled and kicked as they slowly choked to death.

Eventually there was a respite in the slaughter. Peering closer, Matilda watched the Knights of the Swan moving amongst the herd of prisoners clustered before the king. Certain individuals, young boys and girls, were picked out and led from the execution ground. Two of the prisoners tried to resist; both women were stabbed and hacked. Their heart-chilling screams proved too much for Matilda; she had seen enough! She turned and fled blindly from that demon-haunted place.

Burgh by Sands, the Scottish border, July 1307

The sky itself was full of foreboding. Black clouds – war clouds, as the chroniclers described them – had swept in over the storm-tossed Irish Sea. The winds were sharp and cruel, despite the fact that it was high summer. Burgh by Sands dominated the highways north to Scotland and south to the crashing, thrashing sea. During the day, unusual sights were noted: the disappearance of the sun and a murky blood-red moon rising at night. Heaven, or hell, depending on your perspective, was proclaiming its message. Edward, the first of that name since the Conquest, was dying.

God's own warrior realised that the summons had been served to present his soul to divine justice. Lying on his cot bed in the silken pavilion set up in the centre of his camp, Edward threaded Ave beads through his stubby, chapped fingers while he half listened to the patter of the priests and their verbal appeals to the Almighty to spare this great prince. If

He chose not to, then He should at least cleanse the king's soul before he passed to judgement.

Edward, his iron-grey hair matted with sweat, leant back against the bolsters, his craggy, lined face set in a mask of indifference, as befitted a warrior when confronting the final enemy. Nevertheless, his fertile brain and impetuous heart concentrated on matters spiritual as much as they did on the temporal. He knew he was dying. But what then? Who would be waiting for him? A host of demons, savage creatures, dreadful apparitions? Would hell disgorge its hideous hordes to plague his soul as the preachers would have him believe? Or would the ghosts of all those slain, with eyes sewn up and mouths filled with blood, crowd around?

De Montfort, Edward's mortal enemy, had been killed at Evesham by a lance thrust through his throat. The king's chosen paladins, the Knights of the Swan, had crowded around the lifeless corpse and hacked off his hands and feet; his genitals were sliced off and stuffed into the gaping mouth of his severed head, while the rest of his butchered flesh was fed to the camp dogs. Would de Montfort come to remonstrate with the king? Would he be accompanied by Dafydd ap Gruffydd, Llywelyn's brother, executed in Shrewsbury for raising a revolt in Wales and other horrid crimes? Because of his treason, Dafydd had been dragged through the city by a horse's tail to the scaffold. Once there, he was hanged alive for his killings. Next, as the royal herald proclaimed, for having committed his crimes during Holy Week, he was disembowelled, his entrails burnt before his eyes. Lastly, for having sought the king of England's death, his body was quartered and the bloody parts dispatched for public view to the four corners of the kingdom, his severed head being displayed in London on a spike next to that of his brother. Perhaps the ghosts of the Welsh princes would be joined by others, such as William Wallace, torn apart by the executioners in Smithfield. Oh yes, the dead might gather in their thousands!

Edward opened his heavy-lidded eyes and stared round at his personal bodyguard, kneeling on the coarse matting rolled out across the floor as a covering in the great royal pavilion. The Knights of the Swan were garbed in their usual gold-lined black jerkins and hooded cloaks, their personal escutcheon a long-necked white swan, its extended wings emblazoned with diamonds for all to see. Edward studied the faces of these men, knights of the body, comrades in arms. He wondered if the rumours were true. Did they truly serve him as celibate bachelors, or was it just that they were not attracted to ladies of the court, or indeed any women? Not for them the tales of chivalry, of Lancelot fighting for his Guinevere. Did these men have a love for each other more intense than any husband for his wife? Were they like David and Jonathan, those two warriors of ancient Israel, committed to each other in life and in death? Only God knew the truth. Yet they had sworn that if their king died, they would withdraw from public life and dedicate themselves only to the service of God and the memory of their old master.

They would assume the rule of St Benedict and live the life of the black monks, observing vows of chastity and obedience.

'Faithful servants,' Edward whispered through dry, cracked lips, 'keep troth in death as you have in life.'

'Sire.' The knights' leader, Henry Maltravers, spoke up. 'Sire,' he repeated, 'do not trouble yourself. We are here, as we always have been and always shall be.'

Edward nodded and sighed as he stared around the pavilion. Twenty of his most faithful comitatus were there. Once there had been thirty, but death had culled their ranks in so many ways. Reginald Berkley, trapped in a Scottish marsh, pierced to death by the lances of Robert Bruce's horsemen. Walter Dakin, a master bowman, caught in a snowdrift in Wales and savaged by starving war dogs. Edward blinked. Wales! He really must have words with Maltravers.

He closed his eyes, his mind drifting down the galleries and passageways of the past. The doors were being opened. Memories burst through, his enemies and friends, long dead, making their presence felt. He hoped and prayed that his beloved Eleanor would be waiting for him. Surely she would forgive his great sins? His greatest love! She who was so lovely in face and form. Edward crossed himself. He had confessed his sin, his pride of the flesh, his passion to rule, to dominate. He just hoped Eleanor would understand.

He recalled that fateful day at Acre. He and his wife had joined the great crusade against Sultan Babyar. They had been sheltering deep in the fortress of Acre when

Babyar's emissary, who had been with them for days, asked to see Edward on a most private and confidential matter. Edward foolishly agreed, believing the interpreter accompanying him would be defence enough against any treachery. How wrong he had been. The emissary had drawn his curved dagger and lunged, killing the man with one swift slash to the throat. He had then turned on Edward, who managed to defend himself with a stool until he found his sword. He had killed his assailant, but not before the assassin had scored a deep wound in the king's arm. Physicians were summoned to inspect both knife and wound, and immediately declared that the assassin's blade had been thickly coated with a deadly poison, which must now be in the wound. Eleanor had hurried in. Learning what had happened, she had immediately sucked the poison from her husband's wound, to the consternation of all. Eleanor his saviour, his dream queen!

Edward opened his eyes and pointed at Maltravers. 'You still hold the dagger, the one I took from the assassin so many years ago?'

'Of course, sire!'

'Good. When you move to Holyrood, that must go with you in its casket. Eleanor would want that, she would insist. You must take it. You must keep it in a sacred place and in no other casket but where it is now.'

'Sire,' Maltravers replied, 'do not trouble yourself. It will be done. But such matters must wait. Think of Scotland, think of Bruce.'

The king roused himself, pulling himself further up

against the bolsters 'You will keep your oath,' he rasped. 'You will continue the general advance against the Scottish traitors, even though my feckless son will not.'

'We swear,' Maltravers replied in a carrying voice, the other knights loudly affirming their leader's oath. 'We will fight the Bruce and oppose his power. We shall wage war sharp and cruel against him and his kind. If we do not, we shall withdraw from the court and this world. Sire, if you do not lead us, what else is there?'

'As I have said before,' Edward replied, 'take Holyrood, close to Clun, a day's march from Tewkesbury, deep in the Welsh March. It stands near the entrance to the Valley of Shadows, that place of great mystery.'

'Of course, we know it well,' Maltravers replied. 'How can we forget the battle along the cliffs of Caerwent, ferocious and forbidding? My only consolation is that I was able to rescue my beloved squire Devizes. I—'

'Make Holyrood a nest for the Knights of the Swan,' Edward interrupted. 'Create and develop an abbey dedicated to my memory and that of my beloved Eleanor. Pray for the Crown of England.' He paused, gasping for breath, wincing at the pain and tightness around his chest, like a ribbon of steel cutting off his breath.

'And Scotland, sire? You must order a general advance. Lord Pembroke is ready to unfurl your standard, display the royal banners to the Scottish rebels.'

The dying king seemed unaware of Maltravers' question; he was now lost in his own wandering thoughts.

'The casket.' he murmured. 'The casket that holds the dagger my beloved Eleanor saved me from?'

'Sire, it is safe. You know it is.'

'And the prisoner; that young man, God bless him?'

'Masked and hidden away in special chambers at Caernarvon.'

'If I die – *when* I die – he must be moved to more secure quarters.'

'Of course, sire.'

'And you and others of the Knights of the Swan are sworn to this?'

'Sire, we have taken the most solemn oath, but more pressing matters await. Does my Lord Pembroke order a general advance?'

'In a while, in a while.'

Edward stared around the pavilion. He trusted most of these men, yet he suspected some were weak, more accustomed to the luxuries of their silk-clad courts than the iron discipline of battle. He just prayed that Hugh Corbett would reach him in time. Corbett, his most trusted clerk. The one soul apart from Eleanor whom Edward knew lived in the truth and would never concede to the darkness. He wished Corbett was here, but his beloved clerk had withdrawn because of Edward's lies and lack of trust, and that too was a sin the old king had confessed time and again. Eventually Edward had relented and sent the most carefully worded invitation to Corbett at his manor at Leighton, close to the great forest of Epping. Corbett had courteously replied that he would come, yet would he reach Burgh by Sands in time? If he did, Edward would discuss matters, confide what he knew, his doubts about some of these knights, but until then . . .

He beat his hands against the blankets. 'And where's my son?'

Silence answered his question. The old king felt a surge of rage against his feckless firstborn, more interested in his handsome lover Gaveston than anything else.

'Listen,' Edward drew himself up, 'my son is not here, yet we march against the Scottish rebels. Henry Maltravers, you are a knight banneret, but you are also a master of wrought metal. In London you were, like your father, a member of the guild until you flocked to my standard against de Montfort. I knighted you, I gave you great honours.'

'Hurling days, sire.'

'Yes, they were,' Edward breathed. 'Now, Henry, I want you to fashion a great cauldron. Once I am dead and my soul gone to judgement, boil the flesh from my bones, put it in a casket and bury it beneath a slab of Purbeck marble at Westminster, next to my beloved Eleanor. My bones you must put in a chest, and whenever you march against the Scots, take it with you. Let those rebels know that in death, as in life, I am utterly opposed to them.' He stopped, gasping for breath. 'As for my son . . .'

The king felt a spasm of pain deep in his chest. He tried to breathe but could not, and fell back dead into the arms of Maltravers.

Holyrood Abbey, the Welsh March, November 1311

Brother Richard, former Knight of the Swan, a member of the old king's comitatus of knight bannerets, braced himself against the crenellations of Raven Tower, one of the four that formed the soaring Eagle Donjon, the great forbidding keep at the centre of Holyrood Abbey, deep in the vastness of the Welsh March, at least a long day's journey from the market town of Tewkesbury.

Brother Richard loved to come up here and survey this abbey fortress. The donjon lay at the centre of impressive fortifications, protected by an inner wall with a fighting ledge for defenders, its only entrance being through a heavily fortified gateway. Beyond the inner bailey stretched the new abbey, a spacious square of elegant buildings surrounding the principal church and cloisters. The latter was two storeys high and housed the various offices – chancery, exchequer, library, scriptorium, infirmary, kitchen, buttery – as well as chambers and cells for the community. Stables, hog pens, cattle sheds, kennels and similar outhouses stood some distance from the cloisters, separated by the broad abbey gardens, rich in herb banks and flower plots. In turn this outer bailey was defended by a lofty square curtain wall with crenellations taller than a man and broad fighting ledges. Postern gates were built into the four walls, and the main entrance was truly formidable, protected by iron-shielded gates, portcullis, and murder holes that pierced the ceiling of the cavernous gatehouse. This sombre vaulted chamber housed the machinery to lower the drawbridge across a wide, very deep moat, served by underground springs.

Holyrood was a truly impregnable abbey fortress, and Brother Richard rejoiced in its sheer magnificence. After all, he and his colleague Anselm had been controllers of the King's Works, royal surveyors and masons who had played a major part in the building and development of this hallowed place. They had also been instrumental in finding the abbey's strategic location here at the mouth of the deepest valley along the Welsh March.

Brother Richard narrowed his eyes and stared across at the soaring sides of the valley. Both slopes were covered by densely clustered ancient copses and woods, rich in game as well as water, timber and all the other necessities the community might need. He stood and drank in the breathtaking scene. The road towards the valley mouth was broad, but it soon sharply narrowed, almost becoming lost in the undergrowth and trees that grew close and thick, reducing the road to a mere trackway through what seemed to be a veritable sea of dark greenery.

Not everyone liked the valley. Some called it the Valley of Shadows, others the Valley of Tears. A few described it as the Valley of Gehenna, a place of perpetual shadow, a title that evoked the ravine outside Jerusalem where the Final Judgement would take place. Brother Richard did not fully know the reasons for such sombre titles. Nevertheless, as he conceded to Father Abbot, the valley had acquired a sinister reputation. Local lore maintained that a bloody massacre had taken place during the ancient pagan days. That gruesome sacrifices had been staged, human beings being bound on stone altars and offered to the dark lords of the air, the ground beneath soaked by the blood of hundreds of innocent victims. Of course, there was also that truly bloody battle some eleven years ago, in which Brother Richard and others had so fiercely participated. A gruesome conflict that had ended in merciless slaughter. It had taken place at the far end of the valley, along the cliffs of Caerwent.

Brother Richard blinked and crossed himself. It was best to forget a day of such utter terror. Like his companions, he now believed that the very sacredness of this place had expunged all such abominations, making both the valley and its entrance hallowed and holy. The abbey church housed the risen Christ's body and blood. It also contained valuable relics such as the assassin's dagger used against Richard's former royal master and now reserved in a most exquisitely jewelled casket above the high altar. Holyrood was supposed to be a place full of God's own harmony. Yet hideous crimes had been perpetrated in this sacred sanctuary; what one of the brothers called 'the abomination of desolation', as described by the prophet Daniel, who had looked into the visions of the night.

The first victim of such horror had been Father Abbot himself, who now lay grievously sick in his bedchamber in Falcon Tower. He was fully convinced that someone had tried to poison him. At least he had survived, unlike Brother Anselm, a former Knight of the Swan, who had been cruelly murdered in a macabre fashion, a thick, heavy nail driven into his forehead. Who would perpetrate such an outrage? Why and how? The victim had been a veteran swordsman, skilled in dagger play. Nevertheless, he had been found stretched out in his chamber, glassy-eyed, with no sign of a struggle or resistance. Prior Jude had reported this at a chapter meeting and no one could understand it. Brother Crispin, the infirmarian, who had dressed the corpse for burial, had examined the wound most carefully and wondered how any assailant could draw so close to carry out such a hideous crime. Surely Anselm would have fought back, raised the hue and cry?

Brother Richard had mourned deeply for his former comrade, who had played such a vital role in the construction and development of Holyrood. The two of them had been the architects and knew all the great secrets this abbey housed, both above and below ground.

Secrets shared with no one else. They had revelled in what they had achieved and what they knew.

During the last few years, Holyrood had been a place to enjoy the comforts of this life whilst looking forward to those of the next. Now the mood of the abbey fortress had abruptly changed, as if some malevolent demon had swept up from hell to prowl its galleries, corridors and aisles. Prior Jude was certain of this, and the community had grown fearful. The weather hadn't helped. Brother Richard heard a harsh cawing and glanced up at the great ravens, deep black shadows against the lowering skies. Winter was tightening its grip. Isadore, the doorkeeper, learned in such matters was predicting that heavy snowfalls were imminent.

Brother Richard gathered his brown cloak closer, pulling his wool-lined hood more firmly against his face. He really should return to his chamber and read that letter again. A missive from the French envoy, Monsieur Amaury de Craon, enquiring about his health and saying how much he looked forward to visiting Holyrood before winter closed in. Brother Richard murmured a prayer for help. He was, through his mother, a distant kinsman of the king of France, Philip IV, known as 'Philip le Bel' – the Beautiful. 'Philip the Fox', Brother Richard preferred to call him. He disliked the French monarch intensely and regarded him as one of the greatest liars in Christendom. Philip was always eager to remind the former Knight of the Swan how they were close kin, of the same blood and lineage. Brother Richard distrusted such an attitude, as had the old king up to the very day he coughed out his life blood at Burgh by Sands four years ago. Both men believed that Philip used his kinship in the hope that a slip, a mistake, a wrong word might betray some secret enterprise by the English king.

Brother Richard sighed noisily, watching his hot breath form clouds on the icy air. The French king's dogs were clearly sniffing around the English court searching for tasty morsels, and God knows there were enough. The old king was four years dead and his son and heir seemed more interested in his Gascon favourite, Peter Gaveston, than in dealing with problems of government, be it on the royal council at Westminster or resisting the ever-encroaching Scots under their cunning war leader Robert Bruce. Brother Richard, a close confidant of both the former king and Abbot Henry, wondered if the French knew the truth about the assassin's dagger, kept in its precious case above the high altar of the abbey church. Or, more importantly, the identity of the masked prisoner held in comfortable but close confinement in the dungeons beneath Falcon Tower.

He stared across at the tower. Perhaps he should visit the prisoner? He pulled a face, scratching the tip of his nose as he listened to the howling of the war dogs chained in their kennels on the far side of the abbey. There were rumours that Hugh Corbett, Keeper of the Secret Seal, was becoming interested in Holyrood, and that he might be dispatched here. Brother Richard smiled to himself. He hoped so. He had met Corbett on many occasions and liked the clerk's quiet but assured manner. A loyal servant of sharp brain and even keener wits, Corbett might help solve the murderous mystery swirling around this once holy abbey.

Brother Richard suppressed a shiver and opened the door to descend from the tower, taking the first few steps carefully. Yet he never reached the bottom. Two hours later, as darkness fell and the abbey bells rang for vespers, his corpse was found, tumbled on the steps, a thick black nail driven deep into his forehead.

PART ONE

John claimed that he had been taken from the cradle and that the king who now reigned had been put in his place.

Life of Edward II

'Put not your trust in princes, nor your confidence in Pharaoh, nor your hopes in the war chariots of Egypt or the swift horses of Assyria. They will not save you on the Day of the Great Slaughter when the strongholds fall.' Sir Hugh Corbett, Keeper of the Secret Seal and personal envoy of King Edward, sat in the refectory of Holyrood Abbey and listened intently to the chanting from the abbey church. He would have loved to join the choir and immerse himself in the serene melodies of the plainchant: the rise and fall of the music, the dramatic language and colourful imagery of the psalmist. However, he and his two companions were exhausted, frozen and ravenously hungry after their long ride from Tewkesbury.

Corbett rubbed his hands together, his dark, saturnine face composed, his deep-set eyes ever watchful as he stared around the abbey refectory, a warm, welcoming chamber, its walls half covered in gleaming oaken panelling. Above this stretched brilliant white plaster decorated here and there with gorgeously coloured tapestries. These exquisitely woven cloths proudly proclaimed and celebrated all the glories of the Knights of the Swan, as well as depicting scenes extolling St Benedict and his monastic way of life.

'Such comfort, such luxury!' he whispered to his two companions, Ranulf-atte-Newgate, Clerk in the Chancery of the Green Wax, Corbett's loyal henchman; and Chanson, Clerk of the Stables, a man skilled in all matters of horse flesh. Both companions were elated that they had reached the abbey safely. Ranulf's lean, pale face was relaxed, his sharp-slanted green eyes heavy with drowsiness. He fought to keep awake, scratching his head, his fiery red hair freshly cropped by a tavern barber on their journey west so the clerk could pull on his mail coif, even though it made his scalp itch. Chanson was very different. Slow, amiable, he had the innocent, open features of a plough boy, his round, red-cheeked face all smiling as he sleepily chewed the soft meat and slurped noisily from his goblet.

'Such comfort indeed!' Ranulf echoed his master's words. 'But Sir Hugh, why are we really here?' Corbett stared back, tapping a finger against his lips, warning Ranulf with his eyes that they had to be careful with their speech.

Ranulf smiled and glanced away. He secretly admired Corbett's steady nerve. A high-ranking chancery clerk himself, he was always struck by how cleverly his master hid his emotions. The way his face never betrayed him: the unblinking eyes, the strong mouth, even Corbett's raven-black hair, now tinged with grey, neatly tied back in a queue. Always composed, the Keeper of the Secret Seal rarely showed emotion publicly, except for when his long, tapered fingers, their nails neatly pared, would drum silently on the table. He was doing this now as he stared down the refectory, where his retinue of Welsh archers clustered around their captain, Ap Ythel. They too were pleased to reach Holyrood, and now sat feeding their faces, eagerly sharing the deep jug of rich Bordeaux that Brother Mark, the kitchener, had supplied.

Corbett turned back and smiled at Ranulf. 'I have told you a little about why we are here.'

'But not enough, Sir Hugh.'

'That's because at this moment in time I know so little myself.' He leant across the table, moving goblets and platters aside. 'Well, Ranulf,' he murmured, 'this is Holyrood Abbey. You have seen the buildings and forti-fications, most of them constructed with that grey sandstone so beloved of the old king when he built Caernarvon Castle and the rest.'

'Gloomy places!'

'True,' Corbett agreed. 'But formidable fortresses, designed by the same royal surveyors and engineers who built a chain of such castles to keep Wales firmly beneath the heel of the old king's boot. You asked for an explanation on our journey here; I was too cold and tired to reply. Now is as good a time as any, whilst we wait to meet Father Abbot.'

'It has not always been an abbey?'

'True! Holyrood began its existence as a single peel

tower, as they would call it in Scotland. A massive four-square donjon, built on the same design as the White Tower in London's fortress, a truly impregnable house of war.' Corbett swiftly glanced down the refectory, where the captain of his escort was busily organising a game of hazard, borrowing cups from a bemused lay brother.

'And the Knights of the Swan?'

'You may know of them, Ranulf, and about them.'

'I met some at court,' Ranulf replied, 'and I've heard a little of who they are, or more importantly, who they were.'

'You are correct, my friend.' Corbett paused. 'The Knights of the Swan were the old king's bodyguard, knight bannerets who took an oath of the most faithful fealty to stand by him, body and soul, in peace and in war against all enemies both within and without. They were formed during the civil war, when the king and his father Henry fought Simon de Montfort *à l'outrance* – to the very death. The Knights of the Swan searched out de Montfort and killed him. Afterwards they cut his body to shreds and fed the mangled flesh to camp dogs. Now the Knights are all bachelors in the full sense of that word. They did not, and do not, consort with women. Indeed, some gossips whisper that their love for the old king and each other is like that David had for Jonathan in the Old Testament.'

'Ah, I've heard similar rumours,' Ranulf interjected. 'That their love, like David's, is stronger than that of a man for any woman.'

'I am sure you have,' Corbett commented drily. 'The Knights are like a monastic order. Some claim they imitate the Templars, now of blessed or infamous memory. Others, more correctly, say they follow the Benedictine rule. Whatever, during the last years of the old king's reign, they vowed that once their royal master had died, they would leave court and become a distinct religious community. This place was chosen. An entire abbey was built around the great donjon stoutly defended by high crenellated walls, fortified gateways and massive towers. You viewed such fortifications when we first entered. Believe me, Ranulf, this is a true abbey fortress.'

'How many souls does it house?'

'About sixteen or seventeen knights in all, dedicated to the memory of the old king and to each other. They live under the leadership of their abbot, Henry Maltravers, and follow the rule of St Benedict. Of course they are assisted by an extensive cohort of lay brothers. They moved here about four years ago, when the buildings were completed.' Corbett paused, shaking his head. 'I know it's hard to believe, Ranulf, but the Knights of the Swan regard their former king as their supreme lord and master, pope and emperor. In their eyes he sat, and still does, at the right hand of the Power. They were totally committed to him. Once he died, they left the royal service because of their vow to serve no other once their liege lord was gone.'

'Of course,' Ranulf declared. 'They would be only too pleased not to serve the new king. He is losing the war in Scotland and fighting his own great lords, because of his infatuation with Gaveston. But you are not a Knight of the Swan, Sir Hugh. Why have you chosen to come here? You could have refused the royal request.'

'This is a place truly sacred to the memory of the old king, and I took an oath to him, Ranulf. I swore that I would do all in my power to assist and support his successor. Sometimes I wish to God I hadn't, but I did, and so here we are.'

Ranulf stared hard at his master, who sat passively, watching and waiting. 'Sir Hugh, I will be blunt.'

'I know what you are going to say, Ranulf. This may be a sacred place, but it is also lonely and desolate?'

'In God's name, master, that valley! Its steep sides, the trees growing so close that no horseman could safely penetrate!'

'A place of deep and lasting shadow,' Corbett agreed. 'Of perpetual night.'

'Master, now you are frightening me.'

Corbett laughed and shook his head. 'I describe what we saw, Ranulf, whilst what we have to confront here . . .'

'Is murder?'

'Yes, my friend. Murder! Strange though it may be in such a holy place. On our journey here you talked of it being a place of mystery. It is a holy shrine, a hallowed sanctuary containing precious relics such as the dagger coffer.'

'What else?'

Corbett recalled the whispers of the Secret Chancery.

He glanced quickly around, reassuring himself that they were safe from any eavesdropper.

'I don't really know, Ranulf. Remember, I left the old king's service, I was not with him during his final years, but I have heard rumours about a special prisoner, masked and hidden away in comfortable but very close confinement.'

'Who?'

'God knows. It may just be a fanciful tale, the creation of some troubadour or minstrel. Rumour claims, however, that if such a prisoner did exist, he would be confined here in Holyrood, well off the beaten track, and guarded by former Knights, fanatical in their loyalty and allegiance to the dead king.'

Ranulf rested against the table and watched as his master stretched, then rose to walk down the refectory to have words with Ap Ythel. The Clerk of the Green Wax smiled to himself. Corbett had retired from the service of the Crown, losing himself in his family – the Lady Maeve and their two children, Edward and Eleanor – as well as the management of his rich, well-stocked manor of Leighton, to the north-east of London, within bowshot of the great forest of Epping. He had now returned to court, soaking up all the mysteries of the Secret Chancery, which collected information from every part of the kingdom, the whispers and gossip about the lords of the soil, be they Church or Crown.

Corbett and Ap Ythel turned to greet one of their bowmen, who'd been ordered to wander Holyrood and see what he could learn. The Keeper of the Secret Seal questioned the man closely. Ranulf was about to join his master when Corbett turned and came back, retaking his seat. Opposite him, Chanson had put his head down on the table and was snoring gently. Corbett pointed at the Clerk of the Stables and grinned. 'Now there sleeps a man with a clear conscience.' He gestured at the door. 'Which is more than I can say for those who have arrived here to fish in very troubled waters.'

'Who?'

'Ranulf, we have visitors, including no less a person than Monsieur Amaury de Craon, King Philip's most trusted envoy to the English court.' Corbett ignored his henchman's groan. 'I heard rumours that he was coming. Apparently he is here to make enquiries about his master's kinsman, Richard Tissot, former Knight of the Swan, close friend of our late king and the second member of this community to be foully murdered by having a thick, heavy nail pounded deep into his forehead.'

'Sir Hugh, you told me that the deaths had been most mysterious, but—'

'Two,' Corbett whispered hoarsely. 'Both slain in the same barbarous way, a nail driven into the skull. One corpse was found in a cell, the other on the steps of a tower. De Craon, all concerned at the horrible slaying of his royal master's kinsman, has hurried here from Tewkesbury demanding explanations, justice and reparation.' He waved a hand. 'You know the hymn that two-faced fox will be singing, whilst dabbing the false tears from his eyes. De Craon was on his way here anyway. He visited the abbey last Easter, and now he has returned, apparently bringing a promised invitation to Abbot Henry to visit Paris next spring. Our king has also been invited, and even I myself.'

'Why?' Ranulf demanded.

'Philip intends to celebrate his kingship and his victory over the Templars, as well as to portray himself as the new Emperor of Christendom. Three of his sons are married to the richest heiresses, whose estates will strengthen the French Crown.'

'And Philip's only daughter Isabella is married to our own king.'

'Oh yes,' Corbett murmured. 'Philip is beside himself with joy. One of these days his grandson will sit on the throne of the Confessor at Westminster.'

'But we are not here, Sir Hugh, to entertain de Craon?'

'Of course not, but these two murders do trouble our king and his council. Matters are not helped by a possible third victim, Abbot Henry Maltravers himself, who lies sick in bed: he claims to have been poisoned.' Corbett gave a half-smile. 'My friend,' he leant over and touched Ranulf gently on the arm, 'my letter to you arranging the time and place for our meeting could have told you more, but there again, it could always have been intercepted. In truth, we are back to the hunt for these children of Cain, cunning, subtle assassins. I suspect this abbey, for all its sanctity, houses a veritable brew of malevolent, murderous mischief.'

Ranulf nodded in agreement. He had been on royal business in Colchester when he received Corbett's letter, dispatched from his master's manor at Leighton. He had wondered about the cryptic summons and worried at travelling to this place. Having inspected the mouth of that valley, he now nursed a deep dread. Ranulf was a child of the narrow runnels and arrow-thin alleyways of London. He was as comfortable there as any hunting cat, but the countryside was different, especially a place like this: a formidable fortress standing at the mouth of a valley so ill-named. A place of perpetual green darkness, the Valley of Shadows probably housed a veritable horde of demons and malignant spirits.

'Ranulf?'

The Clerk of the Green Wax shook his head, 'I am lost in nightmares, master. A place like this can make the heart skip with fear and the blood turn cold. But,' Ranulf asserted himself, 'you implied that others had come to fish in these troubled waters.'

'Ah, yes.' Corbett glanced down the table. 'Ap Ythel's man is a veritable ferret. No less a person than Lord Mortimer has arrived, full of solicitous concern, a true snake in the grass.'

'A marcher lord.' His henchman nodded. 'A leading light among the Lords Ordainers, those great barons opposed to our new king and his favourite.'

'Oh yes,' Corbett agreed. 'Those same lords are building up their strength, issuing writs of array summoning up their levies. Mortimer and his ilk would love to seize a place like this, as they would all the great fortresses along the Welsh March. His estates adjoin this valley. He is the king's justiciar in these border lands and is using his position to snout out any possible mischief. In fact—'

Corbett broke off as a booming bell rang out the tocsin, a chilling clanging sound that echoed ominously across the abbey. For a few heartbeats he and his entourage sat still.

'In God's name!' Ranulf sprang to his feet, whilst Corbett roused Chanson. The three clerks hastily put on their war belts, donned their cloaks and followed Ap Ythel and his archers out of the refectory and into the cobbled yard, which stretched down to the Great Cloister. The peal of the tocsin had now been taken up by more bells. Lay brothers and other servants of the community had gathered in the yard, looking up at the cloud-packed sky, which hung low and heavy.

'There's a second one!' a voice yelled. Corbett glanced up as the fire arrow, a streaking tail of flame, cut across the sky before turning to tip and lose itself in the blackness of the night. More people joined them, former Knights of the Swan breaking off from their evening devotions; these hurried out of the cloisters, then stopped as a third fire arrow scorched the night sky. Shouts and cries of alarm echoed.

'Three in all,' one of the Knights shouted. 'A warning.'

'What does he mean?' Chanson demanded, rubbing the sleep from his eyes. 'Ranulf, what does he mean?'

'When the English army first invaded Wales,' Ranulf replied, 'the Welsh would warn our troops in the dead of night that raging fire, fierce attack and sudden death awaited them. Each of those fire arrows contains such a warning.'

'But the Welsh princes have been slaughtered,' the Clerk of the Stables protested. 'The power of the tribes has been shattered, that's what you told me.'

'Hush now.' Corbett glanced up at the sky, then beckoned a lay brother to ask him if this had occurred before. The man, visibly frightened, just shook his head.

'Is it a warning to us?' Ranulf asked. 'After all, it occurred just after our arrival.'

'Heaven and all its angels help us!' a servant screamed as he hurried out of the refectory, robe hitched up, sandalled feet slipping on the cobbles. Hands outstretched, he raced towards Corbett, but Ranulf intervened, seizing the man by the arm, pulling him close.

'Master!' the servant gasped, shaking himself free. 'Brother Mark, our kitchener, has been cruelly murdered. He lies dead.'

Corbett ordered the man to show them. They entered the refectory, where more lay brothers milled about like a gaggle of geese, fingers all a-flutter as they gabbled about what had happened. Corbett and Ranulf pushed their way across the cavernous kitchen; its stoves and ovens, fired to the full, exuded a welcoming heat and savoury smells. They entered the buttery yard, where a range of derelict beer barrels stood, now used to hold rubbish and refuse from the kitchen. Brother Mark lay between two of these, sprawled on the ice-crusted cobbles, legs and arms splayed, his bearded face a mask of blood, which had gushed from his nose and mouth, as well as a thick trickle from the gruesome wound in his skull, where a nail had been driven in so hard, only its head protruded. Corbett glanced around, shouting at the lay brothers who had followed them to bring lanterns. In the light of these, he returned to his scrutiny, Ranulf crouching beside him.

'Master, there's nothing! Look around you. No sign of any resistance. No trace of a struggle; just a man stretched out on the cobbles with a nail driven through his forehead.' Ranulf felt the top of the nail. 'How can this have been thrust so deep into his forehead? A victim who is vigorous, a former soldier, skilled in defending himself. How was it done? Why was it done?'

'Why indeed?' Corbett echoed.

'Let me take my brother's corpse.'

Corbett hastily stepped aside as a lean, cadaverous individual, together with two lay brothers carrying a pallet, pushed his way through. He glanced sharply at Corbett and extended his hand. 'You may not remember me, Sir Hugh, but I certainly recall you, in both court and chancery. Crispin Hollister, former royal knight.'

'I remember you well.' Corbett gripped the man's hand. 'How could I forget such a skilled jouster? Victorious so many times in the tourney and the tournament.'

'Those days are past. I am now the infirmarian at the abbey of Holyrood, and I have to collect my sworn brother's corpse.'

Corbett realised that Crispin was deeply upset. He and Ranulf helped the infirmarian and his acolytes to place the corpse on the pallet. Then they followed the sombre procession back into the abbey buildings, where Crispin cleared a way through the throng of brothers. They processed down stone-paved galleries and passage-ways, along dark tunnels where cresset torches burnt. The dancing flames flared in the breeze, shedding light and smoke around the gargoyles, devils, monkeys and goats that gazed grimly down. Ranulf quietly cursed. The grotesque faces carved on the top of the pillars stirred nightmares in his soul. Corbett nudged him, so the Clerk of the Green Wax joined his master in quietly reciting the death psalm. 'Out of the depths I cry to thee, O Lord . . .'

Eventually they reached the corpse chamber, a cavernous room stretching beneath the infirmary. Brother Mark's mortal remains were laid out on a high wooden table with thick tallow candles in sockets on all four corners. The air reeked of pine juice as well as herbal essences stewing in large pots around the dimly lit chamber with its row upon row of mortuary tables. Only one of these, as Brother Crispin wryly remarked, held 'a guest': a beggar man who had staggered into the abbey before he collapsed and died.

Corbett watched as the infirmarian and his assistants stripped Brother Mark's corpse, then he and Ranulf, with Chanson staring furtively from behind them, joined Crispin in scrutinising the body. The cold, hardening flesh was criss-crossed and bruised with old scars and battle wounds, but apart from the gruesome death blow to the forehead, Corbett could detect nothing significant.

Brother Crispin told his assistants to withdraw. Once

they had done so, he brought a pair of powerful prongs from his medical coffer and used these to clasp the nail driven deep into the dead man's forehead. Slowly he pulled it out, the serrated edges of the nail grinding the bone, dark blood slowly trickling out. He held the nail up so that Corbett could clearly view it, then crossed to a barrel of water and washed it carefully with a rag. Next he took a small but heavy mallet from his coffer. Corbett sensed what was about to happen but decided to hold his peace. The infirmarian strode across to stand over the corpse of the beggar man. He beckoned Corbett and Ranulf to join him. The clerks studied the pathetic remains: the beggar's belly skin was discoloured, a filthy froth between his lips.

The infirmarian placed the heavy black nail in the centre of the dead man's skull, its pointed tip piercing the skin. 'Have no qualms, Sir Hugh, this poor creature's soul has long gone to the angels. I mean no disrespect. You know we search for the truth, and this unfortunate, though dead, can assist us in our quest.' He paused. 'I have reflected,' he murmured, 'how long it would take to drive such a nail into a man's skull, and I don't think it could be done swiftly.'

Corbett held his breath as the infirmarian made sure the nail was positioned correctly before hitting it with three powerful blows to drive it as deep into the beggar man's skull as it had been in Brother Mark's. Some black blood trickled out of the wound, and Corbett noticed how both the skin and bone of the man's forehead were ruptured.

'In the name of all that is holy,' he whispered, walking back to Brother Mark's corpse. 'How could this be done? Here lies an able-bodied man, a former soldier, whose skull was pierced, yet there is not a shred of evidence to indicate he was drunk or being fed some opiate to render him senseless. There is no other wound or blow to his head or body, no proof that he was held by another. Nevertheless, he goes out into that kitchen yard and allows his assailant to draw close and drive a nail into his forehead with two, even three blows. There is no sign of any resistance, no protest, no sound. So how? And why? Why kill a refectorian, a man dedicated to God and pledged to honour the name and soul of his dead royal master? Why have two of his companions been murdered in a similar way?'

'So many questions,' Crispin grated. 'Sir Hugh, do you have any answers?'

'The only logical explanation,' Corbett retorted, 'and it's a beginning, not a conclusion, is that a member of this community has turned, like some rabid wolf, on his comrades. But as for the why and the how, that must remain a mystery.'

Corbett's unease only deepened as he left the mortuary and led Ranulf up the steps onto the broad parapet walk that circled the abbey buildings. For a while the two men stood muffled in their cloaks, buffeted by an icy breeze as they stared across at the Valley of Shadows.

'We have entered the forests of the night,' Ranulf

murmured. 'Here on this high wall, I stare into the blackness and confess that I feel truly frightened. Sir Hugh, what is happening?'

'I don't know,' Corbett replied, 'except that some evil has emerged to prowl around this place. God knows why, Ranulf, but I have a nagging suspicion.' He paused at the mournful hooting of an owl carried by the night breeze from the green darkness so close to them. 'I do wonder,' he continued, 'if the evil here is linked to that business in Scotland, that secret society, Satan's own coven: the Black Chesters.'

'I thought we destroyed them. You executed their leader, Paracelsus.'

'I thought the same, Ranulf. You may recall how after we left Scotland, I had business in York and elsewhere before returning to my manor at Leighton. Chanson and Ap Ythel accompanied me. Now.' Corbett patted the stonework and turned to face his henchman. He glanced over Ranulf's shoulder, his gaze drawn by the fire bowls burning fiercely along the wall, their flames leaping up against the night. In the flickering light, Ranulf's face seemed a deathly pale, sheened with sweat. Corbett caught his companion's deep, curdling fear.

'Come.' He plucked at Ranulf's cloak, pulling him closer. 'Let's at least go down to some merry fire. I came up here so we could be alone.'

He was about to turn away when an arrow whipped through the air just above their heads. 'In heaven's name!' Ranulf exclaimed. He was about to lean over the crenellation, but Corbett pulled him down to crouch behind the stonework.

'Keep low,' he hissed, 'and follow me.'

The clerk turned, and was almost crawling towards the steps when he heard a scream further along the parapet walk. He glanced up and glimpsed the watchman stagger, hands going up to the shaft piercing his throat before he toppled to fall like a stone into the bailey below. Corbett and Ranulf reached the steps, straightened up and hurried down. The alarm had already been raised, the abbey bells tolling the tocsin once more. By the time they had reached the cobbled outer bailey, others had gathered. The watchman who had been struck, a lay brother garbed in a boiled leather jerkin, thick woollen hose and sturdy boots, lay sprawled on his back, eyes staring blindly up at the flickering torches gathering around him. His short stabbing sword was still fastened in its sheath, so Corbett reckoned he must have seen nothing untoward; his conical helmet, lying a short distance away, was unmarked.

Corbett ignored the exclamations of those gathering around as he swiftly studied the death wound. The arrow, a slender yard-long shaft, had pierced the man's throat just beneath the chin. 'A master bowman,' murmured the clerk. 'An archer wielding a powerful war bow with long feathered shafts.'

'But so high,' Ranulf replied. 'He would have had to draw close to the walls.' He paused at the clatter of hooves as a postern gate was opened and a hastily arranged party of horsemen dispatched across a make-shift bridge to scour the darkness.

'Too late and too futile.' Corbett shook his head and got to his feet, plucking at Ranulf's sleeve. They pushed their way through the gathering throng. Corbett nodded to Brother Crispin, who was demanding to see the corpse, then led Ranulf back into the deserted refectory. They checked on a sleeping Chanson, head down on the table, before going to warm themselves over the capped braziers.

'Don't be so surprised at what you saw,' Corbett declared. 'What we have just witnessed is the mark of a true archer. I have seen the likes before in Wales. They can take the eye out of a bird and place a shaft through the narrowest cleft. They move on foot, garbed in brown and green to keep them subtly disguised and hidden, but . . .'

'Sir Hugh?'

'Ranulf, these archers are highly skilled, yet this one seems to have moved far too swiftly, which might account for his poor aim. He narrowly missed us because we also moved, a mere heartbeat before that arrow pierced the darkness above us.'

'And . . .'

'He would have had to notch again, take aim and loose at the watchman, yet that poor soul was killed even as we crouched down. Moreover, he was further along the wall than us. No bowman could move so quickly.'

'So there must have been two.'

'Yes, Ranulf, certainly more than one, but who they were and why they attacked . . .' Corbett shook his head. 'What I suspect is that the attack on us was not specific. These enemy bowmen were searching for a target, any target along the parapet wall.'

'And this could be the work of the Black Chesters?'

Corbett was about to reply when a lay brother hurried in, gasping how the lord abbot and others were assembling in the council chamber, and would Sir Hugh be kind enough to join them?

'We have no choice.' Corbett plucked at his companion's sleeve. 'We are invited to the tournament, and battle is about to begin.'

The lay brother led them out through the darkness and into the council chamber, which lay close to the abbey church. Corbett and Ranulf were ushered to their seats. Corbett slouched down, staring around at the guests making themselves comfortable, turning to the lay brothers responsible for the buttery table, telling them what they would like to eat and drink. He himself asked for a goblet of mulled wine and a platter of capon sprinkled with herbs. Once this was served, he ate and drank slowly, as if paying full attention to the meal.

Ranulf smiled to himself. He now knew 'Master Longface', as he sometimes described Corbett, and his little foibles. The clerk was highly skilled at apparently watching one thing when in truth he was closely scrutinising something else; today was no different.

'You know all these guests?' Ranulf whispered. Corbett nodded imperceptibly, and continued his scrutiny of the man at the head of the table: Henry Maltravers, former Knight of the Swan, close confidant and friend of the old king, now abbot of this great abbey fortress. Corbett knew Maltravers of old, and considered him a true warrior. The abbot had sketched a bow towards the clerk as, resting on his canes, he allowed two assistants to help him to sit in the great throne-like chair. He had the face of a hunting falcon, shaven of all hair, which made his narrow eyes seem all the more watchful. His high cheekbones and sunken cheeks told of a man hard as iron, a blood-soaked warrior. The son of a London armourer, he had entered the old king's service as a page, and had fought his way up to become a royal henchman, a knight banneret in the Brotherhood of the Swan.

Corbett watched as the abbot made himself comfortable, wincing at a pain in his stomach, which he kept rubbing with thick, stubby fingers. He turned to speak to Devizes, his master-at-arms, who stood behind his chair, garbed for war in his hauberk, a conical helmet cradled in the crook of his arm. Devizes' mailed coif was pulled over his head to frame a truly handsome, even beautiful face. Nevertheless, both he and his master were true men of war. The abbot even had his sword belt slung over the newel of his chair.

Maltravers was a fine example of the church militant, a warrior who believed in both prayer and the power of his arm. As he glanced down the table, he caught Corbett's eye again and winked, then gave that thin smile that never reached his eyes. He and Corbett had served together in Wales, Gascony and Scotland, and the clerk strongly suspected that Maltravers had asked the young king to send his Keeper of the Secret Seal here to Holyrood to assist on certain matters. On either side of the abbot sat his two henchmen, Prior Jude and Brother Crispin, both veteran warriors, skilled in battle: in their brown woollen robes, the three men looked like blood brothers, stern-faced, yet openly worried about what was happening in their abbey.

Across the table, head down and playing with his food, sat Roger Mortimer. Corbett studied him out of the corner of his eye and quietly wondered what mischief, what villainy, brought this most sinister of marcher lords to Holyrood. Mortimer abruptly glanced up and stared across at the clerk with those glassy blue eyes, so light that Corbett wondered if there truly was a soul behind them. He held the marcher lord's gaze. Mortimer gave a lopsided grin and returned to his food, fingers flicking at the crumbs on his jerkin, lost in his thoughts. Corbett wondered what he was thinking about, then mentally recited the opening verse of a psalm: 'The Lord is my light and my help, whom should I fear.' Certainly Mortimer!

He glanced at the crucifix fixed on the far wall of the chamber. Mortimer was arrogant and deeply ambitious, determined to build his own fiefdom along the Welsh March. He would bully, harass and even kill any who opposed him, yet there was more. Despite his rugged looks and easy charm, he also enjoyed a chilling reputation as a warlock. A dark-souled lord of the midnight rites, with a penchant for consulting conjurors and others steeped in the black arts. Corbett had no proof of this; just the whispered gossip of the Secret Chancery. According to what he had learnt from a lay brother, Mortimer had arrived at Holyrood with a small though well-armed retinue. The marcher lord had been lodged in one of the towers. He had not bothered to change, and was still swathed in a mud-stained travelling cloak, eloquent testimony that he had ridden hard and fast to reach Holyrood. The Keeper of the Secret Seal wondered why.

Corbett heard murmured French behind him. He turned in his chair and stared up at the smiling face of Amaury de Craon, Philip IV's special emissary to the English court, Master of Secrets in the French king's chancery at the Louvre in Paris. De Craon finished thanking the lay brother who'd brought him in before extending a hand, which Corbett clasped. De Craon tightened his grip.

'So good to see you, Hugh. You are never far from my thoughts.'

'In which case, we have something in common.' Corbett withdrew his hand and let it fall to the hilt of his dagger.

'*Pax et bonum*,' the Frenchman murmured with that knowing smile that always infuriated Corbett. 'And it's good to see you too, Ranulf.'

The Clerk of the Green Wax rose and proffered his hand, leaving Corbett to marshal his own thoughts and emotions. The French envoy settled himself, still smirking. Corbett studied this most devious man, a true fox, with his wiry russet hair, moustache and beard, his ever-darting eyes, sharp nose and pointed features. Corbett had crossed swords with de Craon more times than he could remember, and he knew the Frenchman loathed and detested him. A man who would not hesitate in taking Corbett's life if he could do so without any hurt to himself.

'Sad days, Hugh, sad days . . .' De Craon broke off as the abbot, wincing in pain, leant forward and tapped the top of the table.

'Gentlemen, my brothers, cherished guests, welcome.' Maltravers made a face as he rubbed his stomach.

'Father Abbot, are you well?'

'Yes, Crispin, thanks to you, I am getting better. Now we are all gathered here—'

'My Lord Abbot.' Corbett leant his elbows on the table. 'I am here, as you know, on the king's business. I carry his warrants, licences, letters and seals.'

'And?' Mortimer lifted his head, his handsome face wreathed in a smile. He stroked his neatly clipped moustache and beard, which, like the long golden hair framing his swarthy features, were streaked with grey. 'And?' he repeated.

'Precisely,' Corbett snapped. 'I am here to ask questions. So, my lord, why are *you* here? Not to mention,' he turned to de Craon, 'our august envoy from France.'

The abbot stilled objections from his guests, rapping the table and glaring down at Corbett. 'Sir Hugh, Monsieur de Craon brings greetings and messages from King Philip of France. He has hastened here—'

'A truly arduous journey from Tewkesbury,' de Craon

interjected. 'I am here for two reasons, Sir Hugh. First, a kinsman of the French king has been cruelly murdered at Holyrood. My royal master has every right to demand an explanation as well as seek assurances that the perpetrator will be caught and most rigorously punished.'

'As for me,' Mortimer drawled, dismissing de Craon with a flick of his hand, 'as you well know, Sir Hugh, I am the king's justiciar in these parts. I exercise the right of oyer and terminer – to hear and to deal with all matters of law. Moreover, I too was a member of the old king's comitatus, although not a Knight of the Swan. For like you, I am married and the father of children – indeed, many children, some within wedlock, others who are truly bastard.' He gave Corbett a meaningful look, as if both of them knew full well that the love of women was not shared by the Knights of the Swan.

'And your second reason for being here?' Corbett turned back to the envoy.

'Sir Hugh,' Abbot Henry forced a smile, 'I appreciate there may be other business you want to prosecute, but we are gathered here now to discuss the real dangers this abbey faces. We must take action, and soon. Today is the seventeenth of November, the year of Our Lord 1311. We celebrate the feast of St Callixtus, pope and martyr; we too are martyrs to our calling.'

He paused to take a deep breath. 'We are Knights of the Swan, the old king's comitatus. We have wielded our swords for him in fierce battle. We have confronted the spear storm and endured the arrow flood. As pages we followed him in Outremer. As squires and young knights we shattered the war bands and the armed hosts of his enemies – be it the tribes here in Wales, the traitor de Montfort, or those rebels who prowl the rugged hills of Scotland. We hoped, we prayed to follow our king to Jerusalem. We vowed that if we could not do this during his lifetime, we would give up our swords and shields for the psalter and the Ave beads. We also vowed to assume the mantle of the Benedictine order and to follow its rule. The old king accepted our pledges of loyalty. He granted us this abbey and its lands, including the Valley of Shadows, the entrance to which we now guard . . .' The abbot fell silent, rubbing his stomach as he gestured at Jude to continue.

'Our stay here', the prior's hard-clipped voice rang through the chamber, 'has proved to be most successful, but now we sip deep from the cup of sorrows. On the eve of the feast of St Simon and Jude, Father Abbot fell grievously ill after drinking from his goblet in his chamber. He was undoubtedly poisoned.'

'How do you know this?' Corbett interjected.

'I took the goblet and fed the dregs to rats in our cellar; we later found the corpses of three of them, bellies bloated and black. Of course the good Lord is not concerned with rats, and we have prayed for Father Abbot. I have purged him, bled him and poured cup after cup of pure spring water down his throat. We are clearing the evil humours from his body and he is improving – are you not, Father Abbot?'

Maltravers smiled and nodded.

'I have placed a guard, or rather Devizes has.' The prior gestured at the handsome, lithe master-at-arms now sitting on a stool to the abbot's right.

'That is so,' Devizes murmured. 'I now keep constant and close watch over Abbot Henry's chamber.'

'As you have done since you were my page,' the abbot murmured. 'Faithful and true.'

'And you have no knowledge, not even a suspicion, of who is responsible?'

'Brother Mark, who now lies murdered, served the wine, God rest him.' Prior Jude blessed himself. 'He admitted that he filled the cup but then left it standing in the buttery for a while.'

Corbett nodded. What the prior had just said brought everyone in the abbey under suspicion. 'And why should someone poison you?' he asked Maltravers.

'There is no reason that I know of. I have tried to be a good father abbot. I nurse no grudge or grievance against any member of our community, and to my best recall, no one holds a grievance against me. Isn't that so, brothers?'

Both the prior and the infirmarian loudly chorused their agreement.

'And the other murders?' Mortimer asked, moving his goblet from one gauntleted hand to the other.

Corbett wondered why the marcher lord kept his hands gloved, then he recalled a story from the Secret Chancery. How Mortimer had certain marks on the back of his hands connected with his dedication to the black arts.

'As for the other deaths,' Prior Jude shrugged, 'you must now know as much as we do. Three of our company have been murdered, one in his own chamber. All killed by a heavy nail thrust into their skull.'

'Father Abbot,' Corbett decided to enforce his own authority here, 'by your vows as well as your allegiance to the Crown, you and your brothers here' – he gestured at Jude and Crispin – 'know nothing of these deaths?'

'Nothing,' the infirmarian replied, Prior Jude echoing his words.

'I agree,' Abbot Henry added. 'How and why three of my comrades were killed by a nail loosed into their forehead is a mystery.'

'Sir Hugh.' Prior Jude joined his hands together as if in prayer. 'The brothers of Holyrood, members of this abbey, are former knights. Most importantly, we are comrades. We fought hard for the old king. We kept our vows to live in a monastic community after his death. This is a happy, harmonious home. Not only do we have rich memories of the past, but each of us has a skill, a talent, an aptitude we can use to the benefit of all. I have a love of chancery work. Crispin is a born leech, well versed in physic. Father Abbot has always had a love of wrought steel and iron; he is skilled in all matters of the forge. He was our royal master's personal armourer.'

'My brothers speak the truth.' Maltravers drummed his fingers on the tabletop. 'We are old warriors, now in our dream time. We live in peace with each other. We were happy until some demon – and I call it that

— thrust its way into our lives. Sir Hugh, I do not know anything about the root of this evil except that it is embedded deep and has flowered in all its malignancy.'

'And these fire arrows, and the bowman who killed your guard?' Mortimer gestured around the table. 'We have all fought the Welsh, Father Abbot. Are there traitors in and around Holyrood? Do tribes hidden deep in that valley still resist us?'

'The Valley of Shadows is deep, broad and long,' the abbot replied, 'very thickly wooded, the trees close enough to impede even the most skilled horseman.'

'Have you penetrated it?' Corbett asked. 'Do you know who actually lives there, friend or foe?'

'My days of warfare are over, yet the memories are still fresh.' Abbot Henry paused. 'You must know, Sir Hugh, and you, my lord Mortimer, that eleven years ago the king led a chevauchée into the valley to extirpate a coven of rebels, true malignants, who had defied him and taken refuge in caves beneath the cliffs of Caerwent, which seal the far end of the valley.' He made a face. 'Some of the outlaws may have escaped and are still in hiding nursing their hatred, greedy for revenge.'

Corbett watched the abbot intently. Maltravers was blunt, even rude in his directness, yet the clerk sensed he wasn't answering the questions levelled at him. He watched as Maltravers leant back in his chair, staring up at the ceiling, then rubbed his face, 'Come, come,' he murmured. 'My lord Mortimer, Sir Hugh, brothers, we have all fought the Welsh. We will never forget those sombre valleys where the mist never lifts. The sudden ambuscade, arrows whipping like a swarm of hornets from the trees. Silent assassins crawling on their bellies, axe in one hand, knife in the other.'

'And the fire arrows,' Mortimer interrupted. He too was growing impatient at Abbot Henry's determination to call up the past rather than deal with the present. 'Aren't they a warning of things to come? The Welsh were skilled at that. They gave such warnings to numb the mind, chill the heart and fray the nerves. Father Abbot, we saw those same fire arrows tonight. My question stands. Are there tribes still hostile to us deep in that valley?'

'I think there are.' Abbot Henry kept his head down. 'More worrying is that we dispatched a hunting party yesterday and they have not returned.' He sat back in his chair. 'Sir Hugh, will you lead a chevauchée into the valley tomorrow so that we can answer some of the questions posed here? I think we need to do so before the weather changes. See what you can discover. Search for our brothers, five in all, who left yesterday. Will you?'

Corbett glanced at Mortimer, who shrugged and nodded.

'We will,' the clerk replied, ignoring Ranulf's hiss of disapproval. 'Now, Monsieur de Craon.' He smiled at the French envoy, who smiled back equally falsely. 'You said there were two reasons why you were here?'

'Oh, yes. As you may know, the French court is planning great celebrations to honour the magnificent achievements of our king. This will take place in Paris next spring. A time of glory. Brilliant pageants, solemn processions, banquets, feasts and masques are to be held in the city and beyond.' De Craon spread his hands, his face full of smugness. 'Sir Hugh, we have so much to celebrate: achievements at home, glory abroad. Now my royal master has always had the most amicable relationship with Abbot Henry, who as you may know, often acted as emissary between the late king of England and the French court—'

'I know all this,' Corbett interrupted brusquely. 'I've seen the invitations sent to Westminster.'

'And you, Sir Hugh, are included,' de Craon replied primly.

Corbett nodded in understanding as he stared at this French envoy who truly hated him. He knew all about the forthcoming festivities in Paris. Philip of France hoped to emphasise his power both within and without. More importantly, he wished to proclaim to the world that his attack and destruction of the Templar order was complete, fully justified and carried through with the unwavering support of other princes, especially that of the Frenchman Bertrand de Got, who now occupied the papal throne as Clement V. Corbett was determined not to join such celebrations. He had already discussed this with both the king and the Secret Chancery. They were all in agreement. If he travelled to Paris, some evil mischief would befall him.

'Sir Hugh, you will lead a company to the valley after first light?' The abbot's voice now had a pleading tone.

'I shall,' Corbett replied, 'but now, my lord, I do need to have words with you *in secreto*.'

'Devizes will go with you tomorrow.' The abbot seemed distracted. 'And yes, Sir Hugh, you and I need words. Prior Jude and Brother Crispin, you too must stay because . . .' he smiled down the table at Corbett, 'because I strongly suspect what the secret business is. You alone, yes, Sir Hugh?' He stared meaningfully at Ranulf.

'My clerk,' Corbett declared, 'has other matters to attend to. I believe we have been given chambers, comfortable quarters in Osprey Tower?'

The abbot nodded and the meeting ended.

Corbett plucked Ranulf by the sleeve and took him out into an open gallery leading down to the cloisters. A sharp breeze pierced the air. The flames of the cressets danced frenetically and sent puffs of smoke to hang against the encroaching darkness. Corbett stared through the murk and shivered. 'This is a sombre place,' he whispered. 'Look around you, Ranulf, stones and darkness! Gloomy tunnels that twist like a maze, a place of dreams.'

'Bad dreams!' Ranulf replied. 'Sir Hugh, what will you discuss with our lord abbot?'

'In time, in time,' Corbett murmured. 'Go, Ranulf. Prepare our chambers. Place our secret chancery coffer in a most secure place. Chain it to a clasp in the wall. Make sure all its locks are turned and the seals along the rim of the lid have not been disturbed.'

Ranulf assured him he would, and quickly left to get out of the freezing darkness.

Corbett pulled his cloak about him and stared down the path lined with bushes, their black branches stark against the night so that they looked like a line of monsters thronging in the poor light. He closed his eyes and recalled his manor at Leighton as it was last summer: the arms of the apple trees bent down with lush fruit, the nuts all plump on the tips of the branches. He thought of the great meadow, its greenery turning white with flowers. In the morning the grass was wet with the sheen of the dew, whilst blackbirds warbled their matins to the strengthening sun. He would love to see the deep brown of the oaks, the glitter of the fresh saplings, the rich green of ripening fruit and the gorgeous red of full-blooded plums. When he was there he would walk with Maeve, feeling the warmth and rejoicing in the God-given fragrances wafting in from the orchards. They would . . .

'Sir Hugh!' He opened his eyes. Prior Jude was beckoning him. 'Father Abbot will see you now.'

Corbett and the prior returned to the council chamber. Abbot Henry had ordered steaming goblets of mulled wine, and the rich herbs had already created a drifting fragrance. Dishes of sparkling charcoal decorated the table, bowls of fiery warmth resting on pewter platters. Corbett warmed his fingers over one of these, then retook his seat and sipped at the wine. Abbot Henry watched him drink before turning to Devizes standing like a statue behind him.

'Come with me,' he ordered the master-at-arms, 'but no further than usual.'

Devizes nodded. The abbot rose, clutching his walking cane, allowing Jude and Crispin to help him follow Devizes out into the vestibule. Corbett walked behind them along hollow-sounding galleries and passageways. Wall torches flared to provide meagre light, which caught the grotesque faces of the gargoyles clustered at the top of pillars like a host of demons gathering to pounce.

Abbot Henry paused, speaking over his shoulder. 'Sir Hugh, you wish to inspect the dagger? You mentioned that in your sealed letter to me.'

'Yes, yes,' Corbett replied, pulling his hood closer against the bitter cold. 'His Grace wants to be assured that his family's precious relic is safe.'

Abbot Henry turned away, muttering under his breath about not being trusted by the young king, Jude and Crispin murmuring their agreement. They entered the abbey church by a postern door. Corbett was surprised by the hosts of flaring candles and strongly burning torches, which created eye-dazzling pools of light along the nave and transepts. Crispin heard his exclamation of surprise and turned.

'Brother Raphael, our sacristan. You will know him as Sir Ralph Hemery, knight banneret, once one of our late king's leading barons.'

'Son of the principal chandler merchant in London,' Corbett declared. 'A true master of light.'

'The very same,' Crispin agreed. 'Raphael can fashion

wax more skilfully than any member of the guild; he just loves the light.'

'Fetch him,' Abbot Henry grated. 'I feel cold, and the hour is passing.'

Crispin hurried away as Corbett turned and walked into the brightly lit northern transept. Despite the church being recently repaired and refurbished, the transepts were already gorgeously decorated with striking frescoes. In one, a woman stood next to a spring. She held a silver comb ornamented with gold, and wore a shaggy purple cloak of the finest fleece decorated with gleaming bronze and copper studs. Her body was as white as the snow of a single night, her hair as black as a raven's wing. She was talking to an angel painted in the form of a young knight, his hair of burnished gold, his body encased in shining armour: his belt, baldric and sword scabbard were adorned with the costliest jewels. In stark contrast, the painting beside it proclaimed all the horrors of hell. A place of utter desolation, where fiery red showers rained down on the damned clustered together. Loaded with flaming chains, these lost souls were herded by gleeful demons with the faces of monkeys, goats, rats and pigs.

'Sir Hugh?' Corbett returned to Father Abbot, who introduced Brother Raphael, a short, stocky man whose lined, cheery face Corbett recalled seeing in both camp and court. They clasped hands and exchanged the kiss of peace, then Raphael led them through the rood screen, across the choir and into the sanctuary. The high altar stood resplendently decorated with silver-white cloths, the candelabra encrusted with precious stones. On a chain to the right of the altar hung a heavy gold pyx shining with jewels, beside it a winking red sanctuary lamp. On the left of the altar dangled an exquisitely carved coffer, a long, slender casket encased in gold and silver and covered with the most lustrous pearls.

Brother Raphael took a key out of his belt wallet and undid a clasp, allowing him to free the chain and so lower the casket. He threaded the chain carefully, then unlocked three more clasps, each with a separate key. Once the casket was free, he handed it to the abbot, who gestured at Corbett to inspect it. The clerk tipped back the lid and exclaimed at the thick, heavy gold that lined every inch of the interior. In the deep body of the casket, an ivory-handled dagger rested on a silver-fringed purple cushion. At the abbot's insistence, Corbett took this out, holding it up and twisting it from side to side so the Damascene blade could be clearly seen: long, curving, cruelly tipped and sharp as a razor. Then he lowered it, scrutinising it carefully, though he was still distracted by the sheer unalloyed beauty of the casket.

'I was there,' Abbot Henry declared fiercely.

'As we all were,' Brother Crispin intoned. 'All of us young squires, sleeping in a pavilion next to the king's.'

Brother Jude drew closer, tapping the dagger Corbett still held. 'We heard the clamour, the screams of Lady Eleanor, the scraping clash of steel and the cries of the assassin. By the time we entered the royal tent, the attacker was dead, our prince nursing wounds to his right arm and shoulder. The blade you now hold, Sir Hugh, was lying on the ground, stained with the king's blood and a sickening yellow mucus. Our lord took it up and smelt it.'

'As did I,' Brother Crispin interjected. 'The stench was rank, fetid. I recognised the mucus as venomous, some kind of deadly poison. It was then that the Lady Eleanor sucked both wounds, spitting the poison out as she did so. She saved his life. Our royal master grew a little feverish, but that soon passed.'

'He commanded us,' Abbot Henry crossed himself, 'to regard the dagger as a sacred relic, a symbol of God's favour, and of his own courage together with that of the love of his life, who saved our prince from an agonising death. So,' he plucked the dagger from Corbett's hands, 'tell his beloved son, our royal master, that this dagger, this sacred relic, is still safe here in Holyrood.'

The clerk caught the deep sarcasm in the abbot's voice. 'I surely shall,' he replied. 'I can give him every assurance that it is so. However, His Grace did talk of moving the dagger to his personal chapel.'

'That would break the late king's will,' Maltravers declared, 'his dying words as well as our own solemn oaths, but that is for the future. Sir Hugh, you seem more taken with the casket than with what it contains.'

'Too true, too true,' Corbett murmured. 'It is exquisitely beautiful, the work of a most skilled master craftsman, surely.'

'You are correct,' the abbot replied. 'The casket was

a gift from the grand master of the Templar order, now sadly no more. Our royal master truly treasured it.' He ran a hand along the casket. 'Some people claim that these pearls once decorated Solomon's great temple in Jerusalem, but,' he pulled a face, 'whether that is true or not . . .'

As Brother Raphael placed the dagger back in the casket and began to reattach the sanctuary chains, Abbot Henry, snapping his fingers, turned and hobbled off, leading Corbett and his two comrades back down the nave to a postern door, where Devizes stood guard. The abbot had a swift muttered conversation with his master-at-arms, who led them off along paved pathways, passing under arches, rounding corners and crossing gardens and herb plots.

Corbett, muffled in his cloak, fingers not far from his dagger hilt, stared around. Holyrood was a true maze. A warren of paths cutting through dark buildings that seemed to close in despite the many lanternhorns. They approached the soaring Eagle Donjon, which rose forbiddingly against the heavily clouded night sky, and entered the Falcon Tower, where Abbot Henry had his lodgings. Corbett expected to be taken up to what the abbot described as his 'palatial chambers'; instead they went into a cavernous storeroom, where Crispin and Jude pulled away some barrels to reveal a hidden door.

Abbot Henry took a key from under his robe, as did his two companions. Corbett, deeply curious, stepped close. The door was new, its oak of the finest, a thick wedge of wood reinforced with metal studs. It had three locks. Father Abbot opened the middle one, then Crispin and Jude the other two. A set of steps inside led them down into a broad, high-vaulted passageway lit by lanternhorns and oil lamps placed in specially carved wall niches. Corbett hid his surprise. Usually such underground tunnels were dark and filthy, with mouldering plaster and flaking ceilings, whilst the damp flagstones would be thick with lice and fleas. Such runnels ran beneath Newgate, the great White Tower and many of the royal palaces around London. This was a stark contrast. The walls and floor were of clear bright sandstone, the ceiling raftered with polished elm, the air sweet, with large vents high in the walls and pots of smoking herbs lining the stone shelves on either wall.

Corbett's curiosity and surprise deepened as they approached a huge grille-like gate. Again this had three locks requiring the attention of each of his companions. Beyond it was another similar set of gates. At last they reached the end of the passageway. Corbett stopped in amazement. Beyond the bars of a long cage stretched a truly sumptuous chamber: its ceiling was decorated a deep blue with golden stars, its walls were hidden under costly tapestries, the finest arras gleaming with gold and silver thread. Turkey rugs, pure wool matting dyed a deep scarlet, covered the floor. Capped braziers glowed softly and exuded thin streams of perfumed smoke, whilst shuttered vents in all three of the walls allowed in light and air. The furnishings were of richly polished wood; aumbries, chairs, a chancery desk, coffers and caskets and, in the far corner, a small four-poster bed, its blue and silver curtains pulled close. On either side of the bed stood tables containing shimmering jugs and goblets. There was a jakes cupboard in the far corner, pegs for clothing, and a well-furnished lavarium with jug, bowl and small trays for soap, razor and little pots of unguents.

Abbot Henry, leaning heavily on his walking cane, pointed at the door, which Crispin hurried to open, and Corbett followed his three companions into that luxurious yet eerie chamber. The abbot beat his cane on the floor. Corbett heard movement, a cough, followed by exclamations from the curtained four-poster, and its curtains were pulled back to reveal an extraordinary figure sitting on the edge of the bed.

The prisoner – Corbett realised it must be a man – got up and walked towards Abbot Henry. He was garbed in a brown woollen nightgown that covered him loosely from neck to sandalled feet; his head was cowled, his face hidden by a mask. Corbett, hiding his surprise, noticed how the apertures for eyes, nose and mouth were neat and precise, expertly cut and sewn. The leather was probably the best of Cordova or Toledo, supple as wool and easy to manage. From the softness of his ungloved hands and the way he walked, Corbett realised the mystery prisoner must be fairly young. He pulled back the cowl and the clerk glimpsed blond hair, coiffed and neatly cut, with a few strands protruding at the side and back of the mask.

The prisoner bowed to Abbot Henry, and Corbett moved away, walking around him to scrutinise the intricately fitted clasps at the back of the man's head that kept the mask in place, noting the small locks for keys that were undoubtedly held by the abbot.

'What is this?' he demanded. '*Who* is this? Abbot Henry, I have heard rumours, the tittle-tattle and gossip of the Secret Chancery. How a certain prisoner was being held fast, concealed from public view. But I never imagined anything like this. Would you remove the mask?'

'Yes, yes,' the abbot murmured. He opened his belt wallet and took out three very small keys, the type fashioned by the masters of the craft to open the delicate coffers and caskets of high-born court ladies. The masked man crouched in front of him. All was now deathly silent except for Maltravers murmuring to himself. He paused in what he was doing, beckoning at Crispin and Jude, telling them to prepare the chamber. The two men hastened to obey, arranging tables and chairs in a line close to the bed.

When the third clasp was loosened, the prisoner, head bowed, shook the mask off and straightened to stare directly at Corbett, who could only gape in surprise.

'Sir Hugh,' Brother Jude declared, 'what do you see?'

'In heaven's name,' the clerk exclaimed, 'I am looking at the king.'

The prisoner smiled and shrugged. 'Who am I?' he whispered.

'I cannot believe my eyes,' Corbett replied, 'but I would swear that you are the king's own twin, his blood brother.'

'Except for this.' The man turned his head slightly and Corbett could see the scar where his right ear should have been: a grievous wound, but now healed and almost hidden by the golden hair.

The clerk took a step closer. He reckoned the prisoner to be no more than thirty summers old. He was tall, slim, long-legged beneath the gown; his face was handsome, his skin the same tawny hue as that of the old king and his heir. His features were well formed, his blue eyes heavy-lidded – the left one slightly drooping, as with all the Plantagenets – his moustache and beard cleanly clipped and precise. He made a mocking bow, kicking away the mask on the floor beside him: even that gesture reminded Corbett of the old king, who had been free with both fist and boot.

'Monsieur.' The young man pointed. 'You must be Sir Hugh Corbett, Keeper of the Secret Seal. Abbot Henry told me you were coming and that you would be allowed to see me.' He turned to Maltravers, who stood leaning on his walking cane. Corbett noticed how the abbot's two henchmen stood like statues, keen to judge his reaction.

'Enough.' Maltravers tapped his cane on the floor. 'Let us make ourselves comfortable and then we can hold our council of secrets.'

The prisoner sat on the edge of the bed. Corbett and the rest took the chairs arranged to face him. The clerk was still surprised, though the shock of the revelation was now receding as he reflected on what he knew about the old king. Was this young man a true

Plantagenet? he wondered. Or the by-blow of some secret love affair? During the life of his beloved Eleanor, Edward had been faithful, but afterwards . . .

'It's best if we begin,' Maltravers declared harshly. 'Edmund,' he nodded at the prisoner, 'tell Sir Hugh who you are and why you are here.'

'My name, my name,' the young man sang. He paused to scratch the healed scar, and for just a few heartbeats, Corbett wondered if he was slightly awry in his wits. 'My name is Edmund Fitzroy.'

'Edmund, son of the king,' Corbett translated. 'Are you claiming to be the old king's son and heir?' He shook his head in disbelief.

'Tell Sir Hugh your story,' Brother Jude insisted.

'It is not a story,' Fitzroy protested, his lower lip jutting as if he was about to cry. 'It's the truth.'

'Then tell me,' Corbett declared softly. 'Master Edmund, I truly want to know who you are and why you are here.'

'And so you shall. I am the true son of Edward and his beloved wife Eleanor. I was born in Caernarvon Castle on the twenty-fifth of April in the year of our Lord 1284.'

Corbett hid his surprise at the declaration, as well as at the subtle change in Fitzroy's demeanour and speech, the prisoner becoming more confident and assured.

'When I was ten months old,' the young man continued, 'I was crawling across the inner bailey of Caernarvon Castle when I was attacked by a sow, which savaged my right ear. The royal nurse, absolutely terrified at the old king's violent temper, realised she might well hang for her neglect, so she changed me for the child of a thatcher, a baby boy with more than a passing resemblance to myself.'

'You have proof of this?' Corbett demanded. He glanced at his three companions, who sat stony-faced, their hands thrust inside the voluminous sleeves of their robes. He wondered if any of them kept a dagger concealed there. He felt as if he was in a dream here in this luxurious cell, deep in a lonely abbey fortress.

'What proof does he need?' Maltravers murmured. 'For heaven's sake, look at his face and tell me that he is not the old king's son.'

'But is he legitimate?'

'There are those who will say that he is,' Prior Jude declared. 'Think, Sir Hugh!'

Corbett caught his breath as he considered the possibilities. He kept his features schooled, but he recognised the threat implicit in Jude's words. All those who opposed the present king would be delighted to support a possible rival. He could just imagine how the subtle clerks of the great barons would weave their story, pointing out that the king was not fit to rule; that he was more interested in digging ditches and other farmyard tasks than in wearing the crown and ruling like a true prince. They would argue that his weaknesses, foibles and vices were due to the fact that he had been given something to which he had no right.

The clerk moved in his chair, leaning forward. 'So

you,' he pointed at Fitzroy, 'were exchanged for a peasant's son. Then what happened?'

'The royal nurse provided my foster parents with gold and silver, on condition they take me away and hide themselves in the fastness of the Welsh March.' Fitzroy shrugged. 'And so they did. Oh.' He paused and gestured to Abbot Henry. 'Perhaps we could have some ale. I have become quite thirsty.' He smiled crookedly.

'Yes, yes.' Corbett nodded.

Jude rose and crossed to a long polished serving table. He filled tankards from a jug, distributed these and retook his seat. As Corbett sipped at his ale, he forcibly reminded himself that this was no dream, despite the bizarre nature of what he was being told in this eerie chamber by such a mysterious individual.

'We came here to the Valley of Shadows, to its very end,' continued Fitzroy. 'We joined a settlement of foresters, charcoal burners and wood cutters. I had a happy childhood. I grew to manhood and never thought about who I truly was until . . .' He paused. 'Until the old king's soldiers, veterans of his wars in Wales, began to comment on my likeness to their royal master. My father, or rather my foster father, died a few years after we arrived in the valley: his wife always claimed that his death was due to the restless spirits that haunted the place.' Fitzroy narrowed his eyes. 'She was never at peace. She fell ill just after what was reckoned to be my eighteenth summer, a fever, some malignancy of the lungs. But before she died, she confessed to what had happened in that royal bailey at Caernarvon, though she begged me to remain silent, for if I proclaimed my truth to the world, my mouth would soon be stifled.'

'Did you tell anyone?' Corbett asked, aware of how still and quiet the chamber had fallen. He glanced at the others, who sat staring hard at the mysterious young man. He suspected that all three had played some part in the events now unfolding.

'I told Grunewald, one of three hermits who lived in an enclosure at the end of the valley, near Caerwent cliffs. There are a number of caves there, ancient dwellings, deep and broad, hollowed out before even Christ was born, or so they say.'

'And what did this Grunewald advise?'

'The same as my dying mother, but . . .' The prisoner pulled a face and sat blinking as though trying to recall something. 'Time passed,' he continued, fingers going to his lips. 'Then one day a party of horsemen arrived in the village, about ten in number. They rested their horses and asked for food and drink at the village alehouse, a tavern called the Glory of the Morning.' He laughed sharply. 'It was certainly not that. Its keeper, Osiric, however, was kind enough to provide me with work and lodgings after my mother died. I swept, cooked and cleaned.'

'These visitors, who were they?'

'At first, Sir Hugh, I thought little about them: mercenaries, wandering swordsmen looking for employment along the Welsh March. They stayed at the tavern for a few days, sleeping in what chambers and outhouses the hostelry could provide. Sometime later they were joined by another ten. Of course the villagers were surprised at the arrival of so many strangers in such a short time.'

'And you?' Corbett asked, his suspicions pricked. 'These men watched you, yes?'

'Yes, Sir Hugh they did. They also began to describe their lives as wandering swordsmen. I was fascinated and asked to become one of them; after all, there was nothing for me in the valley. I was keen to wander and savour the world they described. They offered me a mount and battle harness from their supplies. Of course I accepted, and became one of their company.'

'But who were they, these mercenaries?' Corbett demanded. He felt a tingle of fear as he recalled certain writs and letters he had studied in the Secret Chancery. 'And when did this happen, how long ago?'

'Eleven years ago.' Abbot Henry's voice was abrupt, incisive. 'You must have seen the letters, Sir Hugh?'

'Yes, yes, I did. Royal licences authorising the Knights of the Swan to ride hard and fast to this valley to apprehend certain traitors.'

'Let him tell his story.' Abbot Henry's voice was hardly above a whisper.

'They proclaimed themselves to be mercenaries.' Fitzroy's tone became a little more cultured, and Corbett wondered if this mysterious pretender was a mummer, ever ready to change masks as his story demanded. 'In truth, I am not too sure who they were. On more than one occasion they mentioned a lord, someone who called himself Paracelsus. To this day I do not know who they meant. I never discovered . . .' Fitzroy paused as Corbett abruptly rose to his feet.

'Sir Hugh?' Maltravers demanded.

Corbett just shook his head as he turned and walked to the door of this eerie midnight chamber. Paracelsus! He felt his mouth go dry. Paracelsus, that dweller in the dark, leader of a sinister coven that had spread its venom throughout the kingdom. A force from hell, dedicated to wreaking mayhem, chaos and anarchy at every turn. He had confronted such malignancy at another time and in other places. He had thought he had destroyed that cohort of hell earlier in the year, but now he wondered. Had those he garrotted on stakes along the shore beneath the towering crag of Tynemouth Priory only been one link in the chain? How far did that chain stretch? He had no proof, no evidence, yet he believed his presence here at Holyrood had something to do with those dark spirits. He took a deep breath and crossed himself; only time would tell.

'Sir Hugh?'

'My apologies, Lord Abbot, brothers.' Corbett retook his seat and pointed at Fitzroy. 'Do continue.'

'We must have travelled a day's journey, riding hard towards one of the ancient Roman roads, when one of the scouts came hurrying back. I was simply a rider in the group, but I realised something had alarmed my companions. We could not go on. We returned to the Valley of Shadows, and the leader of our cohort, a Scotsman called Dalrymple, asked for the villagers' support. What I did not realise until then was that the community my foster parents had fled to was, in the main, implacably opposed to the king of England and all his works. The families who dwelt there, relicts of certain clans and tribes, had fought strenuously for the Welsh prince Llywelyn and his brother David. When these two were slaughtered by Edward and his armies, those who could retreated into the vastness of the valley to shelter from English rule. They were left alone and so held their peace. However, when they heard that an English army might re-enter the valley, they decided to resist and joined the mercenaries in their retreat. Men, women and children, all fled to the cliffs of Caerwent.'

As Fitzroy sipped at his tankard, Corbett tried to recall all that he had learnt about this mysterious valley, which, he knew from the charts he had studied, ended in a soaring wall of rock.

'The mercenaries and the villagers fortified the caves,' Fitzroy continued. 'These could only be approached by goat paths, very steep shale-covered trackways. Both the villagers and the mercenaries believed the caves could be defended. Barricades were set up; from behind these they could loose a veritable storm of arrows and other missiles.'

'And water?' Corbett asked.

'Many of the caves were soaked due to hidden springs. Barrels of food and drink were also filled and taken there. As for what happened next . . .' Fitzroy's voice faltered and he gestured at the abbot.

'Sir Hugh.' Maltravers drew himself up, both hands resting on his walking cane. 'You asked if I, if we, had

ever threaded the full length of the Valley of Shadows.'
He paused. 'Of course we have, and he' – the abbot
pointed at Fitzroy – 'is the cause. Reports were received
at Westminster about a young man who bore a striking
resemblance to both the king and his heir, sheltering in
the Valley of Shadows along the Welsh March. So
concerned was the king that he decided to move his
court to Caernarvon. These reports were mere straw in
the wind, yet it was worrying enough that this young
man was also known to others and might pose a danger.'

'And who were these others?'

'We do not know; enemies of the king either within
or without. God knows, they are legion, be it Philip
of France or Bruce of Scotland, not to mention the
disaffected here in Wales.' The abbot banged his cane
against the floor. 'You know how such rumours can
spread and strengthen.' His tone was now pleading.
'Dust in the wind, yet still irritating. Suffice to say,' he
added briskly, 'the king and his Secret Chancery set up
a watch on all approaches to this valley. We learnt
soon enough about a force moving swiftly, well armed
with all the harness of war. The king ordered us, his
personal comitatus, the Knights of the Swan, to investigate.' He paused as if trying to choose his words
carefully. 'We were to provide what you clerks call *une
tiele remedie*.'

'A suitable remedy,' Corbett translated. 'In other
words, you were to kill that young man, removing the
problem completely.'

'In a word, yes.'

'Sir Hugh, you can imagine the problem.' Brother Jude spoke up. 'How can you attack caves that can only be approached by twisting goat paths? Our archers found it almost impossible to loose upwards at an enemy so deeply concealed.'

'We arrived and pitched camp.' Abbot Henry's eyes closed in concentration, seemingly lost in the past. 'It was autumn, a good season for war. The weather was warm, the ground underfoot firm. Any attack on the caves was soon beaten back, even if we approached with locked shields.' He opened his eyes and smiled as if savouring a memory. 'Edward the king eventually arrived and changed all that, as he did everything. We were not to attack from below, but from above.' His smile widened. 'You are surprised, Sir Hugh?'

'No, not by our old master.'

'Too true,' Maltravers whispered. 'Edward could and would do the unexpected. He brought up siege equipment, catapults and slings to pelt the caves with rocks and fire, though even that proved difficult. Eventually a traitor, a hunter, showed us a path that snaked around the cliffs to their summit. Edward was delighted and immediately ordered wood, ropes, pulleys and carts to be taken up.'

'Carts?' Corbett exclaimed.

'Yes, with their wheels removed. You've seen those war carts, Sir Hugh, planks of wood and iron clasps that can easily be assembled. Once we'd secured the ridge above the caves, we built fighting platforms that could be lowered by pulley from the summit. You can imagine how difficult it became for the defenders. If they came to the mouth of the caves, they would meet an arrow storm.'

Maltravers fell silent. Corbett stared at Fitzroy even as he imagined those fighting platforms being lowered by the king's engineers. So much effort, so much violence and bloodshed. So who really was this young man?

'I know what you're thinking.' Fitzroy declared.

'Do you now?' Corbett replied.

'Yes, yes I do. You are thinking that if I am the king's true son and heir and I was in those caves, I could have been killed.'

Corbett shrugged. 'I would hazard a guess that Edward demanded that the young man he was searching for be taken prisoner. Yes?'

'True.' Maltravers murmured.

'We took those caves one by one,' Prior Jude declared without raising his head, and Corbett felt a shiver. He knew the old king's reputation, his ferocious temper. 'We used long spears with hooks on the end. Those who did not die in the arrow storm, we dragged out for capture or just let them fall.' Jude pointed at Fitzroy. 'He was taken prisoner.'

'And the others?' Corbett demanded, even though he dreaded the answer.

'We took a few.'

'And the rest?'

'They were hanged, men, women and children.'

Corbett closed his eyes. Fitzroy put his face in his hands.

'We hanged them on the trees below the cliffs of Caerwent,' growled Maltravers. 'You knew the old king, Sir Hugh. He saw them all as traitors. He had unfurled his royal banner before the assault. He'd offered them terms for surrender; their only response was a shower of fire arrows. Some of them escaped, but the rest were slaughtered. We tried to plead with the king, but he was obdurate.'

Corbett stared at Fitzroy, who had now composed himself. The Keeper of the Secret Seal knew that Maltravers was telling the truth. The old king was ruthless and, when crossed, bloodthirsty in the extreme.

'I was spared,' Fitzroy said. 'But I saw others die, strangled on the end of a rope.'

Crispin spoke up. 'We were allowed to choose one or two captives to pardon. I took twins, two young boys no more than twelve summers old. I tried to comfort them, but one morning, just before we left the valley, they escaped.'

'I chose a young maid.' Jude murmured. 'But,' he shook his head, 'she died out of sheer grief.'

'And I chose Devizes,' Maltravers declared. 'A truer soul I cannot hope to meet.'

Corbett eased himself in his chair. The chamber had fallen silent. His companions seemed lost in their own thoughts, memories perhaps of those hurling, bloody days when Edward of England imposed his iron will. He closed his eyes and prayed quietly. Time and again he had advised his royal master to show mercy and pardon, but Edward was Edward. When he had fought Simon de Montfort, the king had extended the ban to Simon's entire family. He had seen himself as God's henchman on earth, with the power of life and death.

Corbett opened his eyes, fighting off a wave of sheer tiredness. He pointed at Fitzroy. 'When you were captured, what did the old king say?'

'Nothing,' Maltravers retorted swiftly. 'Isn't that right, Edmund? He said nothing to you except to tell him the same story you have told us.'

'I met him in the royal pavilion,' Fitzroy declared. 'He pitched it on that open ground before the cliffs of Caerwent. He sat slouched in a chair, staring at me in a way . . .' He shrugged. 'He frightened me, Sir Hugh. I was terrified.'

'And then?'

Fitzroy spread his hands as if to encompass the entire chamber. 'I was brought to a place like this, a gilded cage.'

'Tell me,' Corbett demanded. 'Tell me about Paracelsus.'

'I know nothing, Sir Hugh, except that I heard his name mentioned by the mercenaries and some of the villagers. They talked of him as if he was some lord and leader.'

'And the Black Chesters?' Corbett caught an abrupt sense of alarm from the prisoner, as well as unease from the others. Fitzroy's face changed, a fleeting expression of deep fear. 'You are glib and smooth in your speech.' The clerk decided to be blunt. 'But I feel you are not telling the truth, or at least not all of it.'

'I . . . I know of the Black Chesters,' Fitzroy stammered. 'I have been asked about them. Those mercenaries may have been part of their coven, but . . .' His voice rose in a wail. 'I am what I am. I know nothing about secret societies.'

'Who said they were secret?'

'Sir Hugh, do not try and trap me. I will tell you what I know. The mercenaries, as well as many of the villagers, mentioned the Black Chesters. They talked about them with deep respect, especially their leader, Paracelsus. When I first came to the village, I thought what I saw was the truth: men and women trying to live their lives. It was only when the mercenaries arrived that I learnt about Paracelsus, the Black Chesters, but even then it was only murmured words or whispered phrases.'

'Sir Hugh,' Maltravers intervened, 'our guest, this young man, knows very little about politics; he is what he is.'

'And after his capture?'

'As he has said, he was moved from one gilded cage to another, this royal castle or that royal palace, usually in London or places such as Kings Langley. The old king stipulated that the mask be worn, and when he was moved, he was always confined in a covered litter. Our master also demanded that he remain constantly under our watch.'

'And our present king, surely he knows about this?'

'Of course, Sir Hugh, but the hour is now late; night draws on. Perhaps we can discuss such matters in my chamber?'

*

81

A short while later, with the handsome Devizes leading the way, Corbett and the others left the prisoner and climbed the steps of Falcon Tower to the abbot's palatial chamber. A truly princely room, well furnished, even opulent, with thick Turkey rugs on the floor, its walls covered with brilliantly hued tapestries. The air was heavy with perfumed smoke from the fire, and braziers where small pouches of herbs and spices shrivelled in the heat.

Corbett made himself comfortable in a chair set before the fire, as did the others. Devizes served richly mulled wine. The clerk sipped this as he studied the young man, the only known survivor of a hideous massacre. He quietly conceded to himself that Devizes was truly handsome, noting the beautiful oiled skin, the carefully coiffed blond hair, the supple wrists. Devizes' long fingers were decorated with rings, their stones shimmering in the light from the fire and the dancing flames of the pure beeswax candles that Raphael the sacristan had placed around the chamber. At first glance the young man might be regarded as effete, yet there was something dangerous about him. He was a street fighter, probably well versed in dagger play and the clash of the sword. Corbett sensed this just by the way Devizes moved, how his long fingers would fall as if to caress the jewelled pommel of the long, thin Italian dagger hanging in its brocaded sheath from his war belt.

The master-at-arms caught Corbett's stare. He smiled and crouched beside him, jug at the ready to refill his goblet. The clerk allowed him to, smiling his thanks.

'You are staring at me,' Devizes declared. 'You have

seen me before, Sir Hugh?' His voice was soft, pleasant, with more than a tinge of an accent.

'Of course not,' Corbett murmured, toasting the young man with his goblet. 'But I have just learnt of your origins. How you came to be here.'

'Through God's own special grace and the favour of Abbot Henry.' Devizes' smile faded. 'Sir Hugh, I am Abbot Henry's man, body and soul, in peace and war.' The smile returned, the full red lips parting to show even, white teeth. 'But such devotion is not difficult. Abbot Henry is a great lord.'

He fell silent as Maltravers banged his tankard on the arm of his throne-like chair before turning to whisper to Crispin on his right and then Jude on his left. 'Devizes,' the abbot ordered, 'guard the door.' Once the master-at-arms had left, Maltravers leant forward, hands out towards the flames. 'Sir Hugh, you must have questions?'

'I certainly do. And the principal one is who is that prisoner and what will happen to him?'

'You are brusque and I will respond in kind. The accepted wisdom is that our prisoner is a by-blow of the old king or of our former master's brother Edmund Crouchback, Earl of Lancaster, father of the present Lord Thomas . . .' Maltravers let his words drift. Corbett recognised the abbot's reluctance to talk about Lord Thomas, leader of the baronial opposition and the most fervent adversary of the present king and his Gascon favourite Gaveston. According to Lancaster's proclamation, Gaveston was the son of a witch and a catamite, filthier than any whore from the stews of Southwark.

Edward and Gaveston had not overlooked such insults, and everyone recognised that the king's struggle with Lancaster would be to the very death.'

'So,' the clerk chose his words carefully, 'Edmund Fitzroy is illegitimate and our present king accepts this?'

'Yes.'

'And what does he want done?'

'In this vale of tears, Sir Hugh,' Brother Jude cleared his throat, 'the most pragmatic solution would be to kill Fitzroy. Yes, I know that is stark and cruel, but what if the opponents of the present king, or indeed anyone opposed to the Crown, seized that young man and proclaimed him to be our legitimate ruler? This kingdom could dissolve into conflict. So perhaps it is best that one man die than the realm be riven by bloody civil war.'

Corbett stared at the gargoyles carved on each corner of the cavernous hearth shaped like a dragon's snout. One depicted a jester, his stupid face framed by a hood festooned with bells. The other was a monk, fat-faced and cross-eyed. He glanced away as he reflected on what had been said. Was Brother Jude correct? Should he also quote scripture and claim that 'it was best if one man died for the people'? Nevertheless, in the end, neither the old king nor his successor wanted the blood of their possible kinsman – and an innocent one at that – on their hands.

'So what is the remedy?' the clerk demanded. 'Life imprisonment, constantly guarded? But what happens, Abbot Henry, when you and your brothers here have gone to God? Who will care for him then? Surely they will think of a more ruthless conclusion to all this?'

'Sir Hugh.' Maltravers scratched his head. 'That is one question we have also asked but never answered. Perhaps you can offer some solution?'

Corbett tapped his fingers as he stared into the fire. The question of the prisoner was vexing, but there were other matters to address.

'Abbot Henry, brothers, I mentioned the Black Chesters. I sensed your unease.'

'Of course you did,' Crispin declared. 'We know who they are, Sir Hugh: a secret society, a witches' coven dedicated to anarchy and chaos, its adherents implacably opposed to the law of Christ and the way of Holy Mother Church. They can be found in all places, be it a monastery, or a chamber in a royal palace. Our late master talked of them, but during his reign they really never manifested themselves.'

'Except here,' Corbett interrupted. 'They sheltered our prisoner, they opposed our king, and that explains his ruthlessness. But do you know anything else?'

'Once we left the valley,' Maltravers declared, 'we heard very little about the Black Chesters. Indeed, since then, our only news has been rumours that you, Sir Hugh, had a most violent confrontation with them along the Scottish March and utterly destroyed them.'

'I would like to think so,' Corbett retorted. 'But, God be my witness, I am not too sure any more. If the Black Chesters have survived, then they will certainly see our prisoner as a great prize. Now correct me if I am wrong, but I believe you are thinking of transferring that prisoner to my care.'

PART TWO

Even brought face to face before the king himself,
John did not deny what he had already said.
Life of Edward II

orbett and Ranulf sat close to the hearth in the clerk's chamber in Osprey Tower. Corbett had left Maltravers and the others to their deliberations and returned to find Ranulf waiting for him. The Clerk of the Green Wax assured his master that Chanson was fast asleep, and as everyone knew, once the Clerk of the Stables fell into a deep slumber, even the last trumpet would not rouse him. Corbett refused the offer of a drink or the dried meats a lay brother had brought. He still felt warmed by the mulled wine he had recently drunk.

Once he had returned, he had wasted no time. He had sworn Ranulf to secrecy, his hand over a crucifix, before informing him about Fitzroy and the possible dangers that young man faced, as well as those he posed to both Crown and kingdom. When Corbett had finished speaking, Ranulf rose, pacing the chamber, scratching his cropped hair, as he always did when deeply agitated.

'What can be done, master?' he demanded. 'What will happen? Do we spend the rest of our lives guarding such a prisoner? And where? At Leighton? Or do we cart him off to some far-flung monastery in Cornwall, or even better, the wilds of Ireland? If people learn of our secret – and they undoubtedly will – we will be swept up in the tempest! Sweet Lord, help us!' He came back and stood over Corbett. 'Master, you know there are those powerful enough to seize on all this. They would reject our true king as a peasant's son who seems more interested in gardening than ruling. Such opponents would use it as a pretext for civil war, and yet . . .' Ranulf paused. 'Do you think the prisoner is telling the truth? Is he the old king's true heir, our legitimate ruler?'

'Ranulf, I truly don't know. But do you remember Mistletoe?'

'Mistletoe?' Ranulf exclaimed. 'Yes, it's the name given to John Stroman, one of the Secret Chancery's most senior clerks. He always likes to wear sprigs of mistletoe; he believes they keep him safe in body and soul.'

'Yes, Ranulf, you are correct.' Corbett took a deep breath. 'Mistletoe could be of considerable assistance. Chanson will leave at first light. He is to travel as fast as he can to Tewkesbury. He will ask Mistletoe to carry out certain searches on my behalf. Mistletoe used to be a keeper of the records; more importantly, he has a nose for the scandals of the royal family.'

'I could go.'

'I need you here.' Corbett laughed. 'Chanson will go,

with letters from me. He will ask Mistletoe, out of the love he bears me, to divulge to no one else the task I have assigned to him.'

'Which is?'

'The task I have assigned to him in my letters,' Corbett quipped. 'And if he is successful, then I will tell you. Now, let Chanson sleep the sleep of the just: he will need all the rest he can get before his long ride back to Tewkesbury. In the meantime, let us concentrate on the present. We will list what is happening, even though everything seems cloaked and hidden, a deeply murderous mystery.'

He pulled across a sheet of scrubbed vellum and the chancery tray Ranulf had taken from his panniers. He chose a sharpened quill and dipped it into the black ink shimmering in its capped pot, the clasp now pulled back. He waited until Ranulf sat down next to him and made his first entry as he half listened to the distant sounds of this lonely abbey fortress.

'Item.' He spoke as he wrote. 'Holyrood stands at the mouth of the Valley of Shadows; it now houses the old king's personal comitatus, the former Knights of the Swan, who are the reason for this abbey. They are, to all intents and purposes, monks, brothers who have taken vows of loyalty to the memory of their dead master as well as to the rule of St Benedict. They have been joined by others, lay brothers, who are probably members of their former retinues. In the end, Ranulf, these are warriors, soldiers, as skilled in combat as any Templar knight. They live their communal life and, bearing in mind their secret predilections and attitudes, are happy enough in a so-called celibate community. Henry Maltravers is their sworn lord abbot: Crispin, Jude and Raphael his principle henchmen.

'Item. Life at Holyrood was calm and harmonious until recently, when suddenly, without any apparent reason, three of the brothers, all former Knights of the Swan, were brutally murdered. One in his chamber, another on the steps of a tower and a third in a kitchen yard, this last killing occurring on the very evening we arrived here.' Corbett glanced up. 'Indeed, a great deal has happened to mark our arrival. Is that significant? Is Brother Mark's death linked to us and our mission? A show of defiance?'

'You are correct,' Ranulf agreed. 'Much has happened since we came. We must not forget the fire arrows, or the murder of that sentry high on the walls, as well as the attack on us.'

'I don't think we were chosen because of who we are, Ranulf; it was simply that we were in the wrong place at the wrong time.'

'So why was that attack launched?'

'To frighten, to cow the community of Holyrood, the same tricks and stratagems used by the Welsh tribes when they fought Edward and his armies.'

'And the guards and sentries along the walls?'

'To make them more cautious?'

Corbett abruptly rose to his feet and began to pace the chamber. He felt very tired, but also fearful. He was aware of encroaching danger, yet he could not define what this actually was, or where it might spring from. 'What if . . .' He returned to his seat. 'What if a hostile force is slipping into the Valley of Shadows? If you were responsible for this, you would move men by night, yes?'

'Oh sweet Lord.' Ranulf leant forward. 'Sir Hugh, I follow your logic. Those fire arrows and the killing of the sentry, they were not just to terrify but to distract. If the sentries along our defences fear attack, they will seek shelter. They will not be so keen to stare out, to lean against the crenellations and gaze into the dark.'

'So if anyone wished to move soldiers into the valley,' Corbett repeated, 'what better time than at night, especially when the watchmen at Holyrood are no longer vigilant, but hide away, fearful of arrows whipping through the dark.'

'But what hostile force, Sir Hugh, and why?'

'Like you, Ranulf, I can only conjecture, I cannot give any logical explanation. I believe this abbey is being brought under close scrutiny, but as for the why and the wherefore . . .' Corbett waved a hand. 'We do not know, we can only conjecture, so let us return to the matters in hand.

'Item. The murders here are most mysterious. As for their motive.' He shrugged. 'We cannot say. And the how? Well, we have posed this problem before. How can an able-bodied man be slaughtered by a nail driven through his forehead?' He rolled the quill pen between his fingers. 'Brother Crispin showed us how it could be done, but that was on the corpse of an old man. Our three victims were warriors, fighters to their very core;

their resistance would have been fierce and ferocious. Oh, by the way, Ranulf, did you find out anything about that old man whose corpse we viewed? Who was he? Where did he come from? How did he die?'

'Sir Hugh, from the enquiries I made, he was a wandering beggar who presented himself at the abbey gate. He was admitted in accordance with the rule of St Benedict and granted the usual hospitality. He was taken to the guest house and given food and drink. By the time the lay brother returned, the old man had collapsed and died. The cause of his death seems natural enough: old age, exhaustion, the cold . . .'

'He did not look emaciated to me. I recall a sinewy body, but . . . Never mind, we can return to that by and by.' Corbett peered at his henchman. 'Do you know, Ranulf, I heard or saw something today that was not logical, but I cannot recall it because I am so tired.' He tapped the quill against his face. 'It will come back to me. In the end, these killings are shrouded in mystery. And what is their cause? Is there enmity between these former knights? Has something happened to provoke sudden bloody murder?'

He returned to his memorandum. 'Item. We also have visitors here. First, Roger Mortimer, the self-proclaimed justiciar in these parts. Mortimer claims the murders in Holyrood should come under his scrutiny because they occurred in his jurisdiction. In fact, he is stretching the truth. These murders occurred on consecrated ground, church land, in an abbey directly under the protection of the Crown.'

'Hence our journey here.'

'Precisely, Ranulf, so what is the real reason for that sinister marcher lord's presence amongst us?' Corbett glanced across at his henchman. 'I understand he has brought a retinue of ruffians with him.'

'Armed to the teeth,' Ranulf agreed. 'The sweepings of every prison along the Welsh March. Most of them should be decorating gibbets rather than riding horses.'

'They look like veterans, skilled fighters. According to Ap Ythel, they claim to be honest men, not thieves.'

'I would agree.' Ranulf laughed sharply. 'They just find it difficult to distinguish between their property and everybody else's. I would certainly advise our good father abbot to watch anything that can be moved; they certainly will.'

Corbett smiled and paused to choose a fresh quill pen. 'Item,' he continued. 'Just as mysterious is the presence of the French envoy, Monsieur Amaury de Craon. Oh, I know all about his invitations and his so-called deep concern for one of the brothers slain here, but I don't believe a word he says. Why is he really here? To meddle, to plot, to conspire? De Craon is attracted to treachery as a mouse to cheese. Something in this abbey warrants his presence here. And so we come to Edmund Fitzroy. Now that the shock of meeting him has receded, I must confront the issue of that young man's origins, as well as what should happen to him both now and in the future.'

'And as you have said,' Ranulf pointed out, 'we must also consider that our secret is not such a great secret any more. News of our prisoner has seeped out: it could well be the true reason for Mortimer and de Craon's deep interest in this abbey. Sir Hugh, I appreciate that Fitzroy's identity is closely guarded, but we all know there is no such thing as a real secret. I suggest both Mortimer and de Craon are here to fish in troubled waters, or even just to disturb such muddy waters for the sake of the stink.'

'Possibly, Ranulf, and that brings us to the next problem.' Corbett paused. 'Item. The Valley of Shadows. We now know that a hideous massacre took place there eleven years ago, when the old king seized Edmund Fitzroy. The valley still holds secrets and may well house a coven bitterly opposed to this abbey and any semblance of English authority, though that too is still a matter of pure speculation. It could be the haunt of rebels, but it may also be a resting place, a refuge for the remnants of that malignant cohort, the Black Chesters.'

The clerk put his quill pen down and, despite the warmth of the chamber, suppressed a shiver. He rubbed his face in his hands and stared at his henchman. 'We see things,' he murmured. 'We hear things. We feel things but we don't know their origin. In a word, Ranulf, what if *we* are the cause of all this?' He paused. 'Have we been brought here for some great hurt, some deeply malicious mischief? Are all these mysteries like strands in a web spun around this abbey, hoping to draw us in? If that is so, then we must discover, track and kill the spider busy at the centre.'

*

96

Next morning, just before dawn, Corbett led his cavalcade from Holyrood. The clerk had slept well, risen
early and washed at the lavarium. He and his two
henchmen had broken their fast alone in the buttery.
After they'd finished, Corbett gave Chanson sealed
letters and instructions about his swift departure for
Tewkesbury Abbey. Once there, he was to seek out the
former clerk known as Mistletoe, deliver Corbett's
message and bring back his response. Chanson left,
riding one mount, with another galloping beside him.

Corbett's party mustered in the outer bailey. Ap Ythel
and eight of his archers were joined by a similar group
led by Mortimer, whilst Devizes fielded sixteen armoured
hobelars. Corbett demanded that each of these carry a
long kite shield lashed to the side of his high-horned
saddle. He also insisted on breaking out the royal
pennant proclaiming the king's personal insignia of three
lions rampant against a gloriously coloured field of
blue, gold and scarlet. Ignoring Mortimer's mumbled
claims about being the royal justiciar, Ranulf fastened
the stiffened pennant in place, positioning the butt of
the standard pole in a specially fashioned hole on his
right stirrup.

Corbett rode up and down the column, checking that
all was in order, then gave the signal and the cavalcade
clattered out of the bailey, thundering across the lowered
drawbridge and into the stinging morning air. As he
stared back at the abbey, it looked even more forbidding,
a towering mass of stone against an angry sky. He
abruptly crossed himself, raising his hand in salutation

to Abbot Henry and others watching their departure from the fighting platform above the fortified gatehouse. Then he pulled his deep capuchon forward, making sure the woollen coif beneath protected as much of his head and face as possible. He had heard the gossip of the stable yard, dire predictions that a fierce snow storm was gathering. He glanced up at the sky, grey and lowering. The chatter was correct. Heavy clouds were gathering over the Valleys of Shadows, floating like sombre angels towards Holyrood. Corbett reckoned it was certainly cold enough to snow, even as he winced against the icy wind, which cut at any exposed flesh.

Head down, the clerk slouched in the saddle, quietly reciting the Mercy Psalm. He glanced quickly at Ranulf riding beside him and noticed how his henchman had wrapped Ave beads around his gauntleted hand. Three of Ap Ythel's archers rode ahead of them, the rest of the cavalcade behind them, two abreast. The weather was bitter. All conversation died as they entered the mouth of the valley. Despite his years of campaigning in Wales, fighting for his very life on mist-shrouded hillsides, Corbett felt he was crossing a most forbidding landscape. The path they followed snaked along the narrow floor of the valley, and he felt the place, like some living thing, close on them in a deadly embrace.

Both sides of the valley were covered by a dense sea of trees of every kind, ancient forests and copses that had been allowed to grow and spread, tangling into each other to block out the light and create their own special darkness, where any monster or wolfshead could safely lurk, wait and watch. No forester or verderer had even attempted to clear a path. Now, in the heart of midwinter, most of the trees had lost their leaves in the turbulent autumn winds. Stark black branches, swept clean of all greenery, stretched up and out to sway slightly in the wind and so create a constant shuffling noise. Above the trees the hunting birds, hawks and other predators circled and cawed, keeping constant watch for any unsuspecting prey. Occasionally Corbett would glimpse some forest creature, fox, deer or the sloping body of a weasel, flit across their path from one wall of trees into the other. On one occasion he thought his eyes were playing tricks on him. He glanced to his left and was sure he glimpsed a woman garbed in a green robe and hood, a fairly old woman, just standing amongst the trees staring out at them. However, when he looked again, she had disappeared. He crossed himself and murmured a prayer for protection.

Ranulf had now stopped threading the beads and was quietly cursing, muttering how he truly hated such places. Corbett ignored him, turning to nod at Ap Ythel, who raised a hand and shouted an order to two of his bowmen. These skilled hunters slid from their saddles, one darting into the line of trees on their left, the other into the forest on their right, slipping through the darkness but keeping themselves visible to the cavalcade. At the same time both men were deep enough in the forest fringe that they could seek out any threat. This was the usual order of march through such a place; Corbett had done the same during the wars in Wales. He reckoned that any solitary enemy archer or hostile mass of men would find it difficult to hide or prepare an ambuscade unless they first approached the area that Ap Ythel's scouts were now patrolling. The cavalcade continued undisturbed. Nevertheless, Corbett felt a prickling unease at the oppressive silence, an ominous stillness that could not be explained yet which frayed the mind with all kinds of unnamed fears.

After about an hour's ride, Devizes declared that they must be halfway through the valley. Corbett ordered a rest so that the men could drink from wine skins and eat some of the fresh bread and dried meats the abbey buttery had supplied in linen bags. He himself took a gulp of wine and, chewing on a piece of bread, dismounted to stretch his legs, telling Ap Ythel to summon his scouts.

Both men were veteran archers with keen sight and a nose for mischief. They pulled back their hoods and eased the woollen coifs beneath. 'We saw nothing,' one of them declared in that lilting, sing-song voice of the Welsh.

'Aye,' the other agreed. 'We saw nothing, did we, Owein? But we felt something.'

'What?' Corbett turned his face against the sharp breeze, then stared up at the ravens, their black-feathered wings fluttering against a sky that had grown even more sullen and threatening.

'Sir Hugh,' Owein murmured, 'we know the forests of the night. Aye, that's what we call them. In a word, master . . .' He lapsed into Welsh before hastily correcting himself. 'We are not alone.' He gestured at his companion. 'Chelling feels the same. Glimpses, Sir Hugh. Shadows fluttering through the trees. You think all paths, if any, would be blocked, but they are not. Occasionally we stumbled on spindle-thin trackways, like those used by the deer, that wind around the trees and cut through the sprouting gorse.'

'And you suspect these shadows are really hunters?'

'Master, we are being followed. We are being watched, and whoever they are, I don't think they mean us well . . .' Owein broke off as one of the cavalcade yelled a warning, pointing up at the sky.

Corbett glanced up and saw the fire arrows loosed from the trees on one side being answered by two more from the other: flaming shafts streaking across the iron-grey sky. These caused consternation amongst the cavalcade, riders hastily dismounting as their horses, catching the panic, reared and whinnied, sharpened hooves scything the air. Men backed away from them, drawing their swords, archers stringing their war bows. Some of Devizes' retinue began to loosen the kite shields fastened to their saddle horns. At Corbett's request, Ap Ythel, assisted by Mortimer, moved amongst the men insisting on silence, urging them to sheath their weapons and calm the horses. At last, order was restored, the cavalcade using their mounts as a ring of defence against any possible attack. Ap Ythel dispatched scouts to search the trees on either side; these quickly returned, reporting they could detect nothing amiss.

Corbett ordered the troop to mount, and they slowly

continued their journey. In a sense, he was relieved. There was an enemy; it was not just a matter of frayed nerves or fearful thoughts. A hostile force was following them, and sooner or later, their foe would show their hand.

At last the trackway turned sharply and widened. The trees receded on either side and Corbett glimpsed the summit of Caerwent cliffs, a grim ridge of grey stone soaring above the treeline. They reached the village Fitzroy had described, a great clearing stretching either side of the trackway. As they entered, the first snowflakes fluttered down, thick white feathers cascading silently through the air. Corbett pushed on into the centre of the village, noting the ruins either side, wattle-and-daub cottages, their wooden pillars and thatched roofs much decayed. All the doors and lintels had been removed, and he recalled the old king's assault on the caves. He must have seized already-cut timber, both here and elsewhere, to build his fighting sledges and platforms. The tavern the Glory of the Morning stood at the centre of the village, nothing more than a derelict ruin, with only a bare shell of crumbling walls. As with other dwellings, the fencing, pens, stables and outhouses had either collapsed or been wrenched down. Corbett felt he was entering a land of ghosts, a place of devastation and desolation, the haunt and home of birds and wild animals.

'Nothing,' Ranulf murmured. 'Look around, master, nothing but the faded, shattered remnants of what used to be a village, with all of its . . .' He paused as one of the outriders Corbett had dispatched along the trackway came thundering back.

'Sir Hugh!' the man shouted. 'My lord.' He gestured at Mortimer. 'You must see this.'

He turned his horse. Corbett raised a hand at the cavalcade and followed. The snow was now beginning to thicken, a falling sheet of white that would soon cover everything. They left the village and rounded a sharp corner to face a stretch of shale-covered ground that stretched to the foot of the cliffs. The outrider reined in, pointing to five poles in the middle of this open area. The poles had been hammered into the earth, and on each a severed head had been thrust, the faces hidden by straggling, blood-caked hair.

Corbett told the rest to wait as he, Ranulf and Ap Ythel dismounted.

'I'll go too!' Devizes shouted.

Corbett nodded in agreement and walked slowly towards the poles. As he approached, he saw that what had appeared to be mounds of rags were, on closer inspection, actually blood-soaked torsos. Once he reached the gruesome sight, he stood and stared at the pathetic remnants. All five heads had been greatly mauled by the weather, time and the hungry plucking of predators. The soft parts – nose, lips, ears and eyes – had been brutally scavenged, making hideous masks of what had once been the faces of men. Corbett stared pityingly at the abomination and quietly invoked the De Profundis, the church's psalm for the dead. Then he turned and walked round to the bundled torsos, staring down at the arrow shafts that had pierced the chest of each victim. He also noticed how their wrists had been tightly bound behind their backs.

'It's the hunting party.'

Corbett glanced over his shoulder. Devizes now stood before the poles, staring closely at the faces of the severed heads. 'I recognise them still,' the master-at-arms declared. 'Retainers of Brother Raphael, skilled hunters; they will be sorely missed.'

Corbett nodded and turned back, muttering a swift requiem as he and Ranulf walked closer to the cliff face. The snow was now falling heavily. Corbett stared at the bleak landscape before him and fought to control his fears, to quieten the panic curdling within him. This was a desolate place, a wilderness for both body and soul. He glanced up at the cliffs, then at the treeline on either side. Here Edward of England had sacrificed men, women and children to his own implacable will. According to Fitzroy, he had hanged his prisoners from these trees after he had slaughtered others.

Corbett peered up through the falling snow. Now that he had drawn closer, he could make out the mouths of the caves, noting how the rock around them was still blackened by the fiery missiles Edward had launched. He could also make out the arrow-thin trackways that threaded the rock face. He now understood the full story of what had happened here in the Valley of Shadows. Edmund Fitzroy, that mysterious royal prisoner, had been taken here as a child. Slowly but surely, the rumours about his parentage and his close similarity to the old king had leaked out. Fitzroy had stupidly confided in a hermit, and he, possibly because he was an adherent of that satanic coven the Black Chesters, had informed his masters, who would realise only too well the potential for mischief Fitzroy posed.

The mercenaries who had arrived here were Black Chesters, sent to collect Fitzroy; they in turn had been watched by the old king, who had also been alerted about what had happened. Only God knows how long Edward of England had watched and waited. However, once the Black Chesters made their move, he had taken action. The Knights of the Swan had swept into this valley like God's vengeance on horseback. Edward had followed to wreak his anger and utterly annihilate the threat. He had slaughtered the Black Chesters and their adherents, then captured Fitzroy, though he could not bring himself to execute his own blood.

Corbett could not prove that the Black Chesters had returned. Yet what other reason could there be for what was now happening? Was the valley inhabited by Welsh rebels, some tribe who had not submitted to English rule? If so, where were these from and why had they emerged now?

'Sir Hugh!'

'Yes, Ranulf.'

'We should return, get out of here as quickly as possible.'

'I agree, but this is going to be difficult.' Corbett continued to stare up at the caves: sombre, forbidding dark holes in the cliff face. 'Rest assured, Ranulf,' he declared, 'we have had some success. We now know what happened to that hunting party. We have also established that an enemy does lurk deep in this valley of desolation. We have confronted their threat. We have entered easily enough, though I suspect our return will not be so straightforward.'

He glanced across at the fringe of trees where undoubtedly the executions had taken place eleven years ago. He could almost imagine the bodies of men, women and children hanging from those sturdy black branches. Somewhere close would lie the small hummocks, now laced with snow, where the victims had been buried. He wondered who had carried out such an act of mercy, though there again, according to Maltravers, some of those who had taken refuge in the caves had escaped. Did they still haunt this valley? This bleak and terrible place, the wandering ground for vengeful ghosts whose brutal deaths screamed to be atoned for? And would this happen now? Would God's anger spill out against Holyrood and all who dwelt there? Corbett quietly prayed that it was not so, whispering a second requiem for the departed souls.

'Well, Corbett?'

The clerk turned to face Mortimer and Devizes; both had their heads and faces cowled and muffled.

'We will be attacked,' he declared. 'I am sure of it.'

'Why?' the marcher lord demanded. 'What makes you think that?'

'I don't think, I feel,' Corbett snapped. 'We have been

warned. We have been allowed to view the remains of the hunting party. Oh, by the way, they must be buried before we leave. Yes?'

'I'll see to that,' Devizes offered.

Corbett smiled and pointed at the scarlet hood the master-at-arms wore. 'It looks pretty enough, but is that wise? Such a colour will single you out for any bowman.'

Devizes smiled back. 'Forgive me, Sir Hugh, but this is a holy hood, a gift from Father Abbot: it contains a relic, the fragments of a bone from a Welsh saint stitched into the lining.' He touched the hood with his fingers. 'It always keeps me safe, but . . .' his voice turned brisk, 'I agree with you, Sir Hugh. We should return, and the sooner the better.'

'But first the dead!' Corbett declared. 'And Master Devizes, when we leave, I want your hobelars to ring our cavalcade. Make sure the horses are rested.' He wiped the snow from his face. 'At my command, we'll leave and ride swiftly.'

Once the burials were hastily completed, Devizes' men hacking the hard earth to create shallow graves with a crudely fashioned cross above each, the troop reassembled, surrounded by the hobelars, who now held their kite shields to create a moving wall of steel. Corbett lifted his hand, then led them into a canter. The snow was beginning to thicken, turning into a veritable blizzard. The cavalcade thundered through this wall of whiteness, horses whinnying, hooves skittering, men cursing as they lurched on their mounts, hampered by the constant flakes covering eyes and muzzles. Corbett kept his head down, reins held loosely, ready to dismount, his right hand never far from the pommel of his war sword.

The attack, when it came, was almost a relief from the constant pounding of the horses and the clatter of steel. A horn brayed from the trees and arrows whipped through the air. One of Mortimer's ruffians was struck, an arrow clean through his throat; he was dead before he tipped from the saddle, blood spurting, gushing out like wine from a split cask. Corbett screamed at the hobelars to raise and lock shields against another volley even as one of Ap Ythel's men slid from his horse. The archer turned the stricken man over, then declared that he was dead and there was little to be done. Another rider, one of Devizes', was also struck and knocked him from the saddle, to be kicked and trampled under the sharp hooves of other horses.

Corbett, wiping the snow from his face, yelled that they all must follow as he urged his horse into a full gallop. The kite shields were protection enough: they had to keep moving forward. They must follow the trackway and ignore the assault, though he suspected the arrow storm was only a prelude of worse to come.

He was soon proved right. They rounded a bend, following the narrow pathway between the trees. Corbett glimpsed a barricade set up further along the trackway, fallen branches, logs, planks of wood and thorny gorse. Recalling his campaigning days along the Welsh valleys, he reined in, shouting at Ranulf to keep close. He ordered the hobelars to dismount and use their kite shields to form an arc, with Ap Ythel's bowmen and others close behind.

'Whatever happens to me,' he whispered hoarsely to Ranulf, 'keep the hobelars moving forward; they will protect the archers. My lord Mortimer,' he called across to the marcher lord, 'your men should dismount and look after the horses. Bring them up, but only deploy them once the barricade is broken. Devizes,' he shouted at the master-at-arms, already busy organising his shield men, 'keep advancing whatever the cost.'

He glanced up the trackway. The enemy probably hoped the mounted force would charge the barricade, to be brought down by a hail of arrows as they became entangled in the branches and gorse. 'Oh no! Oh no!' he whispered to himself. 'You are in for a surprise.'

The hobelars were now arrayed in a small semicircle, which protected both the front flanks of Corbett's force. On his shouted order, they shuffled forward, then paused as a volley of arrows poured from the barricade; these either flew too high or thudded into the great shields. Archers hidden in the trees either side also loosed, but the shield wall held and then abruptly parted so that Ap Ythel's bowmen could retaliate. A volley of well-aimed shafts to the left and right sent men tumbling, pierced in the face, belly and chest.

The shield wall continued to approach, until they were so close, the enemy had no choice but to climb onto the top of their barricade to attack with sling and arrow, yet this made them clear targets for Ap Ythel's master bowmen, who were now loosing shaft after shaft. The hobelars, using their long spears, began to drag away the hastily assembled obstacle, pulling down logs, gorse and rocks. Corbett glanced over his shoulder to where Mortimer and the rest of Devizes' men were now mounted. A troop of cavalry, impatient to charge. He gestured for them to move forward, pointing to the narrow path that had been cut through the barricade. Archers and hobelars stood aside as he led his horsemen through.

The enemy now realised the growing danger and swiftly retreated, darting figures garbed in the brown and green of the forest. They were desperate to get off the trackway and hide amongst the trees, their only defence against horsemen. Corbett yelled to his troop that they should take prisoners, then they closed with a line of the enemy trying to defend their comrades' retreat.

Like all such clashes, the fighting grew frenetic. Corbett glimpsed dark bearded faces, wild eyes and snarling mouths. The enemy danced to the left and right of the horsemen in a flurry of knives, clubs, swords and axes. Corbett, both hands gripping his war sword, brought the blade down like a hammer, slashing at his opponents. Blood splashed and gushed, turning the snow a deep, soggy scarlet. Screams, war cries and curses rose then fell abruptly silent; the enemy had either fallen or fled. Mortimer and Devizes shouted at their horsemen not to follow their assailants into the treeline. Corbett, wiping his face of snow and sweat, slouched in the saddle, sword down, as he caught his breath and waited for the surge of nausea to subside.

Ranulf called his name, pushing his horse up along-side Corbett's, tapping his master's blade with his own.

'It's finished,' he murmured. 'It's over.'

'It's never finished, Ranulf.' Corbett raised his sword in swift salute, then sheathed it and stared around. Most of the cavalcade had dismounted and were tending to the dead and wounded. Devizes, his face blotched with blood, hurried up to declare that they had lost three hobelars, with about five wounded men, most of them lightly injured.

'And prisoners?' Corbett demanded.

Devizes gestured at Ap Ythel's archers, who held two captives close and bound. Elsewhere Corbett's men moved amongst the enemy wounded, misericord daggers at the ready to give the sorely injured the mercy cut, a slash across the throat to soothe all pain. The snow-covered ground had turned into a red slush, the blood seeping out to form puddles. Two of the horses had also been badly mauled, their legs broken, so these were unharnessed and taken into the treeline for a swift dagger thrust. The air reeked of that strange iron tang that always hung over a bloodletting.

The mad fury of battle was now ebbing away. Men became busy collecting fallen weapons and searching the dead for any valuables. Corbett dug in his spurs and guided his whinnying mount across the battlefield to where the two prisoners stood bound hand and foot, closely guarded by Ap Ythel's archers. He ordered their tarred hoods to be pulled back and stared down at their faces. The captured men were thickly moustached and bearded, their high cheekbones scored and chafed by the cold, their eyes still full of fury from the fight.

'Who are you?' Corbett leant down. 'Where are you from? Why did you attack us?'

One of the prisoners lunged forward, mouth full of foaming spittle, which bubbled through twisted lips: his keeper struck him on the back and the man fell to his knees coughing and spluttering whilst his comrade shouted a tirade of Welsh. Corbett understood a few words, the usual insults and protests at English interference in Wales and their oppression of the tribes. He realised he would get no sense out of the men, at least not yet, and turned his horse away, half listening to Ranulf, who was listing the casualties of the battle, which included at least two dozen enemy killed. Corbett simply nodded and gazed around the gore-soaked snow and the tangled heap of enemy corpses. They would leave the dead to be collected and buried by their own kin. He could do no more than murmur a blessing, then he crossed himself, stood up in his stirrups and shouted that they would return to Holyrood. Mortimer and Devizes swiftly marshalled the cavalcade. Corbett urged them on, eager to be free of the baleful valley and return to some semblance of warmth and comfort at Holyrood.

On their return, Corbett and Ranulf joined Abbot Henry and his two henchmen, Jude and Crispin, in the warm, scented council chamber. Mortimer also attended, with Devizes as usual standing guard behind Abbot Henry's chair. The party had reached Holyrood without further trouble. The prisoners were now held fast in a cell deep beneath the Eagle Donjon, the wounded being tended to in the infirmary. Outside, darkness had fallen and the snowstorm increased in vigour. Corbett, with interruptions from Mortimer, described their journey through the valley to the cliffs of Caerwent, their discovery of the hunting party and the attack. Abbot Henry heard them out, elbows on the table, fingers steepled as if in prayer.

'So,' he sat back in his chair, 'we now know for certain that there is a hostile force deep in the valley. God only knows who they truly are.'

'And our situation?' Mortimer demanded. 'Outside, a blizzard blows. One of my men skilled in reading the weather believes this storm could last for days, with drifts at least a foot deep. Lord Abbot, we are besieged by both the elements and those hostiles who lurk in the valley. So what is our strength?'

'We have a comitatus of about seventy fighting men.' Ranulf declared. 'We could and should dispatch messengers to royal castles along the Welsh March.'

'I have sent couriers to my own estates,' Mortimer declared. 'They left early this morning; I am sure they escaped the storm.'

'We must not forget de Craon.' Brother Jude spoke, his voice tinged with mockery. 'The Frenchman is already protesting as if we are responsible for the snow.'

Corbett was about to ask what supplies the castle held when a furious knocking on the door stilled all conversation. A lay brother entered, whispering to

Devizes, who passed the message to Abbot Henry. Maltravers, head down, listened intently, then glanced up, staring bleakly down the table.

'My Lord Abbot?' Mortimer demanded.

'Your two prisoners, Sir Hugh; they have both been found dead in their cell.'

Devizes and a group of lay brothers carrying flaming torches led the abbot, Corbett and the rest out of the council chamber and into the freezing night air. The snow was still falling, a curtain of white to carpet and cover every open ledge and space. Corbett, hood pulled tight, his cloak wrapped close about him, stared around. He felt this was a place of real danger. Some demon prowled here, turning the abbey into a house of murder. He decided to watch and wait before he moved to any judgement. They crossed the bailey towards a door already opened leading down beneath the massive donjon. More lay brothers clustered there holding torches and lanterns. Abbot Henry, hobbling on his cane, testily demanded to be taken down the steps into the passageway that ran beneath the keep. This was a freezing-cold, sombre tunnel, with fortified doors on either side above which cressets flickered in the piercing draughts. One of the doors had been flung open, its entrance filled with light.

Corbett hurriedly pushed himself forward to pluck at the abbot's sleeve. 'Lord Henry,' he whispered, 'perhaps it's best if I go first.'

The abbot peered angrily at Corbett, then his harsh face relaxed and he gestured at the open door. 'Go alone, Hugh,' he murmured, 'and God help us all.' He turned, telling his companions to wait.

Corbett stood on the threshold of the cell. Lay brothers had set down lanternhorns, and their shifting light revealed a scene of slaughter. The two prisoners lay spread-eagled on the ground, their heads haloed by thick, glistening puddles of blood. Corbett knelt and turned both corpses over. They were sprawled so close it looked as if they had collapsed into each other before falling to the ground; the cause of death was black iron nails driven deep into their foreheads.

Corbett gazed around. The cell was bleakly furnished, a straw-filled palliasse against each wall, a battered stool and a cracked jakes pot. He peered into this, wrinkling his nose at the stench of the urine swilling there, then returned to the corpses, examining their hands and faces. Apart from cuts and bruises probably inflicted during the bloody melee in the valley, he could detect nothing amiss. Both men were still garbed as he had seen them; little had changed. He closed his eyes and prayed. How had these men died? He opened his eyes. The cell showed no sign of disturbance. The threadbare blankets used to cover the mattresses had been pulled back, as if the prisoners had settled down there.

He heard a sound and glanced over his shoulder. Ranulf was standing on the threshold, staring across at him. 'Fetch me the janitor,' Corbett snapped.

Ranulf left, telling others to stay in the passageway, and returned with a burly lay brother garbed in brown with a thick leather apron strapped around his bulging belly. Its deep pockets held jangling rings of keys.

'Master?'

Corbett grasped the man by the shoulder and turned him, pointing first at the corpses and then at the door. 'What happened here? Tell me.'

'Sir Hugh,' the janitor stammered, 'I answer to the lord abbot.'

'You answer to the Crown, and in this place and at this time, that is me.'

'Ah well,' the janitor sighed. 'If you must know, the prisoners were brought down here . . .' He paused, glancing over Corbett's shoulder at the door.

Corbett turned. Ranulf had now stood aside to allow the abbot, Jude and Crispin as well as Mortimer into the doorway. He turned back to the janitor.

'I asked you a question. What happened here?'

'The prisoners were brought down and thrust into this cell. I personally locked the door; only I hold the keys.' The janitor tapped the pockets on his apron. 'I came back once and peered through the grille.'

Corbett crossed to the door and asked the abbot and the rest to stand aside. He then closed the door and peered through the grille, iron bars about an inch apart, a square aperture, unmarked in any way.

'Who else came down here?' he demanded.

'Sir Hugh.' Abbot Henry hobbled forward, his cane tapping the straw-covered floor. He sketched a blessing over the corpses, murmuring the requiem, then stared bleakly at Corbett. 'Hugh,' he repeated. 'We stand

beneath the great four-square Eagle Donjon; there are
tunnels and passageways on each of its sides. They all
lead down here. You have seen the Stygian darkness;
it's hard to see anything! Lay brothers come and go.
Remember, we guard against people breaking out, not
breaking in.'

'And you saw nothing?' Corbett demanded of the
janitor.

'Sir Hugh, I have talked to others, who will go on
oath. They saw and heard nothing untoward, I assure
you.'

'And the door was locked?'

'Of course, and as I have said, only I hold the keys.'

'The Angel of Death is here, dark and cowled,' a
voice bellowed. 'He is steeped in the deepest of shadows,
which are all tinged red. Behold, he comes. He demands:
are you ready? He whispers the words of the tomb so
the grave can open to receive the dead.'

'Shut up!' the janitor yelled, going to the door.

'My time has come,' the voice boomed back. 'I have
looked into the visions of the night; I have seen tribes
of sinners all drinking greedily from the cup of eternal
sorrow. The Angel of Death is here, flown up from the
hideous depths of hell.'

The janitor was now banging furiously on the cell
door opposite.

'Brother Norbert,' Abbot Henry whispered. 'Mad as
a March hare under a full moon. Usually he is quiet,
but he broached a cask of wine, and what you hear is
the result.' He turned back to the corpses. 'I will have

these anointed and buried if we can hack the earth open. Sir Hugh, is there anything else?'

'Nothing, except . . .' Corbett snapped his fingers and pointed to the door. 'I would like that left open.'

'Our meeting is not yet finished,' Mortimer declared.

'For the time being it is,' Corbett retorted. 'Ranulf, let us go.'

The two clerks returned to their chamber in Osprey Tower. Corbett pulled stools close to the glowing brazier; from the top of another one, he lifted a jug of mulled wine, a thick cloth wrapped around its handle. He filled two goblets, placing these on the table between the stools. 'We'll drink this,' he sat down, 'stare into the coals and get warm, then we are going back to that prison cell.' He winked at Ranulf. 'Brother Norbert, whoever he is, however frenetic, may have seen or heard something. I wish to question him.'

'And then?'

'I can only reflect,' Corbett pulled a face, 'and wait for my spy to manifest himself.'

'A spy?'

'Of course, Ranulf. Do you think the Secret Chancery would allow a place like Holyrood to live in peace and harmony without any survey or scrutiny? Oh no, ever since this abbey was founded, we have had our secret representative. However, until he decides to show himself, we can do nothing but wait.'

Corbett paused at a knock on the door. Ranulf went to open it, and Mortimer, all cloaked and hooded, swept into the chamber. Corbett rose to greet him, asking

Ranulf to fetch a stool and offering the marcher lord a goblet of mulled wine, which he gratefully accepted. Tossing his cloak onto the floor, Mortimer squatted down on the stool, staring narrow-eyed at Corbett.

'I wonder,' he murmured, 'why you are really here, clerk.'

'Wonder if you must, my lord. I am on the king's secret business.'

'Which is?'

'If I told you, it wouldn't be secret, would it?'

'Ah well.' Mortimer grinned. 'I have heard rumours about a certain prisoner.'

'Have you now?'

'As well as stories about Templar treasure hidden away here.'

'So that's why you're here? Not because of the murders, but to discover what you can about this mysterious abbey?'

'I am a marcher lord.' Mortimer spread his hands. 'I hear the gossip, the rumours, but . . .' he let his hands fall, 'I am genuinely concerned. I also heard rumours about men, armed and harnessed for war, assembling in the valley.'

'Why didn't you inform His Grace the king?'

'I did, but he is too busy playing with . . .' Mortimer glanced away. 'I did inform the king, but I received no reply. As for Abbot Henry, he knew nothing about such rumours.' He cleared his throat. 'I did my own searches. There was a hermit who lived in a cell close to my manor of Wigmore. I persuaded him, paying him good silver to act for me. I chose a man who could look and speak like a wandering beggar, a hermit, a holy man dedicated to God. Anyway, I asked this man to move into the Valley of Shadows and set up a hermitage. In the end, he did not take much persuasion. He was to discover what he could and, when I visited Holyrood, to meet me here.' Mortimer pulled a face. 'From the little I have learnt, my hermit kept faith. He dwelt in the valley and then came here as arranged, being shown to the guest house. However, a short while later, he apparently collapsed and died.'

'From natural causes?' Corbett queried.

'So it would appear, but one lay brother – in fact the one now chanting like a lunatic in his cell beneath the Eagle Donjon—'

'You mean Norbert?'

'Yes, Sir Hugh, Norbert.' Mortimer grimaced. 'Norbert's a drunk. He told me that when the beggar came here, he asked if I had arrived; of course I hadn't. A short time later, he was found dead.'

'So,' Corbett closed his eyes. 'You send a spy into the Valley of Shadows. You then arrange to meet him here, so the man knocks on the abbey gate and asks for shelter. He does not realise how our enemies press in from every side. He openly admits he is here to meet you, my lord Mortimer. He wants to share with you what he knows.' The clerk paused. 'However, you never learnt what he knew, and you suspect someone here realised who he truly was, why he had come, and so silenced him.'

'In a word, yes.'

'So why have you come to me, Mortimer?'

'Corbett, I am nervous, wary. Here we are sheltering in a desolate abbey fortress. Outside, the devil's own blizzard blows. A mere walk away, a determined enemy lurks deep in the vastness of the Valley of Shadows. This place houses about seventy fighting men, not to mention servitors and others. It's the depth of winter. We have diminishing supplies; certainly enough water from the well, but food?' Mortimer pulled a face. 'I am not too sure. It's a situation fraught with danger. I have already dispatched two couriers to my estates, the nearest manor house. I understand your messenger has also left?'

Corbett just stared at the marcher lord.

'No need for secrecy, Sir Hugh.'

'Oh, my lord, there's every reason for secrecy. I accept your description of Holyrood, but there is more to it than that. We are now in the house of murder, where brothers are slain, the abbot is poisoned, ambuscades are sprung, sentries killed, prisoners cruelly silenced. We are in a forest even more dangerous than any stretch of those dark-clustered trees in the Valley of Shadows, and who can we trust? You, my lord?'

'Of course.'

'Only time will tell.' Corbett rose. 'But now we have other matters to settle. Perhaps when we dine tonight, or some other time?'

Mortimer took the hint and left. Corbett closed the door behind him and sat down, hands out towards the brazier. He glanced at Ranulf, squatting cross-legged. 'So we enter the web,' he murmured. 'Well, Ranulf, let us follow one strand.'

They collected their cloaks and war belts, Corbett also picking up a small wine skin, and went down into the icy bailey and across to one of the passageways beneath the donjon. The row of cresset torches there created a world of fluttering shadows, so that it seemed as though shapes and forms crawled up the walls on either side or darted along the tunnel before them. Silence reigned, an ominous, baleful stillness. They passed the occasional lay brother busy on this task or that and, with the help of one of these, entered the gallery where the two prisoners had been housed. The door to their cell still hung open, though the corpses had been removed.

Corbett went in, wrinkling his nose at the foul smell. Again he could glimpse nothing untoward. He left the cell and went across to where Norbert was imprisoned, peering through the grille at the lay brother sprawled on a palliasse, snoring his head off. He ordered the lay brother who'd brought them to fetch the janitor as swiftly as possible. The man hurried off and returned with the grumbling janitor, who muttered under his breath about taking orders only from the lord abbot. He quickly fell silent when Ranulf drew his dagger and beat its pommel against the cell door.

Corbett heard a clatter from within, followed by moans and protests. He stood back and gestured at the janitor, who opened the door. The two clerks went in.

Norbert, bony-faced and balding, his eyes wet with sleep, his cheeks still flushed with wine, crouched, arms folded, against the wall. Corbett told the janitor to go back to the top of the passage and wait for his sign. Then, with Ranulf standing behind him, he squatted down and offered Norbert the small wine skin he'd brought from his chamber. The lay brother greedily snatched it, and slurped one mouthful after another until Corbett wrenched it from his grasp.

'What do you want?' Norbert gasped. 'You must want something.'

'The two prisoners in the cell opposite, the ones captured in the valley and brought down here, they were killed, murdered. You saw something, didn't you? You must have.' Corbett caught a knowing, cunning look in Norbert's eyes.

'You want the truth, clerk, don't you?' Norbert peered closer. 'Oh yes, I know who you are, and you should be warned. The devil has come to Holyrood, I have seen him. Oh yes! A misshapen creature with a twisted, ugly black shield on the slumped slope of his back. He carries a broad cutting lance against his scaly thigh. I saw him and his minion slip through a postern gate, to be met by another demon, who led them away. Oh yes, I see many things, I do. I creep around, a shadow without a form.' He chomped on his toothless gums. 'I see many strange things in the murk. Ghosts flit here and there. People appear where they should not be, in chambers with moving lights and dancing flames.'

'And the two prisoners?' Corbett lifted the wine skin.

'I can leave this with you, for what it's worth, and look . . .' He dug into his belt purse and brought out a coin, which he held up. 'Listen, Norbert, the snows will soon go. Spring will return. Merchants and travelling traders will visit Holyrood. Keep this coin and buy yourself something nice, yes?'

Norbert licked his lips, one claw-like hand going out.

'No, no.' Corbett put the wine skin and the coin on the ground beside him. 'Now,' he urged, 'tell me.'

'I heard a sound.' Norbert hugged himself. 'I was still full of the strong drink so I knew I had to be careful. I crept towards the door and peered out. The monster carried a mallet in one hand and a nail in the other. Oh yes, I am sure I saw that. Anyway, he turned, so I crouched down like a frog ready to spring, then I heard him hiss, "Are you ready to emulate?"'

'What?' Corbett demanded.

'Yes, clerk, I know it's strange, yet I am sure that's what he said.'

'Emulate – that means to copy, to be like something else,' Corbett murmured.

'He banged his mallet against the door and I heard a cry, followed by another, then he was gone and there was silence. Yes, silence!'

'And Mortimer's man, you met him in the guest house?'

'I passed him when he was sitting there. He was waiting for something to eat and drink. I bade him good day and asked him his business. He did not answer but simply asked if the lord Mortimer had arrived. I told him I didn't think so, but there again, that is not my business. Anyway, that man died too, didn't he? No mark of violence, not like the others with nails driven through their heads. He just died.' Norbert laughed. 'Probably just a lack of breath.'

'Is there anything else you can or want to tell me?'

'Perhaps, master,' again the cunning look, 'if you could leave that wine and the coin for sweetmeats, perhaps I will remember more. Then you can come back and visit poor Norbert.'

Corbett glanced over his shoulder at Ranulf and asked him to fetch the janitor, who returned, still muttering under his breath. The clerk ignored him and, plucking at his companion's sleeve, left the dungeon and returned to his chamber. He pressed a finger against his lips as a sign to Ranulf to remain silent until they were firmly ensconced before the hearth.

'What's the matter, Sir Hugh?'

'I do not trust Norbert and I certainly don't trust this place. Holyrood is a maze of winding stone passages, gloomy galleries and tortuous twisting tunnels where eavesdroppers can lurk like mute gargoyles in the murk. Anyway,' he sighed, 'what can we make of what Norbert told us?'

'Nothing, master. Nothing but the ravings of a lunatic, his wits even more twisted by cups of strong wine.'

'I don't know, Ranulf. Sometimes the mad see things we don't. I will reflect on what he said. Do you know, when we left that dungeon, I am sure we were being watched.' Corbett paused and smiled at a knock on the door. 'I thought so; our visitor has arrived. Let him in, Ranulf, I suspect I know who he is.'

Ranulf opened the door and, hiding his surprise, ushered Brother Raphael the sacristan to a stool.

'Welcome.' Corbett smiled, clasping his visitor's hand. '*Pax et bonum.*'

'And the same to you. Sir Hugh, at last we meet alone.'

'Indeed we do! Ranulf,' Corbett gestured at Raphael, 'our good friend here is . . . how can I put it?'

'Your spy?'

'Better than that, I would say our close ally here in Holyrood. Let me explain. The Knights of the Swan were, and still are, very important men. Once they were lords of the soil. They were our former king's personal bodyguard, his comitatus, his comrades in arms. They were Edward's men in peace and war, body and soul. They knew the royal secrets, or most of them.' Corbett smiled. 'Naturally, when they left the king's service, the Secret Chancery wanted to ensure,' again the smile, 'that everything remained as it should.'

'Hugh, Hugh,' Raphael declared, accepting a goblet of mulled wine. 'Be blunt! The Secret Chancery needed a spy here. I am your comrade, your good friend, but above all I was the old king's constant companion. I owe it to you and our present king to alert you to any mischief or threat to the Crown. If I am concerned, you will be the first to know.'

'And is there such a concern?' Ranulf asked.

'Yes, there certainly is,' Corbett replied. 'Raphael, tell him.'

'Monsieur Amaury de Craon!' Raphael placed his goblet on the table and waved a hand. 'Ostensibly the Frenchman is here because of Brother Richard's mysterious murder, as well as to convey invitations to pageants organised in Paris. Rest assured I think that's all a mockery. Amaury de Craon is here because of the Templars. You see,' he coughed, cleared his throat and then drank from his goblet, 'my father was a leading jewel merchant in London, a creator of beautiful objects. A man who loaned money to the Crown, especially when the old king refused to repay his loans to the Bardi banks of Florence. I entered the royal service and, like my compatriots, climbed the stair of preferment, from page to squire, to knight, to royal henchman and so on. The old king also retained me as his expert on precious stones and other jewels. Now, Ranulf, you must have seen the casket that holds the dagger used against our former king in Outremer: it hangs above the sanctuary in the abbey church.'

'I wasn't present,' Ranulf murmured, 'when you showed it to my master, but I have been in and glimpsed it from afar. They say it's an object of incredible beauty. A fitting container for that dagger.'

'It was not always so.' Raphael's voice became hushed. 'The old king used to keep the dagger in a jewelled box. However, in the spring of 1307, a few months before Edward died, Jacques de Molay, Grand Master of the Templars, secretly visited the English court. He was deeply fearful about what was happening in France. He had heard rumours, gossip, the secretive chatter from the Chambre Ardente.'

'Literally the Chamber of Fire.' Corbett glanced at Ranulf. 'You've probably heard it mentioned. The Chambre lies at the very heart of Philip's Secret Chancery in the Louvre, the centre of that great spider's web, where all kinds of mischief are concocted, plotted and carried through.'

'Too true, too true,' Raphael murmured. 'That's where Philip and his coven – de Nogaret, Marigny, de Craon and the rest – brew their pot of mischief. This time it was the total destruction of the Templar order and the seizure of all its treasures. Now Philip and his coven had heard how the Temple in Paris held a special casket, and believe me, the casket is unique. It is of great age, fashioned out of gold, silver and the world's most exquisitely beautiful pearls, all of which allegedly comes from the Holy of Holies, Solomon's temple in Jerusalem. Such a casket is worth at least a dozen king's ransoms, and of course, many think it possesses miraculous qualities.'

'And de Molay brought it to England?'

'Indeed he did, Ranulf. He entrusted it to Edward in return for guarantees from both the old king and his heir that they would do their very best to protect the Templars in England.'

'But they didn't . . . they haven't,' Ranulf declared. 'The order lies destroyed in this kingdom as it is in others.'

'Ah yes,' Corbett replied. 'But there has not been the wholesale torture and executions that has taken place in Paris and elsewhere. Anyway,' he sighed, 'the casket is now here.'

'It could be stolen.'

'No, Ranulf, it is a sacred object in a sacred place, well guarded by the former Knights of the Swan and their coterie. Moreover, if it was stolen, how could any thief sell it, whilst to break it up would be foolish. All of Europe would be alerted to its disappearance and the felon responsible would not only incur the wrath of the Crown but the full power of Holy Mother Church, who would proclaim the perpetrator excommunicate, worthy of eternal damnation.'

'Except . . .' Raphael interjected.

'Except for Philip of France,' Corbett murmured. 'I am certain that de Craon is not only here to check on the casket, but, if he can, to seize it for his royal master.'

'But that would incur the sanctions you have mentioned.'

'No, no, Philip is unique in this. The present pope, Bertrand de Got, Clement V, resides in Avignon, so he lies within the power of France. Clement will do whatever Philip tells him. Secondly, if he seized the casket, our French king would proclaim that he is no thief; that the casket was originally kept in the Temple of Paris, and, like all the order's goods, is forfeit to the French Crown. Finally,' Corbett rolled his goblet between his hands, 'as you know, Philip of France does not give a fig for either God or man.'

'But how will de Craon seize the casket?'

'I am not sure, Ranulf, and that's the mystery.'

'But that's why you're here, isn't it?' Raphael's tone turned accusatory. 'To collect that casket, as well as the mysterious prisoner we've housed ever since we arrived here.'

'Yes, Raphael, it is. I have in my chancery coffer letters, signed and sealed personally by our king, ordering me to do what is best, as well as instructing all loyal subjects to cooperate with me and support me in every way possible.'

'Father Abbot will resist.'

'Father Abbot, my friend, will do what he's told or this abbey will be occupied by royal troops.'

'And when will all this happen?'

'I cannot say, but at the right time and in the right place, I shall do the right thing.' Corbett paused. 'This snow storm has created new obstacles, new dangers, and will continue to do so. Now, my friend, what news?'

Raphael, who seemed deeply distracted, just shrugged and glanced away.

'The murders, the murders,' Corbett pressed on. 'When did they begin?'

'Brothers Richard and Anselm were murdered during the last few weeks, whilst Brother Mark was killed on the evening you arrived.'

'Raphael, why do you think they were murdered? Was there any grievance or dispute between these former knights?'

'No, much to the contrary. They were, we all are, good-hearted comrades, loyal and industrious. Hugh, remember that the bonds of our community were forged in battle. We have stood by each other over the years.

We became each other's family. We brought to Holyrood all our experience and skill.'

'And these dead brothers in their former lives?'

'Well, Anselm and Richard were master masons, royal engineers. They lived for construction, for developing strongholds. They chose the location for Holyrood, they cleared the site of ancient dwellings and other obstacles. They planned and supervised its construction and development around the great Eagle Donjon. They lived and worked in the mouth of that sombre valley whilst we toasted ourselves before the fire in royal palaces. They enjoyed nothing more than planning and designing this corridor, that gallery, a tower or a gatehouse.'

'So you know no reason for their brutal murder?'

'None.'

'And Brother Mark?'

'Well, as you know, he was in charge of the abbey kitchen, buttery and wardrobe. Mark, God rest him, liked nothing better than food and how to prepare this dish or that, be it lampreys highly spiced or veal cooked in the creamiest butter.'

'And yet he was found murdered, sprawled in his own kitchen yard?'

'God have mercy, yes he was.'

'And when the murders took place, where were the abbot and other Knights of the Swan?'

'Sir Hugh, that is a difficult question. When Mark was murdered, we were all in the abbey church, chanting compline. When Brother Richard was killed on those tower steps, we'd assembled to hear the lord abbot in our chapter house. As for Anselm, God knows when he was murdered; his cell door was unlocked, his corpse sprawled within.' Raphael paused, fingers going to his lips.

'My friend?' Corbett queried.

'Oh, just something about Brother Mark. You may recall how, on the evening of your arrival here, the same time Mark was found murdered, you and your companions were in the refectory. Lord Abbot and the other brothers were in church. I had left the sacristy to give Brother Mark a chest of candles for the kitchen. Anyway . . .' Raphael chewed his lip, 'if I recollect correctly, I was in a hurry. Brother Mark was counting the tankards, and as I passed, he made a strange remark. He said, "He hasn't returned it, and what business did he have taking it in the first place?"' He shook his head. 'No, Sir Hugh, I do not know what he meant. I found the remark strange, yet there again, Mark could be a true fusspot, especially about his kitchen and all it contained.'

He peered at Corbett. 'You asked for news, Sir Hugh. I live in a world of candlelight, both physically and spiritually. I try to keep free of the gossip and the rumours that run through a community such as ours. We do wonder why you're here, but I know that if I asked you directly, you wouldn't give me the full truth. You are a man of secrets.'

'And that's my calling, Raphael. The king expects me to be what I am. I have taken a great oath, a solemn vow to protect the Crown's secrets, yet we are still friends.' Corbett extended a hand for Raphael to clasp. The sacristan then rose, nodded to both clerks and left the chamber.

'Like a mist,' Ranulf whispered. 'The mysteries here are like a mist that crawls, twists and turns as it wishes. I am exhausted. I must sleep.' He made himself comfortable in the chair and closed his eyes.

The abbey bells began to clang the summons to compline. Corbett put a rug over the sleeping Ranulf and joined the community as they filed into the church, along the nave and into the choir. Here the brothers divided, shuffling into the raised benches either side. Corbett turned and went to the right, waiting to be ushered into a stall by a smiling lay brother who handed him a psalter. He glanced towards the sanctuary, where the candles blazed and flamed in dazzling pools of light. Abbot Henry stood in his throne-like stall, hands gripping the lectern as he gazed stonily around.

The leading cantor approached the lectern and intoned the opening psalm: 'In God is my trust, I shall not be confounded.' Corbett joined heartily in the responsive chant: 'I rejoiced when I heard them say, let us go to God's house, and now our feet are standing within your gates, O Jerusalem. Jerusalem is the walled city where the tribes go up, the tribes of the Lord . . .' The chanting continued, rising and falling, creating its own serene melody, in a place where the light shifted, flared and ebbed to gleam in the polished oak of the stalls and illuminate the earnest faces of the brothers, lost in this last great hymn of the day. 'One thing I have asked of the Lord, for this I long to dwell in the house of the Lord all the days of my life . . .'

Corbett, who knew many of the texts by heart, glanced around, his gaze caught by the eerie carvings of gargoyles and the comic faces and expressions they portrayed. Incense smoke curled and twisted around these, whilst the air was so cold that the breath of the chanting brothers could be seen hanging for a few heartbeats. The plainsong rolled on until a clatter further down the nave disturbed the service. A lay brother hastily entered the choir and climbed the steps into the abbot's stall. He whispered to Maltravers, who turned and had a swift word with Crispin and Jude. Both these worthies made to leave, gesturing at Corbett to join them outside the church, where the janitor was waiting, jangling his keys.

'It's Norbert,' the man blurted out. 'Dead in his cell like the rest. You'd best come.' He flailed a hand. 'Brother Crispin, Prior Jude, what is happening here?' He spread his hands as if to embrace the snow, still falling silently and steadily.

'Do not worry, Brother William,' Jude comforted him. 'Let us see this for ourselves.'

The janitor led them off. Corbett was surprised at how deep the snow now lay, a thick carpet that caught the legs and tripped the feet. All the abbey buildings were covered, every ledge, step, cornice and roof hidden beneath a gleaming white blanket. They reached one of the tunnels leading into the basement of the Eagle Donjon, its doorway guarded by two lay brothers wearing mailed hauberks, sword belts strapped around their waists. The janitor explained that similar guards watched the other three entrances. He then led them down a tunnel of deep darkness, a nightmare place despite the flaring torches, until they reached Norbert's cell.

'I didn't open it.' The janitor peered through the grille. 'Look!'

Corbett glanced in. Brother Norbert lay sprawled against the far wall, but the clerk guessed what had happened as he glimpsed the stud of a black nail driven through the victim's forehead. The janitor unlocked the door. Corbett told the rest to wait and went in. The cell was very similar to that which had housed the other two prisoners so recently slain. Norbert slumped dead-eyed against the wall, arms down, legs out. Corbett glanced around, but he could see no mark or sign of violence, no disturbance of the cell. The rickety stool, battered jakes pot and shabby palliasse were undisturbed. He crouched down and tipped the dead man's head back: Norbert's face was contorted in death, eyes rolled up as if trying to glimpse the black iron nail embedded deep in his brain.

'Driven with great force,' Corbett whispered. 'Though God knows how.' He got to his feet and returned to the door, beckoning the janitor closer. 'You know who came down here this evening?'

'Of course, Sir Hugh. Ever since the death of those two prisoners, no one except you is allowed in unless they state their business. You've been outside, Sir Hugh, it's freezing cold. None of our community would want to go out on a night like this to such a place as this. I have questioned those on guard; no one came here.'

Corbett shook his head in disbelief and left the cell. He bade his companions goodnight and ordered some food from the buttery, a servant taking the tray up to the clerk's chamber. Once there, Corbett roused Ranulf from his deep sleep and served the food: fresh chicken broiled and spiced, with the softest white bread from the abbey bakery and a jug of white Rhenish. Ranulf ate hungrily as Corbett told him what had happened. At last he put his horn spoon down.

'Master, how can we resolve all this, and if we cannot, how do we get out of such a benighted place? The snow lies thick; it will get even deeper. We cannot forage, send for help or try to escape. Even if we did, God know what lurks in and around that Valley of Shadows.'

The Clerk of the Green Wax's deepening apprehension was proved to be correct the next morning. Corbett and Ranulf had risen early and gone down to the abbey church, where Father Bernard, a former royal chaplain who had joined the community, celebrated a simple mass on the high altar. He had hardly finished the Ite, Missa Est when the abbey bell began to toll the tocsin, the alarm being taken up by the horns of the guards along the parapet.

Corbett and Ranulf joined the rest surging out of the church, braving the icy-cold breeze, which whipped up the snow. Corbett muttered a prayer of thanks that at least the blizzard had spent itself. They crossed the inner and outer baileys, heading for the steps leading to the fighting platform above the massive gatehouse. Devizes let them through, telling the others to wait. The two clerks clambered up the steps. Thankfully, both these and the parapet had been strewn with sand and pebbles to provide a better grip for their boots. Abbot Henry, Jude, Crispin and Raphael stood leaning against the crenellated wall, staring out across the broad frozen moat at the horrors placed there: two poles, each bearing a severed head, and close by, the mangled torsos almost sinking in a pool of bloody slush.

'Who are they?' Abbot Henry whispered. 'Jude, you have good sight. Devizes,' he shouted over his shoulder, 'silence those bells! Corbett, what do you think?'

'They are my men.' Mortimer came onto the parapet, his face flushed with fury. He leant against the wall, bracing himself as the wind whipped up the ice, then wiped his face and stared out at that sinister, silent abomination. 'They are my men.' He turned to Corbett standing beside him. 'You see, Sir Hugh, that brown and blue jerkin on the torso to the right; you can catch glimpses despite the snow and the blood. I am sure that's Gruffydd, a good man. I am not leaving him there. We have to bring his body back. Look!' Corbett did so. Already the glossy black ravens were circling the expected feast. 'Battle bird to the blood drinking,' Mortimer murmured. 'We cannot let them.' He turned as if to go, but Corbett caught him by the arm.

'Be careful, my lord, it could well be a trap.'

'What?' Mortimer snarled. 'Look to your left and right, clerk, there's no tree, bush or rock to hide behind.'

Corbett glanced across the great stretch of snow leading up into the narrow mouth of the valley. Mortimer was correct. Such open ground afforded little shelter, if any, to a lurking assassin. Yet the clerk still sensed a pressing danger. The poled heads were intended to warn and terrify, but they could also be a lure, the trap it concealed cunningly contrived.

'I will go with you,' he declared. 'No, Ranulf, you stay. Mortimer, order your hobelars to form a battle ring, kite shields locked together. It will be slow, but definitely safer.' Abbot Henry made to object, nervously fingering the pectoral cross hanging on the broad red ribbon around his neck. Corbett shook his head. 'Believe me,' he insisted, 'this mischief is not over yet. Our enemy is counting on us being stupid. He wants to draw us out to inflict murder and mayhem, so bear with me.'

Corbett clattered down the steps and nodded at Devizes, who stood, his scarlet hood pulled close against the cold. De Craon, clustered nearby with his clerks, smiled wolfishly. Corbett just glared back and followed Mortimer into the gatehouse. The marcher lord's hobelars swiftly assembled there. Corbett put on the mailed jerkin Ranulf brought, as well as a conical helmet, its broad nose-guard almost hiding his face. Then he and Mortimer stood in the shelter of the shield ring, along with Ap Ythel and four of his master bowmen. Sacks, rope and sheeting were loaded onto a sledge, pulled by two of the archers. Corbett gave a signal. The portcullis was raised and the drawbridge lowered in a clatter of wood, chain and screeching steel, a strident noise that must have echoed across to the valley mouth.

'If there is an enemy close by,' Mortimer murmured, adjusting his helmet, 'they now know we are coming.'

At Corbett's order, the shield ring moved out, crossing the drawbridge, booted feet shuffling through the deep snow that clogged and hindered their march. As he lurched forward, Corbett recalled Norbert's death and wondered what had truly happened in those cold, grim cells. How could a man be killed in such a way, a nail driven through his forehead? But that was only one mystery. How had the assassin got in? Norbert had been protected by a door, which had not been opened or forced. Nor had the cell inside been disturbed: it showed no sign of resistance or defence, or indeed any vestige of a struggle. Norbert's cell, like that which had housed the other two prisoners, was merely a block of hard stone, with no hiding place or secret entrance. Nevertheless, bloody murder had been committed. The only logical explanation was that the janitor had been involved in these deaths; that he had opened the door for the assassin. Or did someone else hold a key to those cells? Yet in the last resort, such explanations were tenuous. Even if the killer could somehow have slipped into the cells, Norbert and the other two victims would certainly have fought back, but not a shred of evidence pointed to this.

'Keep in formation.' Mortimer's harsh voice made Corbett glance up. They were now approaching the poles, with their hideous declaration. The clerk noticed how the ground around the gruesome scene had turned a frozen scarlet. He could detect no trace of any footprint or disturbance, and recalled how some Welsh tribesmen strapped thin wooden platters to their feet to slide across hard-packed snow. 'Heaven protect us,' Mortimer whispered. He raised his voice and shouted orders, and the hobelars parted.

Corbett and Mortimer went and knelt before the poles, while Ap Ythel helped drag the mangled torsos deep into the shield ring and onto the broad canvas cloth the archers had unrolled. Corbett tried not to look at the ravaged face in front of him. He put gauntleted hands firmly either side of the severed head and pulled it off the pole, a sickening sound, like that of sludge sliding down a sewer. Then he placed it in one of the sacks they had brought. While Mortimer did the same with the other head, the clerk stood, eyes closed, murmuring a prayer. At last he opened his eyes and stared at the two poles, black with the blood that had drenched them.

'Let's go,' he murmured. 'Let us leave this horrid execution ground.'

The hobelars reassembled. They were about to begin their cumbersome march back to the gatehouse when two arrows whirred through the air. One narrowly missed Mortimer's face, but the other struck a hobelar full in the nape of his neck. The shield wall had gaps, some at least a foot wide, that a sharp-eyed enemy could exploit.

'There!' Ap Ythel growled. Corbett followed his

pointing finger and glimpsed just in time what looked like a flapping white sheet fall to the ground. He ordered the shield wall to pause and close, then knelt in the middle with Mortimer and Ap Ythel.

'An old trick, Sir Hugh.' The captain of archers grinned. 'I've played it myself in the snow. Our enemy bowman, garbed completely in white, digs a pit and shelters there. Perhaps he brought a charcoal pot to keep himself warm. He definitely brought a white sheet to cover himself.' Ap Ythel pointed to the fallen hobelar. 'Very sharp, very good, precise, clean and swift: that man would have been dead before he fell. Be careful,' he added. 'There may be more than one.'

Mortimer turned and shouted to a soldier to collect the man's corpse and place it on the sledge so that it could be dragged back to Holyrood.

'We can't keep kneeling here like three nuns,' Mortimer snarled.

'Oh, don't you worry,' Ap Ythel retorted. 'If they can play tricks, so can we!' He winked at Corbett and moved at a crouch to peer through a gap in the shield wall. 'Brancepeth!' he called over his shoulder. One of the bowmen hurried towards him, and Ap Ythel spoke to him swiftly in Welsh. Brancepeth nodded and rose to his feet, rubbing his hands in glee. Ap Ythel then called over the remaining three bowmen. Two knelt, bows strung, on one flank of the shield wall. The third joined Ap Ythel on the other.

'What's happening, Corbett?' Mortimer wiped the snow-encrusted sweat from his face.

'I don't know, my lord, but I have a suspicion.'

'A clever Welsh game.' Ap Ythel grinned in a display of sharp white teeth. 'It's called "hunt the hunter with the hunted". Watch, my lord and you may learn something. Sir Hugh, let me do what I am best at.'

Corbett raised a hand. Ap Ythel notched an arrow and placed three more shafts on the ground beside him. His companions did the same. 'Are you ready, Brancepeth?' he called. 'Can you act the rabbit, the man fleeing from the terror of battle?'

'I am ready as ever, sir.'

'Good!' Ap Ythel gestured forward. Brancepeth moved to the front of the shield wall. 'Now!' the captain of archers shouted.

Brancepeth pushed through, knocking hobelars aside as he lumbered through the snow as if he could no longer stand the tension, desperate to reach the gatehouse. Corbett glimpsed a flurry of white, and an archer seemed to rise out of the ground, war bow in one hand, arrow shaft in the other.

'Brancepeth!' Ap Ythel screamed.

The fleeing man collapsed onto the snow as Ap Ythel loosed his own shaft, and his companion followed suit. Corbett glanced over his shoulder, peering through a gap. Another enemy bowman had appeared, but he seemed disconcerted by what was happening. A blood-chilling scream made him stumble back into the snow. Corbett looked towards Ap Ythel. The master bowman had been successful. The other enemy archer now lay stretched out on the ground, flung back by the two arrow shafts that had pierced belly and chest.

'Sir Hugh,' Ap Ythel crawled back to join Corbett, 'we should move, leave the enemy dead.'

Corbett got to his feet and issued the order, and the shield wall continued its slow, shuffling march towards the gatehouse. Now and again the clerk glanced back. The fallen enemy archer lay soaked in his own blood. Though his companion had decided to remain hidden, Corbett could hear his soul-wrenching screams.

'He is cursing in Welsh,' Ap Ythel murmured. 'The man I killed was his twin brother, but there again . . .' he shrugged, crossing himself, 'they have killed my kin, so I have a blood feud with them.'

The march continued. The small shield ring had almost reached the drawbridge when two more arrows whipped through the air, smashing into the shields. Corbett yelled at the hobelars to move as swiftly as possible. They did so, boots drumming on the draw-bridge. Once they had reached the safety of the cavernous gatehouse, the drawbridge was raised, the portcullis clattered down and the men began to tear off helmets and jerkins, their bodies drenched in sweat. Mortimer supervised the removal of the dead to the coffin chamber beneath the infirmary.

Once they'd disarmed, Corbett, Ranulf and Ap Ythel returned to their own quarters to wash and change before joining the abbot and his three henchmen, Crispin, Jude and Raphael, in the refectory, its doors closely guarded by Devizes and a retinue of lay brothers.

The buttery served bowls of hot oatmeal laced with honey and nutmeg, as well as tankards of morning ale, together with freshly baked bread, butter, and conserves made from the fruits gathered and dried the previous autumn. The abbot intoned the Benedicamus and the meal began.

Corbett, Ranulf and Mortimer ate silently, eager to satisfy their hunger and slake dry throats with refreshing ale. De Craon joined them just as the bread and fruit platters were passed around. The Frenchman bustled in, garbed in a scarlet and gold jupon under a blue and silver robe. His hair, moustache and beard were all neatly combed and coiffed, his eyes rounded in amazement at what he had seen and heard that morning, his mouth crammed with innocent-sounding questions.

'God save us from him,' Corbett whispered to Ranulf. 'A true Judas! He cries all hail when he means all harm.'

'Master, I agree. I wonder what role that French fox played in the bloody events of this morning . . .'

Abbot Henry called for their attention. 'God knows what was planned and plotted this morning,' he declared, looking up at Devizes, who stood, hand on the hilt of his sword, to the right of his chair. 'Sir Hugh, Lord Mortimer, perhaps you could enlighten us.'

'Better still,' Corbett retorted, turning to Ap Ythel, with whom he'd had a brief discussion before they had entered the refectory, 'my captain of archers will explain.'

Ap Ythel's strong, lilting voice echoed through the chamber. 'It was very easy for the enemy to set their snare. My lord Mortimer dispatched two couriers just before the blizzard swept in. Sometime last night, those two unfortunates were taken out onto that stretch of snow and decapitated.' He shrugged. 'Now the enemy, whoever they are – and I suspect they know the valley very well, in all sorts of weather – used the snow to cover their tracks. What they planned and plotted was very clever. The ground stretching out from the edge of the moat is furrowed, it ripples like the waves of the sea; the folds and ridges formed provide both protection and concealment. The bowmen who attacked us were clothed in white and used sheets of the same colour. They dug deep into the snow and waited for us to collect the dead. They expected us to go blundering out. On reflection, they could have killed all of us, one shaft after another. Imagine, my Lord Abbot, men desperate to escape, fleeing towards the drawbridge, lumbering and staggering through the snow.'

For a while Abbot Henry just sat, head down. Eventually he glanced up.

'And what now, Sir Hugh?' he asked. 'What do you propose? Captain Ap Ythel, can you see a way forward?'

Corbett gently tapped Ap Ythel's ankle with his boot, a reminder of what they had agreed before coming here. Neither of them was in any doubt that arrows had been loosed from inside the abbey fortress just before they reached the drawbridge. So there was not only an assassin prowling Holyrood but a dyed-in-the-wool traitor as well. For the moment, however, they'd decided to keep their suspicions secret.

'My comrade and I,' Corbett pushed away his tankard, 'will take careful counsel together, then we shall decide.'

'You'll inform us?' Mortimer barked.

'The other enemy archer.' Corbett chose to ignore the marcher lord. 'Father Abbot, you were standing on the gatehouse; you must have seen what happened.'

'He crawled away like the vermin he was.' Devizes answered for his master. He forced a smile. 'There was little we could do.'

'Leave the corpse to rot,' the abbot declared. 'It can lie as a warning to the rest.'

The meeting broke up, everyone eager to return to the warmth of their own chamber or to toast themselves before the roaring fire in the great hearth, which stood in the centre of the outside wall of the refectory. Ranulf and Ap Ythel followed Corbett up to his room. Once he had closed and locked the door behind them, the clerk carefully scrutinised the chamber, moving furniture, examining the floor and lifting the brightly coloured arras that covered the wall.

'Sir Hugh?'

He grinned at his two companions. 'Someone in this abbey fortress,' he declared, 'loosed those arrow shafts at us. They missed simply because they left it too late. We retreated swiftly to the gatehouse and across the drawbridge, so it would have been difficult for the would-be assassin to position himself properly and aim accordingly. Let's face it, my friends, we face an enemy both within and without.'

'Sir Hugh.' Ap Ythel loosened his war belt and placed it on the ground beside him. 'I can guess what you are plotting. You are going to use that corpse as a lure to our enemy.'

'Of course.' Corbett sat down between his two henchmen. 'I heard that scream of protest at the death of a beloved brother killed so swiftly, so unexpectedly. The archer, whoever he is, will return under the cover of night with his comrades to retrieve the body. Isn't it strange?' he mused. 'Even in the most violent struggle, love plays a part. But that's the way things are. So, how can we trap those who will definitely come? If we leave Holyrood, they may well detect us, and we must not forget the traitor within. We have to slip out.'

He paused at the howling from the abbey war dogs. On their arrival at Holyrood, he had visited the kennels and viewed the massive beasts, ferocious hounds with long legs and cruel jaws: animals trained to bring down any prey they were loosed against. The Knights of the Swan had used such dogs when they had campaigned in both Wales and Scotland, and their ferocity and cunning were legendary. Ranulf had also been fascinated by those huge, ugly brutes, which were only kept in order by their keepers, four burly lay brothers. Garbed in thick leather, these dog-men were armed with daggers and white willow wands, expertly pared so that their sharp edges could sting the backs and legs of the fierce animals they managed. Again the savage howling echoed, shattering the abbey's stillness.

'Sir Hugh?'

Corbett turned and smiled at Ap Ythel.

'Sir Hugh, you are not thinking of leading those dogs in a wild charge against our enemy?'

'No, no.' Corbett laughed and clapped Ap Ythel on the shoulder. 'The howling has provoked childhood memories of my father's demesne, a good, prosperous farm. He owned two mastiffs, watchdogs, whose barking at night always alarmed me. I used to think demons from hell had come to ride the beasts through the dark. Anyway,' he gestured at the jug of mulled wine on the tray, 'Ranulf, please fill three goblets, and while we drink, let us plot. How can we trap our enemy? We need to take prisoners. I want to question them about what is truly happening in that Valley of Shadows.' He paused at a fresh howling from the kennels. 'Something's disturbed them,' he murmured, 'but let us, like keen scholars, ignore everything else and ponder on our problem.'

Ranulf filled the cups and distributed them, then the three men sat discussing the possibilities. At Corbett's insistence, Ap Ythel slipped out to order Brancepeth to keep a sharp but discreet eye on the corpse and report anything untoward. On his return, Corbett questioned him on the most keen-sighted amongst his archers. 'Oh, Brancepeth certainly,' the captain replied. 'At night he can see as well as any owl. Why, Sir Hugh?'

'Look.' Corbett arranged objects on the table. 'Our enemy will undoubtedly return under cover of dark. They will bring a sledge with slats of wood so it can slide swiftly across the snow. They will follow the valley trackway because the snow elsewhere is too deep. At the same time, they will mount a vigil on both our main gate and the postern doors.'

'So what shall we do?'

'A good question, Ranulf, and the answer's obvious. The only place we can hide is the moat. It is a wide two-sided trench: the water is frozen hard and the approaching enemy will not see us until we decide they should . . .'

Corbett, teeth chattering, leant against the snow-covered far bank of the moat. He, Ranulf and Ap Ythel had been informed that the corpse still lay sprawled on the ice. Making sure that no one saw them, they had slipped out by a narrow postern door close to the main gate, sliding down the bank onto the thickly frozen moat.

They had planned well. Armed with war bow, sword, dagger and club, Ap Ythel had summoned five of his archers. They carried small bowls of heated charcoal and were swathed in heavy military cloaks. They had not informed Abbot Henry or anyone in Holyrood about what they'd planned, but gathered silently in the gatehouse, where Ap Ythel instructed four of his archers; the fifth, Brancepeth, would remain on the parapet walk above the gatehouse, keeping close watch. If the enemy approached, he would fashion snowballs and throw them down into the moat as a warning. They had done everything they could. Like the rest, Corbett had eaten a piping-hot stew; nevertheless, he still felt the cutting cold, the deepening freeze, and quietly prayed the enemy would move sooner rather than later.

It was a bleak, hard night. No snow fell, but the skies were clouded, with no moon or stars. An ominous silence weighed heavily, though occasionally Corbett and the rest would startle as some hunting bird floated ghost-like over their heads. Sometimes the predator would plunge, and a sharp, shrill scream meant that some creature had died under its claws. The hours wore on. Corbett's eyes were growing heavy when one, then another snowball fell into the moat.

He roused his comrades, whispering for silence. One of the bowmen scrambled up the frozen bank and peered over. There was no need. Corbett heard faint sounds from the dark: the crack of frozen snow, the slithering clatter of wood, the gasp of voices. He crawled out of the moat and, joined by the others, ran at a crouch through the dark, staggering and slipping. Their enemy was now in full sight: a huddle of dark shapes shifting against the poor light. These shadows turned and started towards them. Corbett and his party had been seen.

The enemy emerged from the darkness wielding razor-sharp swords and daggers. Curses were shouted, war cries yelled, then battle was joined. A clumsy, bloody struggle, blade grating against blade, steel against bone, flesh hacked and gashed. Screaming and cursing, men slashed at each other and, when close enough, grabbed at cloak, belt, jerkin or hair, desperate to gain a grip with one hand so that they could deal a killing blow with the other.

Corbett was confronted by a darting opponent, who slipped and slithered like a snake as he swung club and dagger. The clerk stepped back. He had given strict instructions that this was not about killing the enemy but capturing them. He edged further back; his opponent followed. They were now free of the melee. Corbett yelled for Ranulf. The Clerk of the Green Wax emerged out of the dark to deal his master's opponent a cracking blow to the back of his head. The man slumped to the snow. Ranulf immediately seized him by the collar of his jerkin and started to drag him away. Corbett grasped the hunting horn pushed through his war belt and, following Ranulf from the fight, brayed it long and hard, the agreed sign to withdraw. Two of Ap Ythel's bowmen who had not joined the fray stayed back to cover their retreat.

Slowly, clumsily, Corbett's line moved back. Ranulf alone had taken a live prisoner. Ap Ythel was dragging another, but a shaft from the darkness struck the captive full in the chest and the captain of archers left the corpse to bleed in the snow. Corbett grimly acknowledged that the enemy also realised what was happening. At one point they seemed to be massing for a fresh attack, though it was now too late for any further fighting. Corbett's line was moving faster. Ap Ythel's archers loosed a steady rain of shafts. Holyrood had also been alerted. From behind him Corbett heard a grating crash as the drawbridge was lowered and the portcullis raised. He glanced over his shoulder. Mortimer and his hobelars were massing in the entrance to the gatehouse, but there was no need. The enemy withdrew, melting back into the darkness, and

Corbett continued his retreat into the comfort and protection of Holyrood.

Within the hour, he received a summons to meet the abbot and the others. Corbett, Ranulf and Ap Ythel strolled into the chamber. Corbett nodded at Mortimer, but pointedly ignored de Craon. Once he had taken a seat, he gestured at the French envoy.

'I don't know why he's here. Never mind, I'll be succinct. Father Abbot, you and others may protest that what I did was, in the main, hidden from you. I had good reason for that. This abbey houses a traitor, an assassin, as opposed to you and yours as he is to me.'

'No—'

He raised a hand to still the abbot's protests. 'I am not going to waste your time or mine proving what I said. I don't need to. In my chancery pouch I carry letters from the king, authorising me to do whatever I see fit in any situation I find myself in. I do so now. I can produce these letters if you wish, but I am sure you will take my word. Now,' he rose and bowed, 'we have a rebel to question.'

He turned on his heel and, followed by Ranulf and Ap Ythel, left the chamber, returning to Corbett's room, where two of Ap Ythel's archers stood guard over their prisoner. The captive was small, dark as a mole, with night-black hair framing a round, solemn face, his cheeks chapped and scarred by the cold. He was sitting, hands bound in his lap, staring at the floor. He glanced up as Corbett sat down on a stool opposite, then grinned and muttered something in Welsh.

'He says,' Ap Ythel translated, 'that he almost killed you.'

'Almost!' Corbett replied. 'Almost is a ghost word about what didn't happen. Tell him I shall certainly kill him if he does not answer my questions. So first, what is his name?'

'Olwen,' the prisoner spat out. 'I understand and speak your heathen tongue. I am Olwen.'

'And who are you, Olwen?'

'I am what you see.'

'Are you an adherent of the Black Chesters?'

'I don't know what you mean.'

'I think you do,' Corbett retorted. He pulled the stool closer. 'The Black Chesters? Paracelsus?' He caught a shift in Olwen's eyes. 'Why have they returned? What do they want? Why do they attack us? Why now? Answer me.'

Olwen abruptly pulled his head back and, before Corbett could move, spat out a mouthful of mucus, which splashed the clerk's face. Ap Ythel punched the man in the side of the head.

Corbett took the napkin Ranulf offered, cleaned his face and gently poked the prisoner in the shoulder. 'You threaten us,' he accused. 'I am the king's personal envoy in these parts. I carry the royal standard. I represent the king, *your* king, yet you attack us. Such a crime makes you a traitor worthy of death, and the most dire punishment for treason is being hanged, drawn and quartered.'

Olwen flinched, though he tried to maintain his stubborn expression.

'Paracelsus, the Black Chesters, the tribesmen in the valley? What is happening there?' Corbett demanded.

'You are heathen English. You should not be here. You have no right.'

Corbett straightened up. 'Ap Ythel,' he ordered, 'take four of your men and the prisoner to the cells beneath the donjon, where we will question him more rigorously.'

Olwen was pushed out of the chamber and across the bailey into the towering four-square donjon, where they were met by the janitor. Corbett ignored the man's protests, and demanded to be taken to an empty cell. Once inside, he had a swift conversation with Ap Ythel, who ensured the prisoner was chained to rings in the wall so that each arm and leg was securely clasped.

'You can stay there for a while,' the captain of archers snarled. 'And you, sir,' he pointed at the janitor, 'will come with me.'

Ap Ythel and his four bowmen pushed the janitor out, leaving Corbett and Ranulf alone with Olwen. Abbot Henry came down, escorted by Devizes, who offered to beat the prisoner into submission. Devizes spoke in Welsh and Olwen retorted with a litany of curses and foul abuse. Once the abbot and his master-at-arms had left, a lay brother brought down a tray of food and a wine jug. Corbett tried to force a cup between Olwen's lips, but the man spat it back. Corbett drank and ate a little himself, then returned to questioning the prisoner, but he refused to answer even the simplest question.

Time wore on. Corbett was about to send Ranulf to discover the whereabouts of Ap Ythel when the captain of archers and his escort returned. Ap Ythel now carried a cage containing the largest and ugliest rat Corbett had ever seen, a brute of a rodent with a quivering snout, glittering eyes, long tail, and sinewy body taut with fury at being imprisoned. He rattled the bars of the cage with his dagger, inciting the rat into a fresh spasm of fury, before putting it on the ground. He then took from one of his comrades a quiver, a long, spacious tube fashioned out of leather and used to contain arrow shafts for a war bow. Both ends had been removed, one end being perforated with holes so cord could be threaded through.

Ap Ythel ignored the anguished look in the prisoner's eyes. He knelt down, placing the top end of the quiver firmly against the side of the prisoner's stomach, using the cord to clasp it as tightly as possible so that it dug into the man's flesh. Watched silently by the rest, he then took down a cresset, which he handed to one of his men. 'For the last time, are you going to speak, to confess?' he demanded in Welsh. Olwen just stared back, though Corbett flinched at the terror in the man's eyes as he realised what was about to happen.

'Very well.' Ap Ythel sighed. He gathered a mound of dry straw as close as possible to the end of the quiver. He then picked up the cage, the rat battering the bars with its snout. As he raised the small door, one of his men used his dagger to prick the rat to even greater fury. The rodent now had no choice but to edge forward into the tube. Once inside, Ap Ythel's henchman fired the mound of dry straw. The cage was withdrawn and the fiery bundle used to seal off the entrance the rat had darted through. By now Olwen was jerking, but the tube was held fast by the cords as well as by Ap Ythel's firm grip. It rattled and shifted as the rat, terrified by the flames, heat and smoke, tried to find a way out.

'Olwen, Olwen,' Ap Ythel said softly. 'The rat is hungry; it is frightened of the fire. It can only get out one way, and that is through your belly. You know that. I am sure you have seen this happen before.'

'I will immolate!' Olwen screamed desperately. 'I will speak, but not here. I will immolate,' he repeated, 'but not here. Untie me, please. It's biting, it's biting!'

Ap Ythel glanced at Corbett, who, intrigued by the prisoner's reply, nodded. The captain of archers cut away the tube and the rat darted out, scrabbling across the straw-covered floor and out through the open door. Olwen was dragged to his feet and pushed out of the donjon, following the narrow path dug across the bailey.

They walked slowly, wary of the sheeted ice underfoot. Corbett glanced up and murmured a prayer of thanks. The clouds were breaking up. He could even catch glimpses of blue sky. He was still distracted by the weather when he heard the first shaft whirring in, followed by a second. He spun round. Olwen now stood at a half-crouch, blood already frothing through his gaping mouth, tied hands trying desperately to pull out the yard-long shaft protruding from his chest. The archer on the prisoner's right had fallen to his knees, mouth open in a silent scream at the pain from the arrow wound to his right shoulder. Another whirring sound cut the air, like birds' wing flapping furiously. Corbett could only stare in surprise as a third shaft pierced one of the lay brothers accompanying them, in the throat.

'Run, run!' Ranulf was the first to recover. 'Sir Hugh, run!'

They needed no second bidding. Slipping and slithering, with arrows whipping above their heads, they hurried into one of the towers along the great wall that circled the inner bailey and threw themselves into the cold, musty stairwell. Before he pushed the door shut, Corbett glanced back. Olwen lay where his guards had left him, the lay brother's corpse a few yards away, the blood of both victims spreading an ugly red blotch across the snow.

Ap Ythel shouted at his archers to deploy further up the tower. Corbett leant against the door and peered through its narrow grille. The attack had already alerted the abbey. He glimpsed sentries moving along the far wall. Others gathered in the doorway of the donjon. A deep, sinister stillness had descended. No one dared expose himself to the mysterious assassins; Corbett agreed with Ap Ythel that there must be at least two to have loosed so many arrows in such a short time. Eventually, order was restored. A phalanx of shield men began to edge across the bailey, whilst above, Ap Ythel's archers shouted that they could see no enemy.

'Whoever it is, whoever they are,' Ap Ythel declared, coming down the steps, 'they have gone. In the beginning, it was easy. Our silent bowman could loose through an arrow slit, a lancet or a window with its shutters pulled back. But now every opening is being closely watched. If . . .' He fell quiet as the abbey bells began toll.

Corbett opened the door and almost collided with Devizes, who had hastened across the bailey with a shield above his head.

'Sir Hugh,' he gasped, before turning to shout at one of the lay brothers who had accompanied him. 'You'd best come.' He pointed back at the great donjon. 'Father Abbot needs you.'

Corbett and Ranulf left, protected by the shield men, and hurried across the bailey, where servants, under the direction of Brother Crispin, were collecting the corpses. 'I heard what happened,' the infirmarian shouted. 'I will join you shortly.'

Corbett was tempted to stop and ask what he meant, but they were hastening fast, the shield men very close, whilst Ranulf whispered heatedly that the danger might not be over.

They reached Abbot Henry's chamber guarded by a throng of lay brothers harnessed for battle. Devizes dismissed these, ushering Corbett and Ranulf into the sweet-smelling room. Corbett stared around. Stools and small tables had been tipped over, scattered and strewn across the thick Turkey rugs. Abbot Henry crouched like a frightened old man in his chair before the fire. Corbett and Ranulf drew up stools beside him. The abbot, with Devizes' help, turned his heavy chair to face them. Corbett found it difficult to accept that this was Henry

Maltravers, in former times one of the old king's fiercest
and most cunning warriors. A sly yet redoubtable veteran
who had survived the heat of battle as well as the cold
malice of court intrigue. Now he cowered beneath his
cloak, face slack and pale, hands shaking slightly.

'My Lord Abbot?'

'I was sleeping.' Maltravers pointed towards the great
four-poster bed, its bolsters and drapes all disturbed. 'I
felt tired, I thought Devizes . . .' He waved at his master-
at-arms standing close by. 'I thought he was outside.
Anyway, I lay down on the bed. I was drifting into
sleep. I felt someone squeeze my shoulder. I woke up.
A figure, cowled and visored, was bending over me. A
dreadful shape from the bleakest nightmare. He held a
thin spike in one hand and what looked like a mallet
in the other. He rested the spike here in the centre of
my forehead; look, you can see the mark.' Corbett
peered closer and noticed the small yet angry scar where
the skin had been puckered as if by some needle point.
'I resisted. I struck out. I pushed him back.'

'I came up the steps.' Devizes took up the story. 'I
heard the commotion, Father Abbot crying for help.'

'You were alone?'

'No, one of the lay brothers was with me. I realised
something was wrong, I was about to draw my dagger
when the door to Father Abbot's chamber crashed open.'
Devizes turned and shouted a name, and a lay brother
shuffled into the room. The master-at-arms asked him
if he could describe the attack. The lay brother just
shook his head.

'Like a demon sparked from the flames,' he muttered, pointing back at the door. 'That flew open and the malignant collided with Master Devizes, shoving him aside. I tried to resist, but it was so . . .'

'You did well, Brother Peter.' Devizes walked over and patted the old man on the shoulder. 'If we had not returned, Father Abbot would have been another victim, a heavy nail loosed into his forehead, so thank you once again.'

Once the lay brother had left, Maltravers straightened in his chair and pointed an accusatory finger at Corbett. 'Sir Hugh, as you know, I wrote to our king for help, for protection against these attacks.'

'And he sent me, Ranulf and a cohort of master archers,' Corbett retorted.

'And yet we remain so vulnerable.'

'But why?' Corbett demanded, leaning forward. 'Why these attacks, and why now? Who is responsible? How can they move around the abbey with impunity, loosing death and destruction at every turn? I need some help in answering these questions if we are to resolve the murderous mayhem engulfing Holyrood. The origin of all these troubles, I am sure, lies deep in the Valley of Shadows, yet we cannot enter. It's too—'

Corbett turned at a thunderous knocking on the door; this was shoved open and Crispin walked in.

'My Lord Abbot, Devizes, you had best come.'

They followed him out and down the steps, where a phalanx of shield men had already assembled. Crispin urged Corbett, Ranulf and Devizes to shelter deep, and the phalanx then advanced through the snow towards the abbey church and its adjoining buildings. They entered the cloisters by the southern portal, a great canopied square with broad paved paths. These led round the garth, a grassy expanse, its hedges and rose bushes all covered with dripping snow. Brother Crispin shouted an order and the shield wall parted. Corbett walked out.

The cloisters were gloomy, fitfully lit by torches and lanternhorns. These gleamed, reflecting in the polished elm-wood carrels that lined all four pathways. In summer, these chancery desks were used for study, writing and illuminating. Now, in the depth of winter, with the snow being whipped up by a bitter breeze, they were deserted, giving the cloisters a haunted look: a place where ghosts might muster before they moved to mingle amongst the living.

'Over there.' Crispin joined Corbett, pointing across the garth. 'Sir Hugh, can you see the bench?'

Corbett peered through the murk. He could make out two slumped shapes. He heard a noise and glanced over his shoulder. Ap Ythel had joined them, his yew bow strung, a feathered shaft ready to be loosed. Corbett raised a hand in thanks, then drew his sword and walked slowly around the cloisters. A bench stood along the far pathway; sprawled across it were the corpses of two lay brothers, who must have died instantly from the feathered shafts embedded so deep in chest and belly. A sad, pathetic sight. Both men were old, their shaven pates covered with sharp white bristle, their lined, furrowed faces contorted in agony at the pain and shock of sudden death.

'Sir Hugh, they were just sitting there.' Corbett turned. Crispin had followed, swift and silent as any shadow. The infirmarian's bony, angular face was twisted in a grimace, his eyes sharp and watchful. Corbett abruptly recalled that this man, garbed in simple monkish clothes, was still a warrior, a veteran of bloody conflict and sudden death. A ruthless killer who had slaughtered the king's enemies without mercy or a second thought. Could he be responsible for all these brutal slayings?

'I am sorry.' Corbett crossed himself. 'Brother Crispin, what did you say?' He glanced across the garth. Abbot Henry and others had now gathered there. 'Tell me.' He turned back to the infirmarian. 'What happened here?'

'So swift, Hugh. The devil's own bowman . . .'

'Brother Crispin, the devil does not have bowmen. Tell me what happened.'

The infirmarian sighed noisily as he pointed at the two dead men. 'Brothers Stephen and Isadore were sitting on that bench. They were sharing the warmth of a wheeled brazier; this has now been removed.' Crispin shook his head. 'They were drinking their daily ales. A servitor heard a sound. He glanced across the cloisters. A bowman, masked and cowled, appeared where Father Abbot is now standing. Four shafts, Corbett, all in the twinkling of an eye, and then he was gone.'

Corbett crouched down and stared hard at the two murdered men. 'I'll seek justice for you,' he whispered. 'God's justice will be done, and so will the king's. I swear to that.' He closed his eyes and murmured a requiem. He realised what was happening here. These two unfortunates had done no wrong. They were just the victims of terror, blind terror. Ruthless assassins now prowled this abbey. They were here to kill, to create a deep fear that would seep through the community and sap its strength.

He rose, blessed himself and walked back around the cloisters to join the rest. He pointed to the entrance behind them, the low wall, the pillars either side adorned at the top with carved acanthus leaves, through which the twisted faces of gargoyles peered and leered.

'Brother Crispin,' he demanded. 'The assassin came through here, yes?'

'I suppose so.'

'Ap Ythel, how swift would he be?'

The captain of archers pushed himself through the throng around Abbot Henry.

'Clear this place, Sir Hugh, and I will show you.'

Corbett asked the abbot and his entourage to withdraw, which they reluctantly did. Ap Ythel went out through the portal of the cloisters, shouting at Ranulf to start counting. The clerk had not reached three when the master bowman returned, walking fast, an arrow notched, another held between his teeth. He loosed one shaft, then a second into the darkness with a speed that surprised both clerks.

'Death in a matter of heartbeats,' Corbett declared.

'And that's how it was.' Ap Ythel held up his war bow. 'Our killers must have these; God help us all.'

PART THREE

John stated firmly that he was the rightful heir to the Crown of England.

Life of Edward II

p Ythel's warning was soon proved correct. All the horrors of hell seemed to descend on Holyrood Abbey. No longer was it a house of prayer and community devotion, but a place of devastation, destruction and despair. A killer, perhaps even a cohort of them, now stalked the abbey precincts. Abbot Henry could hold council meetings, Devizes and Mortimer could deploy their hobelars, but Holyrood was a warren, a veritable maze of galleries, passageways, paths, tunnels and corridors, with enclaves, jakes rooms, window embrasures and stairwells. Most of these were shrouded in the deepest darkness in spite of sconces, torches and lanternhorns. The fitful, flickering light these provided only sent the darkness dancing, so it was difficult for people, already panic-stricken, to distinguish between substance and shadow.

The arrow storms continued, confining the community, its servants and guests to their chambers. It became increasingly difficult to cross the bailey to the stables or the various outhouses containing all the essentials of life, be it candles or flour. The attacks were sudden and abrupt. Yard-long shafts with bristling feathered flights and barbed heads would whistle through the air; sometimes just a solitary arrow, at other times five or six, so swift that as one struck another would follow.

Corbett, Ranulf, Mortimer and the Knights of the Swan held meeting after meeting. Devizes' men-at-arms, assisted by Mortimer's retainers, combed the abbey fortress. They would rush to where they thought the arrows had come from, only to find nothing but a broken arrow shaft or a door or window that had been forced. On one occasion, a lay brother had apparently startled someone in a stable; his corpse was found just before dusk, a thin Welsh dagger pushed deep into his heart. Nobody could explain how the assassins could move around and attack with such impunity.

The anxiety deepened. You could not be sure who you were approaching down a corridor or up a flight of stairs. Everybody donned war belts or carried a weapon, be it sword or club. Some of the community argued that they should form a battle column and leave the abbey, perhaps march south to Tewksbury or Shrewsbury. Corbett warned that this would be too dangerous. The snow had not yet melted, whilst they also had no knowledge about the enemy lurking in the Valley of Shadows. Mortimer agreed, declaring that to be caught out in open countryside would be disastrous.

The anxiety turned into hysteria. People began to talk of ghost-walkers, demons from hell, who could move through stone and timber without hindrance. Corbett was desperate that one of the killers be caught, so Ranulf joined some of the searches, but to no avail. On his return, he confessed that it was like threading a maze. Corbett kept to his own chamber, reflecting on the mounting chaos, trying to sift through what he had seen and heard. He would sit at his chancery desk, writing in a cipher only he and Ranulf understood, as he tried to make sense and impose order on the information he had gathered.

By now the common consensus was that there were at least three killers prowling the abbey, and that these must receive sustenance and support from someone within. Nevertheless, this was difficult to determine. As Ranulf declared, where did the assassins lurk? Where did they sleep? What did they eat? They could find no answer to these or other questions.

Days passed. Corbett reached one firm conclusion: the terror in the abbey was somehow linked to the Valley of Shadows, and although he could not go there, he could at least question someone who had. Using all his authority, he insisted that he and Ranulf meet with the mysterious prisoner Edmund Fitzroy. Abbot Henry made to protest, but Corbett was insistent, saying that if necessary, Ap Ythel and his archers would force a way in. The abbot grudgingly agreed: he, Jude and Crispin took the two clerks down to the prisoner's cell, handing the keys to Corbett, who promised that after he left, the doors would be properly secured. He also demanded that he and Ranulf meet the prisoner by themselves: they wanted no one present. The abbot and his henchmen left, the doors were unlocked and Corbett and Ranulf walked in.

Edmund Fitzroy seemed pleased to see the two clerks. Corbett removed the prisoner's mask, and Fitzroy served them sweet white wine in silver-edged goblets. Corbett and Ranulf sipped at the delicious drink whilst exchanging pleasantries with their host.

'Sir Hugh, I have heard there is grievous trouble in the abbey.'

'Yes, there is.' Corbett toasted Fitzroy with his cup. 'Perhaps friends of yours, valley dwellers?'

'I have no friends there.'

'Yes, but you lived there. You mingled with those mercenaries. You ate and drank with them. You listened to their talk. I believe our present troubles,' Corbett again sipped from the goblet, 'are part of a chain that links this abbey to the Valley of Shadows.'

He got to his feet as if he needed to stretch, and walked over to the four-poster bed. As he glanced at the bolsters and coverlets, so neatly placed, so tidy, a memory was sparked: something he had seen but, for the moment, couldn't recall. Something that was untoward, not logical.

'Sir Hugh, are you tired?' Fitzroy joked. 'Are you admiring my bed?'

'No.' Corbett turned and walked back to his chair. 'Paracelsus and the Black Chesters. What do you know of them?'

'Straws in the wind, names and titles I heard mentioned, but nothing else.' Fitzroy's voice took on a pleading tone. 'Nor do I understand the present troubles. Sir Hugh, I cannot help you.'

'When you were in the valley,' Corbett placed the goblet down on the floor beside him, 'you sheltered in those caves. Didn't you ask why the mercenaries were so determined to resist the king and his forces?'

'The villagers I lived with hated Edward of England; they needed little urging to take up arms.'

'And the mercenaries, who I suspect were members of the Black Chesters?'

'They too were implacably opposed to the king and all his power. They were determined to fight to the death, and can you blame them? They had no choice. If they had surrendered, they'd all have been hanged.'

Corbett could only stare back and silently agree. The old king had showed no mercy. Once he caught rebels in arms, there could only be one outcome. Death in the most gruesome manner, or a swift hanging from the nearest gallows or tree.

'I am a prisoner in all of this,' Fitzroy pleaded.

'And do you realise what could happen to you?' Ranulf barked. 'If this abbey fortress was stormed and taken?'

'Of course I am fearful. Sometimes I think of that and I worry. I wish Brothers Anselm and Richard were still alive; they would help.'

'Anselm and Richard?' Corbett demanded. 'Why them?'

'They used to visit me here. We would talk about the future, the dangers to be confronted, the threats that might emerge. They were good men. I think they felt sorry for me, pushed from here to there. They were also present when the caves were stormed.'

'They knew the old king's moods?'

'Naturally.' Fitzroy waved a hand. 'I became fearful, frightened. I still am, trapped here, held fast in the vastness of Holyrood. Outside there is nothing but the gloomy Valley of Shadows and whatever monsters and demons lurk there. Brothers Anselm and Richard would comfort me, especially Richard.'

'Tell us how,' Corbett insisted.

'Very well. I will tell you something I have never shared with the others; Brother Richard made me swear to that. He claimed it was best if what he knew was kept secret.'

'So why are you telling us?' Ranulf demanded.

'Oh, because Brother Richard often talked about you, Sir Hugh. He said you were a man of integrity, one of a very few who attended the king. I think he had a hand in asking you to come here.'

'So what did he say?'

'It was last summer, around the feast of the birth of John the Baptist. Brother Richard came down here to celebrate with a jug of the richest Bordeaux.' Fitzroy scratched his head. 'He certainly drank deep.'

'One thing,' Corbett interrupted. 'Brothers Anselm and Richard were party to the full truth about you; they knew who you were and where you came from?'

'Of course, both were former Knights of the Swan. They devised this gilded cage as well as the others I have been placed in. They insisted that I be kept honourably and comfortably. They knew about this tunnel; it already existed.' He shrugged. 'I suppose it is the most comfortable dungeon in the kingdom.'

'Continue,' Corbett demanded.

'As I have said, it was a feast day. Brother Richard came here. He drank deeply and began to boast about this and that. I remained quiet because,' Fitzroy rubbed the side of his head, 'I still have dreams, nightmares about that ferocious battle of the caves.' He paused at the mournful howling of the war dogs chained in their kennels. 'They also frighten me,' he murmured. 'They always have.'

'Brother Richard?' Corbett insisted.

'He told me not to worry, that if I was in real danger, he and Brother Anselm would come for me and take me to safety.' Fitzroy stumbled over the words. '*Per portam . . . per portam Naiaboli.*'

'Naiaboli,' Corbett exclaimed. 'Through the door of Naiaboli, what does that mean?'

'I don't know.' Fitzroy seemed distracted. He glanced at Corbett, a vacuous expression on his face, then blinked and began to hum softly beneath his breath. Corbett studied him closely and once again wondered if the prisoner was weak-witted, feeble in mind. He glanced at Ranulf, who just pulled a face and indicated with his head that they should go.

'Is there anything else?' Corbett asked. 'My friend,

is there anything else?' Fitzroy did not answer, now lost in his own thoughts, eyes closed, still humming.

Corbett and Ranulf left the cell. They locked the door and handed the keys to Abbot Henry, waiting at the end of the passageway. The abbot snatched them from Corbett's hand, saying he would see to the prisoner's mask. The clerk made a mocking bow and left the donjon, whispering to Ranulf that Father Abbot would certainly ensure that the prisoner was safely locked away.

They returned to Corbett's chamber. Ranulf busied himself with the contents of a chancery coffer, wondering aloud how Chanson was faring and whether the snow storm had crossed the Welsh March. He fell silent as the abbey hogs began to squeal, stridently protesting at the mournful, bell-like howling of the war dogs. Corbett felt restless. He bowed his head and prayed three Aves for help. He opened his eyes, glanced up and stared at the small triptych fastened to the far wall beneath a crucifix. The painting depicted an angel going into a church whilst the devil left through the opposite door. He studied this carefully.

'Of course,' he whispered. 'Not *Naiaboli*, but *diaboli*; through the devil's door.'

'Sir Hugh?'

'The door in the north wall of many churches is called the devil's door,' Corbett explained, 'through which Satan flees after a baptism or exorcism, to be away from Christ and all that is sacred. I just wonder . . .'

'Wonder what?'

'No, Ranulf, let us wander rather than wonder. Bring a kite shield and be armed.'

They slipped out of the chamber, down the steps and into the bailey. A killing had taken place earlier in the day. Some hapless scullion had wandered out and paid for his carelessness with his life. The corpse had been removed, but blood still smudged the snow, an ugly spreading stain, eloquent testimony to the horror that had caused it. Corbett and Ranulf walked prudently. Once inside the main abbey buildings, they met Jude. Corbett asked to be shown to Anselm and Richard's chambers.

'Of course, of course,' the sharp-faced prior murmured. 'But what do you seek?'

'The truth.'

'What is the truth?'

'Pilate asked the same question of Christ, Father Prior. At the moment, all I want is to search those rooms.'

'Yet they have been emptied; I myself supervised it. There's nothing there now.'

'I still want to search both chambers.'

Corbett had his way, though Jude was proved to be correct. The two clerks inspected both rooms but discovered nothing of note. Once they had finished, Corbett returned to the cloisters and entered the scriptorium and library, two chambers adjoining each other, only a short walk from the carrels in the cloisters. He openly revelled in such places of study, breathing in what he called 'the fragrance of the chancery'; the sweet smell of scrubbed parchment, leather, ink, vellum and sealing wax. Both chambers were fairly busy. Members of the community were sheltering from the cold as well as from the 'ravenous wolf', as one lay brother called the assassin prowling the abbey. Corbett introduced himself to the Master of the Books, Brother Roger, and said he wished to study any manuscript connected with the construction and development of Holyrood. He was tempted to pose other questions, but as he had whispered to Ranulf in their walk through the cloisters, he did not wish to alert anyone to a suspicion forming in his mind. A possible solution to the attacks by the silent assassin and any coven he might be leading.

Brother Roger showed Corbett and Ranulf to a chancery desk, then brought two tomes bound in calf-skin and closed with leather thongs, as well as tubes crammed with documents. Corbett first sifted through the latter, admiring the skilled calligraphy of the clerks who had devised the plans and maps. These described in great detail how Holyrood had been constructed over ancient dwellings, as well as how the abbey could be developed both as a monastic foundation and a fortress to house former warriors. The manuscripts listed the necessary buildings: stables, granges, outhouses, barns and forges. Corbett noticed how well the latter were furnished, bearing in mind that the abbot was a skilled smith and armourer who had personally worked for the king. There were plans for gardens, a mill pond, herb plots, flower beds, stew ponds and a warren close to where the cow byres, hog pens and kennels stood on the far side of the abbey. Other folios described towers, walls, fortifications and gateways. Corbett took careful note of these, tracing with his finger the narrow postern doors and recalling the rantings and ravings of Brother Norbert.

'I wonder,' he whispered.

'I wonder what?' Ranulf, leafing through the drawings of the abbey church, glanced up.

'I wonder,' Corbett leant closer, 'if our perhaps not so mad lay brother Norbert had a glimpse of our secret assassin. Remember he talked about seeing a demon enter Holyrood, how he was armed with this and that. Now Norbert might have drunk until his wits, mind and eyes were truly addled. However, did he see one of the assassins being allowed in, all hooded and cowled? Is that what he meant by the demon having a hunched back? Was he in fact describing a bowman with all kinds of weaponry concealed beneath his cloak? A jutting war bow, a bulky quiver crammed with arrows?'

'All possible,' Ranulf replied. 'But if an assassin was allowed in, who is responsible, and more importantly, where in God's name is he hiding?'

'About that, I have my suspicions.' Corbett tapped the manuscript on the table before him. 'But let us keep searching.'

He pushed the chancery tubes away and turned to the tomes. The first simply listed all the movables the abbey would need: desks, chairs, benches, stools, kitchenware, Turkey rugs, crucifixes, paintings, curtains, as well as the detailed furnishings for both the church and the sanctuary. Corbett quickly leafed through these before turning to the second volume. At first this proved disappointing because it simply contained the Regula, the rule of the Benedictine order, especially adapted 'for the common life of the former Knights of the Swan at Holyrood'. As he read the introduction, however, one item caught his eye and he gasped in surprise. He pulled the book closer and read the introduction more carefully before asking Brother Roger if the library held a copy of the Benedictine rule in general. The Master of the Books smiled, took the manuscript Corbett was studying and leafed through the pages to the centre, pointing to the title 'Regula Sancti Benedicti – The Rule of St Benedict'. Corbett read this and his curiosity deepened. When he glanced up. Ranulf was staring fixedly at him.

'Sir Hugh?'

'For the moment, nothing, my friend. Let us return to my chamber.'

They did so safely and without incident. Corbett locked the door and sat in his chair, staring at the triptych, before turning to his henchman. 'Be as careful as you can, Ranulf, but go and find Ap Ythel and bring him to me.'

'Where?'

'To the devil's door in the abbey church. I will meet you there.'

Ranulf strapped on his war belt and, armed with a kite shield, left the chamber.

Corbett waited for a while, and then, similarly harnessed for combat, followed, slipping out across the inner bailey, keeping to the shadow of the wall. At one point he paused and stared up. The sky was clearing and there were blotches of blue, whilst the weather was not so cold. 'If it rains,' he prayed, 'O Lord, let it rain hard and warm.' He reached the abbey church and, still gripping the kite shield, made his way through a side door. The nave stretched before him, empty but glorious, with its vaulted ceiling and majestic pillars along each side. The transepts beyond were filled with the light from a host of candles. The air had that special rich smell of burning charcoal and smoking incense, whilst the beeswax candles provided their own pleasing perfume.

Corbett stood, ears strained for any sound, but there was nothing except a restful silence. He crossed into the south transept and paused to examine the magnificent wall paintings, all celebrating the exploits of the former Knights of the Swan. The frescoes were a glorious array of gorgeous colour depicting chevaliers, lances couched, horses richly caparisoned and harnessed for war, charging across the greenest of fields: above these, wings extended, floated alabaster-white swans, their beaks picked out in gold, their yellow eyes ringed with black kohl. Banners, standards and pennants boasting the royal colours of blue, scarlet and gold as well as the personal insignia of the king rippled and curled around the royal host. The knights were charging an army of demons, grotesque, ugly figures garbed in chain mail, gargoyle faces twisted and contorted in rage. Corbett smiled at the way the artist had subtly integrated into the painting the arms and insignia of Edward's enemies: the de Montforts and others of their coven.

He stiffened as he heard a sound behind him. He was sure of it. The soft shuffle of a boot, the scrape of leather against stone. He moved slowly back till he stood close to a pillar, then stepped behind this as he tried to place the noise he'd heard. If there was an intruder in the church, an assassin lurking here, he reasoned that he too would also use the pillars as concealment, creeping up along the transept, waiting for the best moment to strike.

Corbett drew his sword and gripped the leather clasp of the kite shield, sliding his arm through it so he could move the shield as he wanted. He whispered an Ave as he recalled his training, and all the times he had confronted silent, deadly ambuscades. If he stayed still, he would become an even easier target. The safest way was to abruptly confront the enemy. Drawing a deep breath, he lifted the shield and, with his sword blade resting on the top, charged down the transept.

He felt a twinge of foolishness at screaming a war cry while running through an empty church. Then he saw a shape, shadowy and indistinct, move from behind one of the pillars. The intruder stepped into a pool of light thrown by one of the cressets and knelt, arrow notched, bow up. Corbett did not flinch, but continued his charge even as he felt the arrow thud into the shield. He peered above the shield rim to see that the kneeling figure had risen and was fleeing back down the transept.

Corbett stopped. Gasping for breath, he moved to the protection of a pillar and waited there. He was about to go forward, wary of any further trap, when he heard voices. A door opened and closed; his name was called. He heaved a sigh of relief and stepped out of the shadows as Ranulf and Ap Ythel came striding up the nave. They soon realised that he had been attacked, but he assured them that he was unscathed, whilst it was futile to pursue or make any search.

'Leave it.' He handed his shield to Ap Ythel and re-sheathed his sword. 'Come.' He gestured at a wall bench in the north transept. 'Let us sit down whilst I share my suspicions with you. First, whilst I catch my breath, make sure all is in order.'

Ranulf and Ap Ythel quickly patrolled the church, ensuring all doors were closed and bolted from within. Once finished, they joined Corbett, sitting either side of him on the wall bench.

'Very well.' Corbett patted each on the shoulder. 'The only two men I trust in Holyrood. Let us begin. We must concentrate not so much on the murderous tapestry before us but on one motif on that tapestry, the enemy within. The assassin, or should I say assassins, how do they move? Where do they hide?' He paused. 'In a word, I suspect Holyrood is built over a maze of secret passageways. Some ancient building preceded this abbey. Brothers Anselm and Richard were royal engineers and master masons. They recognised the unique position of Holyrood and acted accordingly. I believe they were men who loved secret tunnels, hidden passages, disguised doorways and enclaves. I have now been through their records, the manuscripts describing the building and development of Holyrood. Strangely enough, there is no mention of hidden tunnels or secret passageways.'

'Why?' Ranulf interjected.

'Perhaps they wanted to hog such secrets to themselves.'

'Sir Hugh, I agree,' Ap Ythel declared. 'I follow the logic of what you say. Here we have an ancient site, men who love to build and are given free rein to do so. They act as they please and delight in having a secret plan.' The captain of archers grinned. 'This has the making of a Welsh poem. But Sir Hugh, what proof do you have for your theory?'

Corbett rose. 'Come,' he murmured. 'Ap Ythel, you are correct. The truth lies in fact, not just fable. Let me show you.' They walked along the north transept to the devil's door, narrow and small. 'Brother Richard told our prisoner that if he wanted to escape Holyrood, he could do so through the devil's door. Now we all know where that leads to.' He drew the bolts and pushed the door open to reveal a waste of snow-covered grass and gorse, which formed part of God's Acre.

'Is it out there?' Ranulf demanded. 'Could the secret entrance to a hidden tunnel lie somewhere beneath those bushes and yew trees?'

'I don't think so, Ranulf. It must be concealed yet

easy to open in a way that cannot be seen.' Corbett
closed the door. 'So where would you build a secret
entrance close to the devil's door? Ap Ythel?'

The captain of archers pointed to the wall. 'You won't
find it there – the walls are thick, yet not broad enough
to conceal a secret place – so it must be in the floor.
Look at the paving stones, Sir Hugh. Fairly new, but
which one is the most likely?' He squatted down, dagger
out. 'Right! When you open the door, it covers *this*
paving stone.' He turned his dagger and beat its pommel
against one paving stone, then another, and finally the
one he had selected. Lifting his hand to hold their
attention, he beat again on all three and Corbett felt a
surge of excitement. The third blow had a slight echo.
Ap Ythel now inserted the blade of his dagger along
all four sides of the paving stone and prised it up.
Helped by Ranulf, he slid the slab to one side, then
took the sconce torch Corbett handed over and thrust
the flaming end down into the darkness. The blazing
light danced and fluttered to reveal a narrow staircase,
its roughly hewn sandstone steps leading down into
total blackness.

'We'll go down,' Corbett declared. 'But be careful.'

Ap Ythel went first, holding the spluttering torch,
followed by Ranulf, then Corbett, who, when he turned,
found that there was a grip carved into the underside
of the paving stone so it could be easily lifted and pulled
back into place. He positioned it carefully, then
continued down. The steps led directly into a tunnel.
The rock ceiling hung just above their heads; the walls

on either side, also hewn rock, were about two yards apart. Corbett, holding his hand up for silence, stared into the inky darkness.

'We cannot go forward,' he murmured. 'I suspect every sound will echo loudly and the torchlight will betray us. Nevertheless, my friends, rest assured, along galleries such as these, murder prowls and chooses its victims.'

'Were these laid out when the abbey was built?' Ranulf whispered.

'No, no!' Corbett replied. 'Think of a great London mansion built over a maze of cellars and passageways, one chamber leading into another, one tunnel twisting into a gallery. So it is here. But enough for the moment. Let us return.'

They climbed back up the steps and into the nave. Once they had slid the paving stone into place, they collected their kite shields and returned to Corbett's chamber.

'What shall we do?' Corbett asked as he locked and bolted the door behind him. 'We now know how the assassins work. They use those tunnels and passageways to scurry here and there.'

'And that would be simple enough,' Ap Ythel remarked, sitting down on a stool, his war bow across his lap. 'You're not talking of something difficult to open, stone and wood sealed by time and dirt. Holyrood is of recent origin. Any secret doors, hatches and openings will still be very easy to move. They will also be cleverly constructed and cunningly positioned. Take the paving stone we moved. When the devil's door stands open, it hangs above that particular paving stone and cleverly obscures it so it doesn't even deserve a second glance. Dust and dirt blown in by the wind fill the gaps on all sides so it looks as if the stone is as firmly cemented in place as the others.' He unstrung the cord on his bow, rolling it into a ball before slipping it into his belt pouch. 'Sir Hugh, we have found one entrance, but what now? Surely others must know about this. There must be plans, diagrams. The workmen who built this abbey, or at least some of them, would be party to such information.'

'Not necessarily,' Corbett replied sitting down in his chair. In truth he felt a little weak, sick to his stomach after that sudden attack in the church. 'Let us say, for sake of argument,' he tried to regain his composure, 'that there are at least six to eight such entrances. In the grand scheme of things, that's not many. Brothers Richard and Anselm could have reserved these matters to themselves. You know how it would be: the fashioning of a certain slab in a particular place, the construction of a stretch of panelling or the ceiling of a hatch. Of course, there might be others party to such information, but I dare not make enquiries because I do not wish to alert anyone else to what we have discovered.' He gratefully accepted the goblet of wine Ranulf thrust into his hands, though he caught the Clerk of the Green Wax's anxious look. 'Don't worry, my friend.' He toasted both Ranulf and Ap Ythel with his goblet. 'The shock of battle will soon pass. So come, let's drink.'

His two companions returned the toast, and for a while they sat chatting about what might happen next. Corbett listened, feeling himself relax as the warmth of both the wine and the chamber loosened the cold grip on his heart and mind. For a short while he dozed, then woke at the baying of the war hounds in their kennels on the far side of the abbey. 'Soon enough,' he whispered to himself. 'We will need you soon enough.'

'Sir Hugh?'

'Ranulf, let us collect our thoughts. Ap Ythel, go find your archers, make sure all is well. See if you can discover what is happening elsewhere, but be careful, promise me.'

Ap Ythel did so and left. Ranulf opened the chancery coffers and laid out long sheets of scrubbed vellum as well as Corbett's chancery tray containing quill pen, ink pots, pumice stone and sander.

For a while, Corbett just sat staring down at the parchment, before picking up the quill pen and dipping it in the blue-black ink. 'So,' he murmured, 'let us begin. I shall speak as I write. Item. The Knights of the Swan. These are former members of the king's old bodyguard. They took a solemn oath that once their royal master died, they would live a community life, adapting the rule of St Benedict. They and their royal master had publicly promised to make pilgrimage, to go on crusade in Outremer. In the end, they could not. With the passage of the years, they realised that this vow was impossible to fulfil. So with the permission of the Pope, they commuted it, once their royal master had died, to living the Benedictine life. In a sense, that was not difficult. They are knight bachelors in the full sense of that word.'

He glanced up and smiled. 'These are lords of the soil who have decided to avoid the world of women and so reject the prospect of betrothal and marriage. They are warriors dedicated to each other and to the memory of their master. They are also self-made men, passionately devoted to the memory of the old king, who promoted and enhanced their careers. In the main, they are the sons of powerful city merchants, skilled in their fathers' business, be it Raphael, whose family was deeply involved in the trade of precious stones, or our worthy abbot, son of a London armourer. The same description could be applied to the careers of the rest.

'Item. The Knights of the Swan planned their withdrawal from life and from the court. They chose a suitable location, and so we come to the Valley of Shadows, a sombre, lonely place, haunted not only by dire echoes of the past but also by fresher, more recent bloody sins. The valley is desolate, but a boy child grows up there with more than a passing resemblance to the old king. To cut to the chase, this young man eventually claims to be the king's son and rightful heir, who was brutally exchanged for a peasant's child and hidden away in the Valley of Shadows.

'The years pass. Rumour and gossip thrive about this individual. Eventually it reaches the court, but it is also taken up by those passionately devoted to dabbling in treacherous mischief. A secret malignant coven, the Black Chesters, dispatches a war party, posing as travelling mercenaries, into the Valley of Shadows. They persuade the young man to join them. However, the old king also learns about what is happening and orders his comitatus, the Knights of the Swan, into the valley. The Black Chesters, together with the villagers, many of them former tribesmen who had strenuously resisted the power of England, take refuge in the caves on the cliffs of Caerwent. A bloody battle ensues. The caves are stormed. The young man is captured. The rest are either killed in the battle slaughter or summarily hanged afterwards. A few escape this final punishment, including the abbot's master-at-arms Devizes. To all intents and purposes, the valley is left desolate, and our prisoner is removed, being cleverly placed, as he said, in one gilded cage after another.

'Item. Time moves on. Fortune spins its wheel. The old king eventually dies. Holyrood is ready and the brotherhood moves here, with Henry Maltravers as abbot. He in turn is assisted by a number of senior former knights. The community gathers and apparently goes from strength to strength. Now I suspect the abbey's location was chosen for many reasons. It can keep an eye on the Welsh March, which is always troublesome. It also has a watching brief on the Valley of Shadows, whilst the very loneliness of the place and the riches of the resources around make it ideal for such an establishment. To many, Holyrood must have appeared an Eden on earth: a happy, harmonious community. A house of prayer as well as the repository of precious relics from the old king's reign, including the jewelled casket containing the dagger the assassins used against Edward in Outremer. The abbey also holds a mysterious royal prisoner, but that should pose no problem, for the place is heavily guarded from within, whilst few if any people will visit it.

'Item. If Holyrood is Eden, then it also has its serpent. Brother Anselm lies murdered in his cell. Some time later, Brother Richard's corpse is found on the steps of a tower. Both were former knights, leading members of the community, and both were killed by a nail driven into their skull.' Corbett shook his head and glanced up.

'What is the matter?'

'Nothing, Ranulf, just a memory of something I saw or heard. Something that doesn't fit the logic of events.' The clerk tapped the side of his head. 'I cannot recall it, but perhaps, in time I will.' He smiled thinly. 'I am tired, Ranulf, as tired as you look. Anyway, let us continue.

'Item. We don't know how these murders occurred. We have already discussed how an assassin could get so close as to drive a nail through his victim's forehead with no trace of a disturbance, struggle or resistance. Why these men, former warriors, were killed is as much a mystery as how. Vague suspicions may form, as they do about the slayings of Brother Mark, Norbert and those two prisoners. Nevertheless, any clear thought is hidden by a deep cloud of unknowing. Indeed, the three killings down in the cells of this abbey are shrouded in mystery. How can men imprisoned by hard rock and a stout wooden door be slaughtered in such a way? How did the killer get in, do what he did and get out?'

'Secret passageways?'

'I don't think so, Ranulf. I scrutinised the walls and floor of both cells. I asked Ap Ythel to go back and do the same, but we found nothing significant. Let us continue. Item. Undoubtedly an assassin is loose in Holyrood. Now is this offspring of Cain a member of this community, or has he—'

'Or they?'

'Yes, there probably is more than one. Have they been admitted by an enemy within? But who could that be? No doubt we are all marked down for destruction. I was attacked in the church, Abbot Henry in his own chamber, and we must remember that was the second attempt on his life, as he firmly believes he was deliberately poisoned. So, Ranulf, who could be the spider at the centre of this murderous web? Who profits from all this turbulence?

'Item. We now come to our two visitors. First, Amaury de Craon, envoy of the French king. He arrived here all a-bustle, full of false concern about his royal master's murdered, but very distant, kinsman. He also brought personal invitations for our good abbot to the so-called festivities planned in Paris next spring. Is he here for those reasons, or is there a more sinister motive for his presence?' Corbett paused, as if listening to the sounds of the abbey.

'Such as?'

'Why, Ranulf, the seizure of our prisoner and the theft of that precious casket.'

'But how could de Craon do that? It would be construed as an act of war, a heinous crime against the English Crown. Abbot Henry, not to mention Lord Mortimer and ourselves, with any force we could muster, would defend both Holyrood and all it contained to the very death.'

Corbett just shook his head.

'Sir Hugh, I appreciate de Craon has war cogs at Bristol and battle galleys as far north as Tewkesbury on the Severn, but if he is here to wreak mischief, he would face a violent, bloody confrontation and our two kingdoms would slip into war.'

'True, true,' Corbett replied. 'And so we come to our last visitor, Roger Mortimer of Wigmore. He could seize the casket. He might even try and take our prisoner, yet we all know that would be very foolish and truly reckless. Mortimer would be proclaimed a traitor, a rebel, a wolfshead, condemned by both Crown and Church, a man to be hunted down and killed on sight. No, no.' The clerk tapped the feathery quill pen against his cheek. 'I suspect our devious marcher lord is here out of sheer curiosity. Oh, he'll meddle and he'll interfere, as long as he emerges unscathed. He has pushed his boat out into the deep and he is fishing for whatever he can catch.'

Corbett cleared his throat. 'What else do we have? Brother Norbert talked about how the killer who murdered those two prisoners asked them to emulate. Of course he had it wrong; it was immolate, which means to sacrifice oneself. The prisoner we captured shouted how he would immolate himself, offer himself up. We took him out and he was killed, murdered. What does all that mean?

'Item. Why was Brother Mark slain in his own yard? What did the kitchener imply by telling Crispin that he – whoever he is – hadn't returned it and what business did he have taking it in the first place? Or words to that effect? Then there was the sentry, killed high on the walls by a deadly shaft, and those fire arrows on the night we arrived here. What is the significance of that? And what really did happen to Mortimer's man, the self-proclaimed beggar who appeared before the gates of Holyrood? He was received and admitted to the guest house, where, I now deduce, he made the dreadful mistake of asking if Lord Mortimer had yet arrived. Now that beggar had been in the Valley of Shadows. I am certain he was bringing information back to his master. The enemy within, whoever he is, realised this and so silenced him. It's all a mystery,' Corbett sighed, 'and yet the good Lord can so easily confound the subtle plans and cunning plots of men.'

'What do you mean?'

'Ranulf, we wonder why the sentry was killed and so on and so forth. We speculate why Mortimer and de Craon are here. I am sure,' Corbett pointed the quill pen at Ranulf, 'that our two worthies are plotting. Indeed, there is something about what is happening here that reminds me of a mystery play, of someone directing events, a master of the masque, a lord of the revels. Whoever this is, like Mortimer and de Craon, they have overlooked one very serious eventuality.'

'Sir Hugh, please!'

'Ranulf, you roll the dice and sometimes you cheat poor Chanson. No, no, I don't want to discuss that, but do you remember playing a game called "the jester in the pouch"?'

'I certainly do.'

'And?'

'The players have a purse containing dice and they must pluck two out at random. They are not allowed to look into the pouch. Most of the dice are regular, but a few have no points, just a jester's hat on all six sides. God help you if you pick out a jester, or worse, two of them, because all your opponent has to do is roll a one and he has won.'

'Precisely, Ranulf, and the jester in this game of hazard is the snow. No one planned for that, so it will be interesting to see what happens next, whilst I am keen to plot my own way forward.'

'Which is why you dispatched Chanson to Tewkesbury?'

'Yes, it is. As you know, the Secret Chancery sits at Westminster, but of course it has outposts across the kingdom where information and gossip can be collected, sifted and, if necessary, sent back.' Corbett shrugged. 'Offices of the Secret Chancery can be found in the great abbeys, such as Fountains, Rievaulx, Canterbury, even in Holyrood, where Brother Raphael acts on our behalf. On our journey here, I learnt that Monsieur de Craon was also travelling to Holyrood. He left London and came up the Severn accompanied by a small flotilla of French war galleys. You've seen the like, narrow and long, with sails and oars, so they can navigate the shallows.

'Now the great Benedictine abbey of Tewkesbury holds a corrody, a pension, for John Stroman, popularly known as Mistletoe, who once worked in the Secret Chancery at Westminster and who has now retired to enjoy his twilight years in reasonable comfort. As you know, Chanson has been sent to him to collect certain information. Mistletoe is under strict instructions to assess the situation and act accordingly. I have given him a few hints. I can only pray that he uses his God-given wits. However, to return to "the jester in the pouch", I just hope that the rains come and the thaw quickens.'

'But as we've said, de Craon cannot make a move against us here.'

'True, true,' Corbett agreed. 'But that fox is hunting, desperate to break into the hen coop.'

'How do you know that?'

'How do I know a fox will attack a hen? It's in his nature, Ranulf, he cannot do otherwise.'

'And so what now?'

'Oh, I am ready. Go as safely as you can and find Ap Ythel. Tell him to go to the abbey kennels and bring the keeper of the war dogs here.'

'Sir Hugh?'

'Please, Ranulf, do as I say, but do it discreetly. No one else is to know.'

Ranulf left. Corbett sat staring at the candle flame dancing in the draughts that seeped between the window shutters and beneath the door. He closed his eyes and called upon the dead: his father, mother and beloved brother, all gone before him into the light. He summoned them and begged in prayer for their assistance. He dozed for a while before Ranulf and Ap Ythel knocked on the door and led in a burly, balding lay brother. The man was garbed in boiled leather from head to toe; he carried a whip in one hand and a goad in the other. He was cheerful enough, patting his jerkin, which gave off the reek of the kennels.

'You are the keeper?' Corbett got to his feet. 'You manage the dogs, a pack of mastiffs?'

'Eight war dogs, my lord, we use them for hunting. They can bring down a boar or an antlered stag. Magnificent beasts!'

'I am sure they are,' Corbett replied. 'I want you to show them to me, but you are to mention this to no one, from this moment to eternity. You understand what that phrase means?' The kennel master gazed blearily back.

'It means,' Ranulf drew his dagger and held the tip just beneath the man's chin, 'that if you talk, if you discuss what happens here or elsewhere, indeed, anything to do with the lord Corbett, you will be judged a great traitor, worthy of death.'

The man swallowed hard, his Adam's apple bobbing in his loose-skinned throat.

'So.' Corbett fastened on his war belt and cloak. 'Let us see these hounds, but most prudently. Keep a sharp eye for any sudden movement.' He waved to the door. 'And so we go.'

He led his small cohort out across the abbey precincts. It was cold and dark. He prayed that the deep greyness would lift and provide some relief from the constant murk. They left the outbuildings, passing by the stinking hog pens and into a long barn-like building of rugged sandstone. Wooden pillars were built into the walls, and from these hung blazing lanternhorns. The air stank of dog and dirt, and as they entered, they were greeted by a howling from the eight dogs, each in its own massive cage. Corbett crouched before one of these, staring at the fearsome war hound. The beast was long-bodied and short-haired, its silky tawny coat rippling as it growled at Corbett before suddenly leaping forward, crashing against the cage. It then squatted down on its muscular haunches, reddish eyes glaring with fury, ears flat against its bulbous head, lips curled to reveal dagger-like teeth in massive jaws. Time and again it surged forward, growling deep in its throat. The other dogs also became increasingly restless, pacing their cages or sitting back on their hind legs, snapping and yelping.

'I have seen enough.' Corbett got to his feet and pointed at the far wall, where iron-spiked collars, chained leads and thick leather muzzles hung. 'Now listen, sir.' He turned to the keeper. 'The dogs are not to be fed tonight or tomorrow morning. Just before first light, as the bells chime, you are to bring them, all muzzled and harnessed, to the devil's door of the abbey church. Do you understand? All eight dogs, unfed, and muzzled so tightly they cannot bark and howl for their food. Yes?'

The keeper made to object, but fell silent as Ranulf and Ap Ythel both drew their long Welsh stabbing daggers.

'I understand, master,' the keeper mumbled. 'But why?'

'To stop these attacks on your innocent brothers and save this abbey from further bloodshed. What I have told you, keep to yourself, or face the penalty . . .'

Corbett returned to his chamber. Ranulf and Ap Ythel headed for the buttery for something to eat. Before they left, Corbett gave the captain of archers precise instructions to deploy his bowmen both near the main gateway and at all postern doors. He was to accept no objections from whoever else mounted a guard. Ap Ythel nodded his understanding.

Corbett was fairly pleased at the progress he was making. On his journey back from the kennels, he realised the sky was clearing and the air felt a little warmer. He hoped for rainfall to hasten the thaw. He was tempted to visit the church, light some tapers and pray for Maeve and their two children, as well as all the others he loved. In the end, he decided it was more prudent to stay where he was, recite the psalms and retire to bed.

*

Ranulf-atte-Newgate, Clerk of the Chancery of the Green Wax, drank deeply with Ap Ythel before staggering back to his chamber in Osprey Tower. He first checked on 'Old Master Longface', but the door was locked and bolted. 'Fast asleep, God bless him,' Ranulf muttered. Head down, he carried on up the steps; he didn't even glimpse the shadow that darted out of a dark enclave. The resounding blow to the head immediately felled him, and he slumped against the stairwell wall before sliding into unconsciousness.

When he awoke, shaken and shoved, a pannikin of icy water thrown into his face, Ranulf didn't know where he was. Hands and feet bound, he was squatting in a tunnel, black as night with only one flaring torch battling against the murk. It was cold, bitterly cold, whilst the cords lashed around his wrists bit hard and deep into his flesh. He wondered if he was alone, because he was certain he heard a groan further up the passageway. He took a deep breath as he recalled the events of the previous evening: visiting the kennels, drinking with Ap Ythel, leaving with the captain of archers, who was determined to ensure that all the postern gates were closely guarded, and now this . . .

He began to be aware of where he was and what was happening. He felt a shiver of fear. Corbett was planning to release those war dogs through the secret entrance near the devil's door, and Ranulf was certain that he was now in one of those hidden tunnels. Would Corbett search for him? He heard a sound and glanced up. A figure emerged from the dark and a fist slammed into Ranulf's face, badly bruising his lips. The clerk struggled against his bonds as his attacker roughly slapped his cheeks time and time again.

'Who are you?' he shouted, as he tasted the blood bubbling between his lips. 'Where am I? Who are you?' He jerked at another stinging slap across his face.

'I am your death,' a voice grated. 'And how you die and how fast you go is a matter for me.' The voice had that sing-song cadence of the Welsh, though its tone was harsh. Narrowing his eyes, Ranulf could make out a hooded face, glittering eyes above a bushy moustache and beard.

'Now.' The face drew closer. 'You and Corbett were down in the kennels. You were visiting those war dogs. What is going to happen? Will Corbett use the dogs to sniff us out? Or have you found a secret entrance? Will those mastiffs be dispatched down here? We have heard their howling. Have they deliberately not been fed, their blood fired to seek out the blood of others?' He struck Ranulf hard, knocking the clerk's head back against the wall. 'Answer my questions. Why does the Welsh traitor Ap Ythel have men watching the postern doors? Tell me.'

'My death may be coming,' Ranulf replied through bloodied lips, 'but yours is definitely on its way. The hunter is about to plunge, so look up my friend. Corbett is a true hawk and he will catch you in his talons.' He flinched at another stinging slap, then his assailant rose and walked away. Ranulf watched him go, disappearing into the darkness. He strained his ears for any sound.

He thought he heard movement, but that was only an echo from somewhere deep in the tunnel. 'Ah well,' he whispered, grimacing at the pain and soreness of his face, 'they never do what they should.'

Moving his bound hands, he felt down to the inside of his right riding boot, fingers scrabbling at the narrow leather pocket. Eventually he drew out a small, needle-thin knife. He twisted this carefully, for its edge was razor-sharp, and began to sever the rope between his wrists . . .

Corbett was roused early the next morning by a thunderous knocking on his chamber door. He rose and opened it to a lay brother gasping for breath as he stammered how the lord abbot needed Sir Hugh in his chamber as swiftly as possible. Corbett drew on his boots, fastened his war belt, wrapped his cloak about him and followed the lay brother out across the inner bailey. Dawn was about to break. The sky was clear, tinged with a strengthening glow in the east. The weather had turned decisively warm, whilst it had rained long and hard during the night. The snow was now rapidly turning to a sludgy mess, sliding off roofs, sills, cornices and corners. The lay brother, slipping and slithering before him, carried no torch or lantern less they attract the attention of the mysterious assassin dealing out death in Holyrood.

Abbot Henry, Devizes, Crispin and Jude were already gathered in close council as Corbett strode into the abbot's chamber. He paused just within the doorway as he heard clear across the abbey the howling of the war dogs, which were now being muzzled.

'I understand.' Abbot Henry pulled himself up in his chair. 'I understand you have been across to the kennels. You have given the keeper certain orders. Why? By what authority—'

'By the king's,' Corbett snapped, and took a stool. 'By the king's own authority. Assassins, traitors, one or more, prowl the precincts of Holyrood. I believe they are using a maze of secret galleries and tunnels beneath the abbey to move around without revealing themselves.'

'Ah,' Jude gasped. 'I did hear rumours of such a possibility, but I never . . .'

'Brothers Anselm and Richard spoke of it,' Crispin agreed. 'I thought it was all gossip, I never gave it a second thought. Until these present events, we had no reason to believe there were hidden galleries beneath us.'

'And you, Father Abbot?'

'Again, Sir Hugh, rumours, but no one ever stumbled over any secret door or hidden entrance. Now you claim to have discovered such places?'

'I have, and I intend to use them.' Corbett paused at a knock at the door. Mortimer, without a by your leave, swaggered into the chamber, took a stool and sat down. He then lifted a hand and cocked his head at the renewed howling of the war dogs. 'Something is happening.' He forced a smile. 'I went down to the kennels: the beasts are furious at not being fed, whilst their keepers are getting muzzles and harness ready.'

'Something is happening,' Corbett agreed. 'So listen . . .'

The Keeper of the Secret Seal then described in brief, pithy phrases what he had discovered and what he intended to do about it. He told Mortimer that he had no choice but to help him in these important matters. Mortimer did not object, but rubbed his hands in glee.

'The dogs will be taken from their kennels,' Corbett continued, 'and on my order released down a tunnel near the devil's door. The passageway will then be sealed. Once that happens, the assassins – and I am sure there must be more than one – will have to either flee or fight. Of course, they will try to escape through any secret passageway or tunnel within the inner or outer bailey. Ap Ythel will deploy his bowmen. You, Lord Mortimer, and you, my Lord Abbot, will place your hobelars and men-at-arms where I command; they will act under my orders. They are to be harnessed for battle and, where possible, carry war bows or arbalests.' He glanced up at Devizes. 'Do you understand?'

The master-at-arms nodded.

'And you, my lord Mortimer?'

'I await your orders with relish.'

'Good, in which case . . .' Corbett made to rise, gesturing at the marcher lord to follow.

'Sir Hugh,' the abbot declared. 'The casket has disappeared.' Corbett sat down again. 'That's the real reason for summoning you. The precious casket and the dagger it contained have vanished, and just as mysteriously, so has our sacristan Raphael. A lay brother preparing the sanctuary for service noticed the casket had gone. Quite wisely, he did not raise the alarm. I do not want members of our community rushing out to expose themselves to more arrow storms. Instead, he went to Raphael's chamber; the door was off its latch, with no sign of anyone inside. More worrying is that his weapons, boots, pannier and travel cloak have also gone.' The abbot crossed himself. 'We must consider the possibility that Brother Raphael has stolen the casket and fled. The thaw is deep and swift; trackways and paths will soon be clear.'

'But I have all the postern doors closely guarded.'

'Ah yes, Sir Hugh, but for whom?'

'Assassins who are hiding deep in this abbey but who will soon try to get out.'

'So you are looking for an enemy,' Abbot Henry retorted. 'Not for a member of our community, a senior official wanting to leave. We have not questioned all the guards, but it is possible Brother Raphael has gone, though the reasons why will remain a mystery until we speak to him again.'

'Could he have left through the secret tunnels?' Mortimer asked.

'If he did,' Corbett replied, 'then he too is our enemy.'

Crispin waved a hand. 'Raphael is our comrade! He is brave and true; we cannot judge him until we discover the truth. Now, Sir Hugh, is it possible that these secret tunnels run outside the walls of the abbey?'

'Possibly, but I do not think so. The two architects, Anselm and Richard, built and developed Holyrood to include the foundations of previous buildings. I suspect the tunnels, if they really do exist, run the length and breadth of this abbey fortress but no more. Like you, Abbot Henry,' Corbett continued, 'I am deeply worried about the disappearance of Raphael and the casket. However, first we must deal with the enemy within. My lord Mortimer, Master Devizes, it is time we did so.'

When Corbett and his two companions reached the devil's door, Ap Ythel had already lifted the paving slab, members of the community crowding round to peer down and excitedly discuss what this could mean. Corbett abruptly imposed order, dispersing the spectators and dispatching Mortimer and Devizes to fetch their men. As soon as they'd gone, he sent Ap Ythel to the keeper of the kennels, waiting deep in God's Acre to bring his dogs in.

'Once he's here,' murmured the clerk, 'the hunt begins.'

'And I will deploy my men,' Ap Ythel declared, 'arrows notched, bows at the ready for any stranger to appear in the abbey precincts, though we also need Mortimer and Devizes's retainers.'

Corbett nodded his approval. He watched Ap Ythel go and began to wonder where Ranulf could be. He felt agitated, and tried to compose himself as he stood in the shadow of the devil's door, a few armed lay brothers nearby. The keeper of the kennels and his assistants brought the war dogs across: the muzzles on the hounds were firmly clasped so they could no longer bark or howl, though their eyes blazed with fury and their muscled bodies rippled as they strained against the leads fastened to their spiked leather collars. Corbett could see their handlers were finding it increasingly difficult to restrain them. The beasts were famished, eager to be free, and could not be safely restrained for much longer.

He ordered the keeper to take the mastiffs down the steps. At the bottom, their muzzles and leads were removed and the hounds sped off into the dark, their bell-like howling even more terrifying as it echoed back down the gallery.

'Sir Hugh.' Corbett turned. Ap Ythel, his bow strung, arrow notched, walked into the church. 'It's Ranulf, Sir Hugh.' The clerk caught the anxiety in the Welshman's eyes. 'I don't want to worry you, but I went to his chamber and his bed has not been slept in. What could that mean? Ranulf should be here. He would want to be here, but there is no sign of him. We know he has not left the abbey, so where could he be?'

Ap Ythel paused at a blood-chilling scream down the nave. He and Corbett hurried towards it, but then stopped. A paving stone close to the entrance to the rood screen had been pulled back, and a figure was clambering out, sword and dagger at the ready to drive away the hound attacking him. The man was screaming, jabbing with his weaponry. He tried to pull the slab across, but the hound burst up after him, snarling and lunging, and caught the screaming fugitive by one of his legs. The man thrashed about in his own blood as the war hound savaged him time and again, dragging him down into the darkness from which he had tried to escape.

Chanson, Clerk of the Stables, sat in the cavernous inglenook of the majestic hearth that warmed the even more majestic tap room of the Angel, Tewkesbury's finest tavern, a hostelry famous for its good cheer, savoury food and delicious drink. The tavern chambers were most comfortable, the mattresses shaken and the sheets changed every month. The floors had been carpeted with clean rope matting and the air was warmed and sweetened by capped braziers crammed with herbs sprinkled over burning charcoal.

Chanson had arrived there three days previously and was now firmly ensconced. He had heard all about the snow storms sweeping the Welsh March, and he thanked God that the blizzard had not spread across the border shires. His journey had been hard and freezing cold, but he had made good progress and arrived safely in the great market town. He had determinedly rewarded himself with all the comforts the Angel could offer, including the charms of Beatrice, the cross-eyed chambermaid who cleaned his room and entertained him in the evening, when the light faded and the lanterns were lit.

Following Corbett's orders, Chanson had visited the great abbey of Tewkesbury and met the clerk Stroman, popularly known as Mistletoe. In the reception chamber of the abbey's incense-fragranced guest house, he had immediately recognised Mistletoe from his days in the Secret Chancery: a small, ever-smiling man with the round face of a red-cheeked cherub, thinning silver hair and watchful blue eyes. Mistletoe had taken the sealed letters Chanson had pushed across the table, deftly slipping them into a pocket of his pure wool robe. 'I'll see to these soon enough,' his smile widened, 'and when I do, I will visit you at the Angel.' He gestured at the pewter goblet on the table before Chanson. 'Drink your mulled wine, my friend, it will fire your blood and warm your bones.'

Chanson had spent the rest of his time at the Angel waiting for Mistletoe. He had eaten and drunk to his heart's content and bounced Beatrice time and again. He knew that something was going to happen, but what? He had brought messages to Mistletoe and the clerk would respond, but how and when was a matter of time. Chanson had busied himself. Imitating Sir Hugh, he took careful note of his surroundings and who came and went. He had noticed a new arrival at the Angel, a man who, by his own admission, had travelled hard from London. Chanson was struck by the stranger's singular appearance. He was garbed from head to toe in black leather, with a war belt of the same colour. A strange-looking creature, with a pointed, clean-shaven face, white as the purest snow, framed by lank reddish hair, he reminded Chanson of a hunting ferret he had owned as a boy on his father's holding south of Mapledurham. The man was very precise in his movements, eating and drinking carefully, keeping to himself, though sometimes he was accompanied by two ruffians garbed in the royal livery. This precious pair would sit or slouch at a nearby table whilst their master dined by himself. The more he stared, the more Chanson became convinced he had seen the man before, though for the life of him he could not remember where.

Chanson half dozed as he wondered about Corbett and Ranulf, locked away in that forbidding abbey fortress. In truth, he was relieved to be away from Holyrood's oppressive atmosphere, though he knew he would have to return. Travelling tinkers and chapmen were bringing tales of how the blizzard had receded and a deep thaw had swiftly set in, turning paths and tracks to a slushy mess. The Severn and its tributaries had swollen, breaking their banks. Nevertheless, the roads were being cleared and would pose no real difficulty for the journey back to Holyrood.

Chanson closed his eyes and slept for a while until he was gently shaken awake by the ever-smiling Mistletoe.

'Come, Chanson.' He waved to a window seat, where the black-garbed stranger was also sitting. 'Join me and my friend in a dish of the softest, sweetest pork, cooked in garden spices, with a sprinkling of ground black pepper. We will drink the finest ale, rich and matured.'

Intrigued, Chanson left the warm hearth. He clasped hands with both the stranger and Mistletoe, then sat down, taking his horn spoon from his pouch and polishing it with a napkin. They all sat in silence until the food and drink were served and eaten, then Mistletoe put his own spoon down and patted the stranger on the arm. Chanson noticed how the man kept his gloves on even when eating.

'Master Chanson, Clerk of the Stables to Sir Hugh Corbett, who as we know is Keeper of the Secret Seal and Master of the Secret Chancery. This, my friend, is the Ravenmaster, held over the baptismal font as Ralph of Ancaster, now popularly known by his title, for certain services to His Grace the king in the royal fortress of the Tower of London.'

Chanson gaped at the stranger, then smiled. 'I have heard of you,' he muttered. 'You look after the great ravens that nest in the Tower. You also . . .' He paused to choose his words carefully.

'I interrogate prisoners.' The Ravenmaster's voice was low and cultured.

'No, sir.' Mistletoe intervened. 'You torture people.'

'Sometimes that is necessary, Master Mistletoe.'

'You also execute those found guilty of high treason and crimes akin to that.'

'A well-deserved penalty. I am skilled in the use of both the rope and the axe, but my real passion,' the Ravenmaster's eerie face broke into a smile, 'is my flowers. I tend all the gardens in the Tower, together with my lady wife and thirteen children.' He closed his eyes and smiled. 'All cherubs,' he whispered. He opened his eyes and stared at Chanson. 'Do you know, in this strange weather we have noticed the appearance of rock samphire?'

'Quite, quite.' Mistletoe glanced quickly at Chanson and raised his eyes heavenwards.

'Master Chanson.' The Ravenmaster poked the clerk in the arm. 'You will be returning to Holyrood?'

'Yes.' Chanson nodded.

'I will accompany you.'

'Why?'

'Because I have to.' The Ravenmaster's voice was so soft Chanson could hardly hear it. 'As our friend here will inform you, I carry the king's own writ, signed under the signet seal. Holyrood holds a mysterious prisoner. My orders are most explicit. I am to execute that prisoner as a traitor and a pretender.' He smiled. 'Though I would much prefer to be tending my garden and herb plots with my wife and children.'

Chanson blew his cheeks out. He caught the warning look in Mistletoe's eyes, telling him not to object, his head shaking slightly as if to confirm the need for silence.

'So,' the Ravenmaster picked up his tankard, 'I will be returning with you to Holyrood to carry out the king's orders.'

Chanson nodded, hiding the cold chill that abruptly gripped him. He had eavesdropped on conversations between Corbett and Ranulf and had learnt how Holyrood housed a mysterious prisoner, but he knew no more than that.

'I too will be making preparations for your return,' Mistletoe declared cheerfully, trying to lighten the mood. 'And I am intrigued,' he added, 'about Monsieur de Craon.'

'Why?' Chanson demanded.

'Well, shortly after he left the galleys, a troop of his rowers led a line of pack ponies out of Tewkesbury.'

'Where?'

'I don't really know. However, one of the galleymen told Beatrice, the chambermaid here at the Angel, that they were taking weapons – arrows, bows, swords and clubs – somewhere along the Welsh March. Beatrice also discovered that another such comitatus is about to leave for Holyrood, ostensibly to escort the envoy of Philip of France back to his galleys. Now isn't that interesting, Master Chanson?'

Ranulf-atte-Newgate, Clerk of the Green Wax, was deep in the grip of a living nightmare. He had cut his bonds and staggered along the tunnel. At first there was nothing except darkness and a ghostly, brooding silence, until he heard the howling of the hounds of hell echoing like the bells of the underworld.

He moved cautiously, his back to the wall, the stiletto gripped firmly in his hand as he edged through the darkness. Soon he glimpsed a shifting pool of light, which grew stronger. A figure rounded the corner and Ranulf sprang, knocking the flaring cresset to the ground. He jabbed time and again at his opponent until the man crumpled, his blood sticky on Ranulf's hands and face. The clerk picked up the torch and bent over his fallen victim. The man was shuddering, trembling, legs kicking, arms flailing as he stared up at Ranulf. The clerk ignored him. He noticed the arbalest hanging from a hook on the man's war belt. He roughly undid this, then strapped it about himself and primed it in the dancing light of the torch. The ghastly howling grew clearer, drawing closer.

'Mercy,' the man spluttered. 'Mercy.'

Ranulf leant down like a priest whispering absolution into a penitent's ear. 'Tell me where the secret entrances are and I will give you the mercy cut. If not, I'll leave you to the tender care of the war dogs.' He stared at the man's dark face, almost hidden by straggling hair, moustache and beard. 'Tell me,' he urged, 'or I'll be gone.'

His victim gazed back, eyes glazed with terror. The howling grew closer.

'Your choice, my friend.'

'Look for the white swans,' the dying man gasped. 'You will see them painted on the walls. I was going towards one when—'

'When you met me. *Pax et bonum*, my friend. May the Lord bless you on your journey.'

Ranulf tipped the man's head back and delivered the mercy cut, a neat slash across the throat from ear to ear. Then he sheathed his knife and, with the arbalest in one hand and the cresset torch in the other, got to his feet. He took deep breaths to calm himself before hastening back the way he had come, passing the place where he had been tied. A tunnel ran to his left. He paused at the hideous howling to his rear; this was answered by a growl that echoed along the gallery he intended to enter. He reckoned the war hound behind him had found the corpse of the man he had killed. Ranulf, his body now coated in sweat despite the freezing air, crept down the tunnel, holding the torch up, staring to left and right. He almost sobbed with relief when he glimpsed a crudely painted white swan, wings extended, high in the wall to his left. Rough steps hacked into the stone led up to it.

He was about to start climbing when a deep-throated growl echoed into the darkness stretching in front of him. He crouched and raised the arbalest. A shape emerged from the murk, a war hound, head forward, belly down, sloping carefully, quietly, as graceful as a dancer, muscles gathered at the base of his neck. Ranulf stilled his panic and waited. The dog raced forward, then gathered itself and sprang, only to meet the bolt Ranulf released, a barbed quarrel that smashed between its eyes, digging deep into the animal's skull. Jaws gaping, legs flailing, the hound turned in its leap, rolled and crashed to the ground.

Now aware of furious barking and hideous screams, Ranulf hurried up the steps and pushed at the wall in front of him. He felt both stone and wood. Peering closer in the light of the torch, he realised that a square window had been cut in the stone. This had been cleverly disguised with panelling, the wooden surface painted and marbled so it looked like part of the wall. To his right, he felt two small rolls of oiled leather. 'Hinges,' he gasped. 'Hinges!' He pressed hard on the wood and it creaked. He pressed again and the hatch swung open.

He threw both torch and arbalest before him, then scrambled out, dropping down into the darkness. He lifted the torch and stared around. He was in an enclave built into one of the galleries. He turned and grasped the hatch, pushing it closed, then crouched, gasping for breath, before shuffling to the edge of the enclave. He placed the still blazing cresset on the ground before him and peered to his right and left. He glimpsed cell doors, grilles high in the wood, and realised he must have emerged close to the dungeons beneath Falcon Tower. He could still hear the snarling of the dogs and started at a heart-freezing scream. Voices echoed further down the gallery. Creeping forward, he peered to his left, then jumped back as an arrow whipped by his face. He glanced to his right and glimpsed Ap Ythel's bowmen sidling along either side of the gallery, arrows notched, bows at the ready.

'*Pax et bonum*, my friends!' he shouted. 'I am Ranulf-atte-Newgate, clerk to Sir Hugh . . .'

A short while later, his bruised face washed and tended by Crispin, Ranulf joined Corbett in the inner bailey, only a short walk from Falcon Tower. The morning was bright, but still very cold, even though the thaw was in full flow. So was the blood seeping and curling around the corpses laid out in the snow, their bellies and chests still carrying the arrows and bolts that had brought them down.

'Four in all,' Corbett declared. 'Though I suspect others have been mauled and savaged by the dogs. You look as if you met one yourself, God save you.' He extended a hand and pulled his companion closer. 'I did worry, Ranulf,' he whispered. 'I was concerned, but there was nothing I could do. By the time I realised you had been taken, the war dogs had been released.' He held Ranulf out at arm's length, gripping his hench-man's shoulders. 'Down in those tunnels, those sewers of blood, as I call them, I knew that Ranulf-atte-Newgate was back in his old hunting ground, the alleys and runnels of London, and if you could survive those, you can survive anything, so . . .'

He paused as a lay brother hurried over carrying goblets of mulled wine. Corbett raised his cup, clinking it against Ranulf's. 'My friend, I truly missed you. Now, thank God, I can give praise that you are still with us. So tell me what happened.'

Ranulf did so. Corbett heard him out, whistling under his breath. He then informed his henchman about the theft of the casket and the disappearance of Brother Raphael, before pointing to the corpses. 'They broke cover and paid the price. So far we have lost one of Mortimer's hobelars, but the hunt goes on.' Ranulf stared down at the four corpses, their chapped faces almost masked by long hair and thick moustaches and beards. 'As I said, there are others,' Corbett came up beside him, 'their corpses mangled by the dogs. We know that; we heard their death screams.'

'How many in all, Sir Hugh?'

'Perhaps ten, certainly no more, yet enough for the mischief they perpetrated. As you yourself discovered, the tunnels and galleries below us were cleverly constructed. Imagine, Ranulf, an underground town with hills, paths, winding trackways. Apparently some of these are steep and lead up to openings as high as the second storey of a tower, or run deep into the storerooms and cells beneath. Armed with torches and informed about the white swans, it must have been easy enough for our assassins to move around, sliding in and out like a cloud of ghosts. Now their hunting grounds have trapped them. I have asked for prisoners, though I doubt we will take any alive: if we did it, would be one way of discovering something about the enemy within, the reprobate who assisted this coven of assassins, who must have given them sustenance and support, be it candles, torches or food.' Corbett clutched Ranulf's arm. 'We have so much to resolve here, my friend, a truly tangled web of deceit, murder and treason.'

'And Brother Raphael?'

'God knows.' Corbett glanced away as one of Ap Ythel's bowmen brought a heap of weapons and threw them on the ground beside the corpses.

'Sir Hugh.' The man pointed at the tangle of steel. 'This is what the attackers used.'

Corbett walked over and stared down, sifting the weapons with the toe of his boot, a mixture of swords, daggers and small maces. 'Well I never.' He crouched and picked up a dagger, turning it to examine the hilt more closely. 'See this, Ranulf, the finger holes in the hilt, the serrated blade?'

'I have seen the like before,' Ranulf joined his master, 'though only now and again.'

'So have I. You are looking at good steel, fashioned not in this kingdom.' He let the dagger drop and picked up a short stabbing sword. 'French.' He squinted up at Ranulf. 'Steel from the foundries of Dijon in Normandy. I do wonder,' he let the dagger drop, 'if Monsieur de Craon had a hand in all of this. Remember the fire arrows, the sentry killed on the parapet walk? Was that mere mummery to cover men slipping into the Valley of Shadows with pack ponies carrying arms and other munitions of war? Well, well, well.' He softly clapped his hands. 'Ranulf, have all this taken to the abbey forge. Search out the smith, Brother Dunstan, I believe. Ask him to examine these, then hide them away.'

Corbett and Ranulf stayed in and around the Falcon Tower, directing the bloody conflict being waged whenever an assailant appeared from some secret place. Four more corpses were dragged out, weapons seized and inspected. Ap Ythel believed at least three of the enemy had been destroyed by the mastiffs, while the same number of war dogs had been slain. The struggle continued for the rest of the day and into the night. Corbett ignored pleas and requests from Abbot Henry. He insisted that he would maintain the search until the hounds fell quiet; only then could peace and harmony be restored and the abbey return to its usual placid horarium.

By dawn the next morning, the mastiffs were silent, and although tired and weary, Corbett insisted that they must still finish the task to his satisfaction. The keeper and his assistants were summoned, along with muzzles, leads and goads, as well as an escort of shield-bearing hobelars. They gathered near the devil's door and went down into the passageways and tunnels. The dogs were now exhausted and sated, and their keepers easily managed to chain and muzzle the survivors, whilst others dragged up the three killed. The dead mastiffs were taken out to be burnt in a furiously flaming pyre in the outer bailey, a veritable furnace fed by dry wood and oil. For a while, a stinking black cloud drifted over the abbey, though by midday this had dissipated, and the charred remains were gathered up and thrown into the icy moat. Only then did Corbett allow a respite for the garrison to wash, eat and rest before insisting that the hunt should continue.

Most of the able-bodied men in Holyrood were drawn into the search through the great maze beneath the abbey. Corbett, Ranulf and Ap Ythel also threaded their way along the tunnels. Having inspected them closely, Corbett and Ap Ythel reached the conclusion that tribesmen had once cut a maze of trenches through the rocky earth as some form of defence to guard and protect the approaches to the Valley of Shadows. Over the years, dwellings had been built over these to form tunnels, galleries and passages. Time passed and the site became deserted and desolate until the arrival of Brothers Anselm and Richard. These clever masons, in a mixture of mischief and building ingenuity, exploited the trenches for their own use, constructing and developing Holyrood over and across the ancient maze.

Corbett insisted on walking the labyrinth again with Ranulf as his scribe, noting all the secret entrances decorated with a white swan. He had almost completed this when an agitated Crispin came hurrying across the inner bailey to where the clerk stood discussing matters with Ranulf and Ap Ythel. The infirmarian's face was pallid and sweat-soaked. He was so agitated he even ignored the slush and ice beneath him and the pelting rain that saturated his robe.

'Sir Hugh, please.' He grasped the clerk's arm to steady himself on the icy ground. 'Please, please.' He turned, lifting his other hand, fingers curled like a claw, towards Ap Ythel and Ranulf.

Realising the infirmarian was in shock, Corbett clasped the man's cold hand, nodding at his two companions to follow them back into the abbey buildings. Crispin led them to a corpse chamber close to the infirmary, now a very busy place where those slain in the bloody struggle were laid out in all their gruesome state. Still deeply agitated, he took Corbett and his companions into a narrow side room with only one mortuary table, its contents covered by a heavy canvas sheet, though this was now blotched and stained, the blood dripping down to puddle on the floor. The room reeked with the foul stench of corruption, but further horrors awaited them.

Crispin pulled back the corpse sheet and Corbett

gagged at the sight of the mangled, gory remains of what had once been a human being. Hands shaking, the infirmarian turned the head so that Corbett could recognise what was left of the face. The clerk closed his eyes as his two companions turned away. He murmured a requiem, then left the chamber, striding out into the welcoming fresh air, the others close behind.

'The searchers found his torn remains, what was left of my brother's body.' Crispin huddled close, trembling violently. Ap Ythel made him drink from the wine skin he carried. 'It wasn't until I peered close that I recognised him.' He started to cry.

'And we,' Corbett declared grimly, 'must now decide if Raphael was the enemy within. If he was, did he steal that precious casket, and more importantly, where is it now?'

Corbett withdrew all the men from the tunnels except for Ap Ythel's archers: they were to scour the maze – indeed, the entire abbey – for the precious casket, though secretly Corbett really wondered if they would ever find it. A conviction he shared when he and others gathered in the abbey council chamber, where Abbot Henry, much recovered and stern-faced, sat enthroned like a prince in his great chair. Along either side of the table were Corbett, Ranulf, Ap Ythel, Mortimer and de Craon, with Brothers Jude and Crispin. Devizes, as usual, stood stone-like in full battle harness close to Maltravers. The master-at-arms bluntly reported how he had done what he could, searching the abbey, the church and surrounding buildings without discovering any trace of either the casket or the movements of Brother Raphael on the evening he disappeared.

'Was he the enemy within?' Abbot Henry repeated the constant question. 'After all, he was the abbey's sacristan, with the keys as well as the authority to go where he wanted and do what he wished. Indeed, on the evening Brother Mark was murdered, Raphael was not in church with us as usual; he had excused himself for a variety of reasons.'

'He held the keys to every chamber,' Crispin agreed. 'But we must remember he was also well liked and popular.'

'True, he could draw close to those brothers who were slain.' Jude spoke up. 'Surely that is something we must not forget.'

The prior's words created a pool of silence: a brooding stillness as people reflected on what might be.

'So,' Corbett tapped the table, 'every room here has been searched. Does that include yours?' He pointed at de Craon.

The French envoy glared back venomously.

'Well?'

'It has been.' It was Devizes who replied. 'I was accompanied by Brother Jude. Father Prior and I have been into every chamber, Sir Hugh, except yours.'

Corbett smiled thinly. 'Once this meeting is finished, we shall soon rectify that.' He leant over and whispered to Ap Ythel, who nodded in agreement. 'Good, good,' the Keeper of the Secret Seal murmured. 'Ap Ythel will go with you, Master Devizes. You and he can search my chamber and that of Ranulf immediately. You'd best join him now.'

The master-at-arms sketched a bow, then he and the captain of archers left the council chamber.

Corbett turned to Mortimer. 'My lord, I must ask you to deploy your men again. One final search of all the abbey outbuildings. More than that we cannot do.' He rose to his feet, Ranulf likewise. 'Until the casket is found,' he rapped the table noisily, 'you must accept me for what I am, the *custos* of Holyrood. I am its keeper, acting with the full authority of the Crown. There must be no dispute over that or anything I decide. Abbot Henry,' he bowed, 'gentlemen.'

Corbett and Ranulf left the chamber. Once the door closed behind them, Corbett raised a finger to his lips for silence, beckoning Ranulf to follow him down the steps. Out in the inner bailey, he asked a lay brother clearing away the detritus of the recent battle to come back with him and wait in the stairwell for Brother Crispin. When the infirmarian appeared, the lay brother was to ask him to bring the individuals Corbett described to the abbey church, where the two clerks would be waiting.

'Well, Sir Hugh, what do you think?' Ranulf asked as soon as they were seated in a small chantry chapel in the south transept of the abbey church. 'Do you think Raphael was the enemy within?'

'I am not sure, Ranulf, but let's wait.' Corbett pulled his cloak about him and pointed at a crackling brazier.

'Fire burns. Time is the same: it flickers, it dims and flares, but it also cleans and purifies. Time burns through all the nonsense and lies of men. Believe me,' he gripped Ranulf's wrist, 'I have my suspicions, but first we must resolve the falsehoods spun about this place.'

He rose, walked to the far wall and peered at a painting depicting David the warrior boy killing Goliath with one well-aimed shot from his sling. Above God's hero floated a white swan, wings extended. The struggle below was narrated in vigorously coloured frescoes – David whirling his sling, Goliath falling, a bolt to his forehead. 'I wonder,' murmured the clerk, 'if our killer got his idea of murder from this painting?'

Ranulf rose and came to stand beside him.

'One thing it doesn't tell us, Sir Hugh, is how those murders were perpetrated. We all know the victims were killed with a nail to the forehead. But how was it done?'

'In the end, Ranulf, the killings were carried out with sheer cunning. It's just interesting to speculate whether this is how our assassin views himself – a David confronting a giant Goliath – but if so, who is David and who is Goliath? I mean . . .'

Corbett fell silent as a door opened and Brother Crispin strode up the nave with two lay brothers, their harness all stained, boots caked in a disgusting sludge. The clerks left the chantry chapel to greet them, Corbett indicating that they should follow him into a pool of light thrown by a cresset.

'Thank you, Brother Crispin, gentlemen.' Corbett opened his purse and took out two coins. He pressed one into the callused palm of each of the lay brothers. 'So it was you two who found Raphael's corpse?'

'Yes, Lord Corbett, it was.'

'Brother Crispin, I have viewed the corpse. When he was killed, Raphael was garbed in the simple robe of this community?'

'He was.'

'He wore no armour, a mailed jerkin, for example?'

'He did not.'

Corbett turned back to the lay brothers. 'Gentlemen, when you discovered the corpse, did you find any weapons or baggage close by?'

'None whatsoever,' one of them replied flatly. 'Only the pathetic remains of a hapless man.'

'Tell me.' Ranulf stepped forward. 'Where did you find the corpse? I appreciate you were searching a labyrinth, but can you recall if it was discovered in an enclave on a passageway that turned abruptly left, along which you may well have come across the corpse of a war dog?'

'Yes.' The man spoke slowly. 'We were going down a passageway. I was in front, I'd already turned a corner. I lifted the torch and saw the dead mastiff. I was about to hurry forward to inspect it when Matthew here called me back. I returned, and he beckoned me into an enclave.' He shook his head. 'Truly terrible. The torn, bloody remains of one of our brothers. I knew Raphael, I liked him. He was loved by us all. So who would kill him, and why?'

'I wish I could give you satisfaction, but at this

moment I cannot.' Corbett thanked both the infirmarian and his companions, then watched them leave. 'Ranulf,' he murmured. 'Why did you ask that question?'

'Remember what I told you, Sir Hugh, when we first met after I escaped? I was held prisoner. When I woke from the blow to my head, I had my back to a wall with a tunnel stretching in front of me. I'm sure I heard a groan from somewhere ahead. On reflection, I believe that was Raphael, and that he must have been a prisoner like myself. Only he did not escape. Once the battle began, his captors left him to the mercy of the dogs.'

'Some mercy,' Corbett replied. 'I tell you this, Ranulf, Raphael was not the enemy within, though it was made to appear that way. Our opponent intended to seize both the sacristan and the casket and hide them away in that labyrinth of darkness. Raphael would eventually have been murdered and the casket concealed. But what then? How was this supposed to play out? Ah well, let us see.'

Corbett and Ranulf left the church and returned to their chambers. Corbett settled down with sheets of vellum and a tray well stocked with parchment, knives, quill pens, sanders, pumice stone and ink pots. He recalled what he had seen, heard and felt and, using his secret cipher, swiftly wrote down the conclusions he had reached. He half listened to the sounds of the abbey as it returned to its normal routine, the wounded being tended, the dead prepared for hasty but consecrated burial in God's Acre. The nave and sanctuary of the church had been cleansed, purified and blessed so that ceremonies could still be performed and divine office recited.

The two clerks joined the rest around the high table in the refectory when supper was served. At first the conversation was desultory, until de Craon, who had been playing with his food, announced that he really must dispatch one of his clerks back to Tewksbury, though he was worried about the weather. This was discussed; the general opinion was that the thaw was deep-set and swift, so roads and trackways would be open. Abbot Henry offered two lay brothers as an escort. De Craon gratefully accepted this, adding with a sigh that he too must leave in the very near future. Corbett, watching the envoy carefully, wondered what mischief de Craon intended, even though his opponent acted as if greatly deflated.

The next morning, the French envoy's clerk and his escort left. Corbett, standing on the steps of Osprey Tower, watched them go. He was about to return to his chamber when the bell above the great gateway began to toll, a sign that someone was approaching Holyrood. He and Ranulf joined the rest in the outer bailey. The rider had already entered, the drawbridge rising behind him. The new arrival provoked guffaws of laughter, as he looked too big for the mount he rode, feet hanging down well beneath the horse's withers. Corbett smiled as the rider dismounted.

'Chanson!' Ranulf called. The Clerk of the Stables patted his horse on the neck, handed the reins to an ostler and came sliding and slithering over to Corbett.

The three men met in a clasp of hands and murmured assurances that all was well before retiring to Corbett's chamber.

Once the Clerk of the Stables had made himself comfortable, his belly full of bread, hot stew and a jug of ale, he handed over a chancery pouch, saying that it contained a letter from Mistletoe, with what intelligence he could offer. Corbett broke the seals, opened the letter and read its contents with deepening gloom. He handed it to Ranulf, who, when he had finished, groaned and passed the letter back. Corbett then briefly but bluntly informed Chanson about the mysterious prisoner. He emphasised the need for secrecy and silence, making the Clerk of the Stables solemnly vow that he would never divulge to any living soul what he was being told. Chanson spluttered his agreement, adding that he'd heard rumours before but never imagined the truth behind them.

'So what do we do?' he pleaded, wide-eyed. 'In God's name, Sir Hugh, the Ravenmaster is coming here to execute the prisoner. Is that right?'

'In law, yes,' Ranulf replied. 'You see, the prisoner claims to be the late king's son and heir. Such an allegation is a clear case of high treason, since it accuses our present king of being a pretender. The prisoner has convicted himself out of his own mouth. There is no need for a trial, for evidence or proof. Just by making his claim, the prisoner has condemned himself to death. The Ravenmaster is also here to seize the casket, which has now been stolen.'

'But why the Ravenmaster?' Chanson asked. 'Sir Hugh, why didn't the king send his orders direct? You have been given full power to act as his envoy.'

'You are correct, Chanson, but . . .' Corbett pulled a face, 'the king knows I would not lift a hand against a hapless prisoner. I cannot drag him out of his cell, put his head on a block and sever it. The king knows that, Lord Gaveston knows that, and I know that. As for the casket, the king also suspects that I am most reluctant to seize such a treasure from the sanctuary of an abbey church and carry it back to London. I would have the deepest scruples over such an act. The Ravenmaster does not share my reluctance. Myself, Abbot Henry, Lord Mortimer and all the merry crew in this benighted place will be expected to cooperate and comply with the Ravenmaster as a matter of loyalty to the Crown.'

'So what shall we do?'

'Ranulf, I truly don't know, but let me think, let me reflect and let me pray.'

Corbett shut himself away for the rest of the day, but early the next morning he roused Ranulf and Chanson, telling them to join him in the refectory. Once they had broken their fast, he moved to the business at hand.

'Chanson,' he began, 'I know people laughed at you when you arrived here yesterday, but you are a wonderful judge of horseflesh.'

'They can laugh their heads off, master. That mount is a garron. It is swifter, more nimble and more sure-footed than any mountain goat. I requisitioned it from mine host at the Angel in Tewkesbury and it certainly proved its worth. The thaw may well have set in, but it's the sheets of ice that pose the greatest danger: that garron moved as if it was crossing a meadow on a summer's day.'

'Good, good,' Corbett replied. 'You are rested and fed, and so is your worthy mount. You are to return today.' He stretched across and gripped Chanson's wrist. 'You must hasten back as fast as you can to Tewkesbury, seek out Mistletoe and give him this letter.' He pushed across a small leather case, which Chanson seized and placed in his belt wallet. He then rose and clasped hands with Corbett and Ranulf, assuring them that he'd be gone within the hour.

PART FOUR

He said certain and shameful things about the king.
Life of Edward II

The normal bustle of life at Holyrood returned, the daily horarium imposing its own order and harmony. Mortimer dispatched a small cohort into the mouth of the valley, but the only person they encountered was an old woman pulling a sledge who said she wanted to seek shelter in Holyrood for a while. The horsemen brought her back and she sat on a ledge in the inner bailey, her paltry possessions piled high on the sledge, while she sipped from a blackjack of mulled ale a servant had brought.

Ranulf came down on some errand and the woman deliberately pulled her sledge so that the clerk slipped and knocked into it. He turned to offer his apologies.

'Keep calm, Ranulf of the Red Hair,' the woman hissed. 'Give no sign of recognition or surprise. I need to speak urgently to Sir Hugh Corbett.'

'Many people want that, lady.'

'About the prisoner kept here?' she asked archly.

Ranulf immediately returned to the tower and

brought down Corbett, who squatted in front of the old woman. She now pulled back her hood to reveal iron-grey hair and a strong, fair face that still exuded some of the beauty she must have enjoyed in her youth.

'I remember you.' Corbett offered his hand to her; she clasped it, then raised it to her lips and kissed it. Corbett smiled his thanks. 'I remember you,' he repeated, 'when we first invaded the Valley of Shadows. You were standing amongst the trees, not far into the valley. When I looked again, you were gone.'

'Sir Hugh.' The woman removed a wisp of hair from her face. 'Are we to freeze here? I must insist that you take me into your chamber. It's the only place someone like myself will be safe. I need not tell you that death stalks this abbey, busy with its scythe.'

Once in Corbett's chamber, his visitor settled herself in a chair before a brazier with the two clerks sitting on stools beside her. She sipped at the mulled wine and ate the bread, cheese and dried meat Ranulf served. She dined delicately like any court lady, using forefinger and thumb, wiping her hands and mouth on the napkin provided. Once she had finished, she stretched out her hands to the warmth.

'My name,' she began, 'is Matilda Beaumont. I am from a noble family, though a descendant from the wrong side of the blanket, so I have no pretensions to nobility. I was born here, the only but beloved daughter of John and Margaret Beaumont, who owned a small farm deep in the forest though close enough to the mouth of the valley.'

'Your family farmed?'

'No, Sir Hugh, my father was a verderer, a forester, given royal licence to hunt and to use forest wood. He had a prosperous business taking produce down to Tewkesbury or the merchant barges that ply the Severn. My mother was a seamstress, and a very good one. From spring to autumn she and I would accompany my father to the markets further south, where she could sell what she had stitched and woven.'

'Mistress, what does this have to do with—'

'Oh, Sir Hugh, everything. One autumn day, I left my father's house. I must have been about seventeen or eighteen summers old, a true wide-eyed maid. In my dreams, day and night, I lived the life of a courtly princess being worshipped by a knight resplendent in gorgeous harness and livery.' She smiled, and Corbett caught the former beauty of her face. 'My heart fed on the tales that travelling minstrels, troubadours and songsters performed or narrated when they visited our farm for safe lodgings. My parents were trusted, respected and well known to those travelling up and down the Welsh March.

'Anyway, on that autumn day – it must have been around the feast of St Matthew, when the seasons change – I journeyed deep into the forest, to my own special cave, a great hollowed chamber in a rocky mound overlooking the loveliest of woodland glades, a sanctuary of warm green darkness where the trees did not cluster so close and the sun broke through like lancets of light in a church. Nearby bubbled a spring of fresh water, lovely to the taste. Inside, the cave was comfortable and dry. When I first discovered it, I found traces that someone else used to visit it and play there: pieces of cloth, the tattered remains of a girl's toys, an empty jar of unguent. On that particular day, as I approached the cave, I heard voices and the strident screams of a baby.'

She paused and stared into the fiery coals. 'I will not talk for the sake of talking, Sir Hugh. I appreciate you are a very busy man. I will keep what I have to say as stark and clear as possible. I made myself known to the three people hiding in the cave – and they *were* hiding! In their desperation, they told me the truth, and startling though it was, I knew they could not be lying. The man and one of the women were dressed richly, like high-born courtiers, in gorgeously brocaded jerkins and soft woollen robes.' She took a deep breath. 'One of the women was a nurse called Eleanor Bridges; the other was Joanna, a royal princess, beloved daughter of the late king, sister to the present one and the mother of the bastard child she held wrapped in swaddling clothes.'

'And the man?' Corbett asked softly. 'Though I can guess his name. Ralph Monthermer?'

'Yes, a Welsh marcher lord. You know something of him, Sir Hugh?'

'I work in the Secret Chancery. I have heard stories, tales, whispered gossip, but little else. Fragments of the tale I believe you're going to tell me.'

'To cut to the chase, Sir Hugh, Ralph and Joanna

had fallen deeply in love. By moving from one royal manor to another, this palace or that in Gloucestershire and elsewhere, Joanna had managed to keep her secret safe: that she was pregnant, heavy with Lord Ralph's child. She and her lover had struggled to keep both the pregnancy and the birth well hidden.'

'And she confessed everything to you?'

'Sir Hugh, listen, I learnt all this on that day and the days following. Joanna and Lord Ralph truly liked me. They trusted me. They had to; there was no one else. They were desperate. The king's rage against them ran deep and dangerous. Now, their baby was injured, sorely wounded.' Matilda waved a hand. 'I shall come to that in a while. They had no choice but to accept my offer and go to my house. My parents, good and kindly, welcomed them warmly. Indeed, my mother recognised Eleanor as one of the valley people. Eleanor used to go to the cave as I did, when she was a green stripling. She knew the valley, even though she had left to serve in the royal manor at Tewkesbury. It was obvious that Joanna trusted her implicitly. A few years earlier, she had taken Eleanor into her household as her personal lady-in-waiting.

'Joanna and Lord Ralph begged us to keep matters as secret as the confessional. The princess produced a crucifix with a relic of the sacred Veil of Lucca. We all took a solemn oath on our immortal souls. My mother, helped by Eleanor, tended the baby, who had been sorely wounded on the right side of his little head.'

'Oh sweet Lord,' Corbett breathed.

'Princess Joanna,' Matilda continued, 'eventually told us how the old king must have learnt about the birth. He swept into Tewkesbury like the Furies on horseback, and his daughter had no choice but to tell him the truth. She and Lord Ralph met the king in the manor solar. Joanna hoped her father would accept both Ralph as her husband-to-be and their child as his grandson.' She shook her head. 'Nothing of the sort.'

'Of course, of course,' Corbett whispered. The old king would never accept either. As I said, mistress, I have heard rumours about Lord Ralph and Princess Joanna. Indeed, I asked a clerk now retired from the Crown's service to search his memory for stories, rumours and gossip about one of the old king's daughters. Now I know the true source of such rumours. I can guess what happened. Edward, even on a summer's day, with all things running smoothly and harmoniously, could lose his temper, and God help anybody who came within range of his fist or his boot.'

'He was furious,' Matilda agreed. 'He physically attacked Joanna, tearing at her face and head. He even threw the silver crown she wore into the fire. Lord Ralph tried to intervene, but he too was pummelled and kicked. Nurse Eleanor, holding the baby, offered it placatingly to the king, but he was so deep in his rage, he drew his dagger and slashed at her. Eleanor moved back, but the knife sliced the baby's ear. The infant shrieked. Joanna and Eleanor were beside themselves. The king, overcome by what he had done, collapsed to his knees, sobbing and cursing. Princess Joanna and

Lord Ralph thought it best to flee. Locking the solar door, they left the king to his anger and grief, took horses from the stables and fled for their lives. The only place Eleanor considered safe and secure was my cave in the Valley of Shadows.' She fell silent, stretching her hands out towards the heat.

'And then?'

'Oh, we gave them comfort. My mother was as skilled as any leech, more learned than any apothecary when it came to the knowledge of herbs and their properties. She could not save the infant's ear, but she cleaned away the scraps of flesh and kept the wound clean and the baby as comfortable as possible. Joanna and Lord Ralph knew they could not stay in hiding forever. They decided to return to court, but to leave the child with us, in Eleanor's care. They would give out that he had died. The latter was not too difficult to believe; the hideous wound he had suffered at the hands of the old king was proof enough. We also hoped that Edward, deeply ashamed at what he had done, might be reconciled with his daughter, which is what eventually happened. A conspiracy of silence over the old king's murderous attack on his own grandson ensured that Lord Ralph and Princess Joanna suffered no further punishment. They would be kept safe, as would the full truth about their child.

'Joanna thought it would be best if her son was entrusted to Eleanor, though both she and Lord Ralph conducted secret visits to see the boy. Of course the princess is now dead, whilst Lord Ralph is grievously ill, suffering from some disease that will eventually take his life. The years passed. Eleanor raised the child as her own. She married a valley man, as I did, but he died.' Matilda smiled grimly. 'As the seasons turned, the rumours and gossip began. Chatter about Eleanor's strange boy and how he had the look of the old king. Nothing serious until the riders came, a cohort of mailed men sweeping into the valley. By then, I was a widow, a virtual recluse in my parents' house. However, when the riders appeared, I sensed that life had taken another savage twist.

'I suspect you know what happened. The riders belonged to a coven of magicians who called themselves the Black Chesters. Apparently such malignants gather both in this kingdom and beyond. You see, I was trusted and respected by many of the valley people. I was one of them, a wise widow; consequently I was party and privy to all kinds of rumours and gossip. I also heard about you, Lord Corbett. It is common knowledge that the king's special envoy to these parts fought in Wales. You know the result of that conflict. The tribes might have been defeated, but they were not shattered. There were many who would resist the English Crown, especially back then, when the deaths of Wales's princes, Llywelyn and David, were still fresh in people's minds and hearts. Many of the valley dwellers were of that persuasion, so they joined and supported the mercenaries, the Black Chesters or whatever other nonsense they called themselves. The old king was also alerted. Rumours about the child had spread, but this was different. Like the old fox he was, Edward sensed a growing danger. He brought his power into the valley, and you know the outcome.'

'The fierce battle of the caves,' Corbett replied. 'Yet I thought, as do my masters in London, that the battle settled the matter.' He made a face. 'Of course, the prisoner, the man who now calls himself Edmund Fitzroy, was captured in that struggle though not executed. He was brought to the old king, who could only stare at a grandson he thought he'd murdered. Perhaps the realisation that the child had survived comforted him, and he could not bring himself to try again; hence the prison he is lodged in at Holyrood.'

'As I said, I am respected, I listen to the chatter. The gossip has grown that Fitzroy is here.'

'But not for long,' Corbett replied tersely. 'And I shall tell you why after I have reflected. Now, as for the present troubles?'

Matilda shook her head. 'Sir Hugh, the abbey of Holyrood has always been fiercely resented. Situated on an ancient site, it dominates the valley entrance. True, once the battle of the caves was over, the troubles receded and peace and harmony returned. Over the last month or so, this has changed. Mercenaries, wolfsheads, outlaws and members of the coven have crept back into the valley. Someone calling himself Paracelsus is organising them, enticing them to come here and fight. I also believe that the French have a hand in this. There's gossip about French gold and weapons.'

'Are you sure?'

'Oh yes, Sir Hugh! Nothing talks more eloquently than money. Just as importantly, this Paracelsus is not of the valley. From the little I have learnt, he resides like some spider in the dark here in Holyrood, spinning his web both here and beyond.'

'And how does he communicate with his followers?'

'Why, until very recently, people could come and go as they wished.'

'True,' Corbett agreed. 'People could slip in and out through the postern gates.' He sighed. 'That's how the assassins were allowed in, probably one or two at a time. You have heard rumours about what has happened here?'

'Yes, men have been killed, others have disappeared. Holyrood is now as dangerous as any battlefield.'

Corbett stared at Matilda; he chewed the corner of his lip and wondered where all this was leading. Deep in his heart he was convinced that the present troubles were a deadly charade to hide something else.

'What proof?' Ranulf demanded, pointing at Matilda. 'What evidence do you have for your tale?'

'For the truth?' Matilda retorted. 'I speak the truth! Fetch me my sack.'

Ranulf rose and dragged across the battered leather bag Matilda had pulled on the sledge. She rose, opened it and sifted among the contents, bringing out a dagger in a brocaded sheath boasting the colours and arms of the royal family, then a thin leather chancery tube and a square bejewelled casket. Corbett inspected the dagger, and then shook out the contents of the tube. The scroll was of the finest white vellum, a letter to all royal officials and servants of the Crown proclaiming 'the widow woman Matilda Beaumont' to be a faithful and loyal retainer of Princess Joanna, daughter of the king, and declaring that all servants of the Crown should provide her with any help or sustenance she required. The princess had signed the letter and sealed it with her own personal signet ring. The small casket contained items of jewellery, all bearing the royal insignia, together with copies of the signet seals of Joanna and Lord Ralph.

'The letter,' Matilda tapped the parchment, 'as well as the keepsakes were given to me just before the princess died. She had journeyed to Tewkesbury for one final meeting with her beloved son, but . . .' Her voice faltered and her eyes filled with tears. Corbett took her by the hand and gently guided her back to the chair.

'All this is proof enough,' he reassured her, 'of your close ties to the princess.'

'Is there any chance I can see Edmund?' she pleaded. 'He will recognise me, which is proof enough of what I say. I used any pretext to visit Eleanor, who pretended to be his mother till her dying day. Indeed, I was regarded as her closest friend. I watched the boy grow and mature; it was the principal reason I stayed in the valley. I wanted to do what I could to oversee and protect him. After Eleanor's death, he told me the tale she had shared with him: that he was the son of the king and had been exchanged for a peasant's child after a sow attacked him in a royal courtyard.' She smiled thinly. 'Even on her deathbed, she refused to give the true story, to betray the trust Princess Joanna had placed in her.'

She paused. 'Oh, I had concerns. Sometimes Edmund could appear weak-witted. However, I remained deep in the shadows, watchful, ready to help him if I could. I grew frightened and concerned as the stories spread about his true parentage. Sometimes I would visit the tavern, the Glory of the Morning, and give him some coins, but apart from that, what more could I do? Tell me, Sir Hugh, is he well? Is he in good health? Does he suffer? I would dearly love to see him.'

'Oh, he is robust enough, and kept most comfortable.' Corbett paused and closed his eyes. He wondered whether he should inform Matilda about the Ravenmaster, but decided that would do little good. She might well panic and share such information with the prisoner, who could do nothing to protect himself.

'Sir Hugh?'

'Stay here.' He opened his eyes. 'Stay here with Ranulf.' He pointed to the far corner. 'There is a garderobe over there, a lavarium to wash at, a bed to sleep in, whilst Ranulf of the Red Hair, as you call him, will ensure you are given good food and drink. On no account leave this chamber. You said as much yourself when you first arrived, and I think it for the best.'

Corbett gathered Ap Ythel and four of his bowmen in full battle harness, their bows strung, and demanded to see Abbot Henry and his two henchmen in the refectory immediately. Once gathered, with the archers guarding the door, the clerk rose from his bench and confronted the three men sitting on the opposite side of the table.

'The keys, Lord Abbot.' He stretched out his hand. 'I want all the keys to the prisoner's cell and the gates leading to it, as well as those that undo his mask. Indeed, I insist that all keys connected with our prisoner be handed over to me immediately, along with any copies. I am demanding this because I think it is the right thing to do at this time. No,' he rapped the table at their cries of protest, 'I will suffer no opposition to my demands. In addition, I shall place a close guard on the approaches to the prisoner's cell, both within and without. Ap Ythel's archers will be under strict orders to kill anyone who tries to enter that passageway beneath Falcon Tower without my permission. I am the Keeper of the Secret Seal, the king's special envoy. I carry all the necessary documentation and warrants. Lord Abbot, I will have my way on this.'

Maltravers, urged on by Jude and Crispin, reluctantly agreed. The keys were handed over by all three and assurances given that Corbett's wishes would be followed. The clerk brusquely thanked them and left, ordering Ap Ythel and his archers to keep close.

The day was now drawing on. Corbett moved swiftly. He returned to his own chamber to collect Ranulf and Matilda, and led them across to Falcon Tower. Devizes' armed lay brothers clustered around the entrance and in the stairwell. Corbett peremptorily dismissed these and posted his own guards under Ap Ythel's supervision. Once satisfied, he led Matilda and

Ranulf down the tunnel through the various gates to that of the prisoner.

Fitzroy was sitting at a chancery table, poring over a manuscript, which he cheerfully declared was a chronicle from Holyrood's library recounting the 'Tales of the Great Hound of Ulster'. Corbett greeted him, then produced the keys to remove the mask, throwing this into a corner and adding that it would never be used again. Fitzroy did not recognise Matilda at first, but when she pulled back the hood of her gown, he cried out in delight. Corbett urged him to remain calm. He showed Matilda how to use the keys to the cell door, insisting that this remain locked.

'Even when I leave?' she asked anxiously.

'You are not leaving.' Corbett smiled. 'You will stay here for a while with Edmund; there's room enough. You have a garderobe in the corner, a lavarium, and a recess for food to be stored. The braziers are primed and they'll provide both heat and scent. You will stay?' Matilda nodded. 'Ap Ythel's bowmen,' Corbett continued, 'will keep strict watch. Only two people will be allowed down here, myself and Ranulf. Our Clerk of the Green Wax will bring food, drink, oil and all other necessities.'

Once he was assured that both of them understood, Corbett wished them goodnight and he and Ranulf left Falcon Tower. Outside, darkness had fallen, yet despite the gathering gloom, Corbett felt it was getting warmer, and the thaw had definitely broken the power of the blizzard. The cobbled baileys were now free of snow, leaving only a rain-soaked sludge over slivers of ice.

'What now?' Ranulf asked.

'We have other matters. Ranulf, you visited the blacksmith Brother Dunstan?'

'I certainly did. He promised to inspect all the weaponry seized from our assailants.'

Corbett nodded and gazed up at the sky. 'God calm the weather,' he murmured, 'and God speed Chanson's return. Let's visit our blacksmith.'

They reached the smithy in the main stable yard, a great open shed with a roaring furnace close to a huge anvil resting on a stone. The walls were decorated with the usual tools, whilst the place smelt of scorched horsehair, tar, pitch and the pervasive odour of burning wood. Logs piled upon logs blazed fiercely in the furnace; close to this stood a great cauldron of icy water where the molten metal was plunged to freeze it firmly into shape. Brother Dunstan looked the part. Despite the cold, he wore nothing but breeches pushed into sturdy boots under a great leather apron, which hung down to just above his knees and protected both his front and back. Above the hem of the apron were deep lined pockets bulging with nails, pliers, prongs and other tools of his trade. A jovial giant of a man, he welcomed his guests to his 'fiery kingdom', waving both clerks to a wall bench and picking up a battered stool to face them, his round, bewhiskered face wreathed in a smile.

'Stirring times, eh, Sir Hugh? Battle royal here in Holyrood, both above and below.' He laughed at his own joke. 'Conflict in heaven and hell. Well, I understand that the demons have been exorcised and dispatched to their proper place, whilst we have their weapons.' He pointed to a large chest. 'They are all there waiting for you.' He leant closer, as though he was a fellow conspirator. 'They were definitely forged in France, that is a fact, but that does not mean that Frenchmen wielded them. Remember, Sir Hugh, the king of France and his minions like de Craon draw heavily for their soldiers on the cities of northern Italy: Venice, Milan and especially Genoa. So if allegations are made, the envoy will wash his hands and claim he knows nothing of such dreadful mercenaries.'

Corbett smiled at the clever mimicry in the blacksmith's voice. He excused himself, rose and walked over to the chest, opening it and sifting through the contents. In a heap of rubbish piled beside the chest was an unfinished arbalest, a small hand-held crossbow. He studied this curiously, then put it back and was about to return to the bench when the abbey bells began to toll the tocsin, the harsh sound clanging threateningly across the abbey.

The three men left the smithy. Ostlers and grooms were already gathering in the cobbled yard, panicked from their duties by the constant tolling. They were all staring up. Corbett followed their gaze and watched the fire arrows curve across the darkening sky, seeming to come from all directions. Streaks of flaring flame, they scarred the night before dipping to disappear into the blackness. Dunstan exclaimed noisily at this impudent threat, but Corbett now realised that such mischief was rooted in a desire to demonstrate that Holyrood Abbey was not safe.

Ranulf tapped him on the shoulder. 'Sir Hugh, shouldn't we dispatch riders?'

'No, no.' Corbett shook his head. 'This is a Yuletide masque, maypole mummery. Why loose such arrows? What harm can they do? No, the great killer, the assassin behind all this, is preparing a way forward, and God be my witness, Ranulf, I intend to trap him. Don't worry about arrows burning the sky. Stay calm and reflect. Ask yourself: how many archers would you need for such a show? Three or four on each side of the abbey, no more than a dozen in all. So let this matter rest. Keep an eye on the prisoner and let us prepare. In the meantime,' he passed Ranulf a piece of parchment, 'read that and ask Brother Dunstan if he can do what I ask.'

'And what will you do?'

'What I do best, Ranulf: sit and plot.'

Corbett spent the rest of that day and the following one locked in his chamber. He divided his time between analysing the murders committed in Holyrood and pondering those things he had seen, heard or felt that seemed illogical and out of context. To clear his mind, he wrote list after list, setting out his thoughts in brief, terse notes, in a cipher that made sense only to him, talking to himself as he wrote.

'Item. The coverlets on a bed, the state of the bolsters. Item. Loosed, not driven. Item. The game of the five peas. Is this a solution to the missing casket? Item. The rule of St Benedict and the declaration of Holyrood. Item. Fire arrows in the night sky. Item. Why confusion

PAUL DOHERTY

for the sake of confusion? Item. Why the murders of Anselm and Richard? What reason? Revenge? To silence them? To seize what they knew? Item. Why was Brother Mark killed for seeing something that disconcerted him? What was this? What do his words signify? Item. The murder of that beggar man, Mortimer's spy from the Valley of Shadows? Item. Immolation? Warriors offering themselves to be killed? The consequence of some blood oath amongst those mysterious assailants in the Valley of Shadows? Item. Who would know about the secret maze of tunnels, and how? Item. How and why is de Craon so deeply immersed in this murderous mischief? Item. Lord Mortimer. What is the real reason for his presence in Holyrood? What does he know, and how? Something Matilda said. Item. Those assassins who slipped into Holyrood. Why? What was their purpose? To take the abbey fortress from within? To seize both the casket and the prisoner? Item. What is to be done about Edmund Fitzroy? The Ravenmaster will soon be here carrying fresh authority from the king that even I cannot ignore. Item. Can Matilda Beaumont be fully trusted? Item. How can all this be resolved?'

Corbett felt like a physician drawing poison from an abscess, a truly malignant abscess that must be brought to fullness before being pierced. But how and when would this take place? He returned to his list.

'Item. The tangle of weapons kept by Brother Dunstan, and that unfinished crossbow with its strange grooves. Item. Above all, when will Chanson return, and will Mistletoe faithfully carry out his orders?'

*

Corbett's speculation about Chanson was resolved two days later. The thaw was complete, helped by a watery sun, when the gatehouse bell rang proclaiming an approaching rider, and Chanson, grasping the reins of his little garron, trotted into the outer bailey to be greeted by his comrades. Safely ensconced in Corbett's chamber with Ap Ythel guarding the door, he handed across Mistletoe's letter. Corbett broke the seals, read the contents and smiled.

'Sir Hugh?'

'Ranulf, Chanson, I have reflected prayed and fasted. I have at last reached certain conclusions that must be the truth. Now I must set the trap, bait the lure and entice our enemy forward. Ranulf, go tell Lord Mortimer I need urgent words with him here, by himself. I trust you, but Mortimer won't. Chanson, spread the news that de Craon's galleymen are close by, marching on Holyrood to escort their master back to his boats moored along the Severn.'

The marcher lord seemed only too pleased to be closeted with Corbett.

'You sent for me, Sir Hugh, and here I am.'

'So you are.' Corbett leant closer. 'And why are you really here?'

'I am the king's—'

'Oh, stop that nonsense! Let me hazard a guess. You are a kinsman, are you not, of Ralph Monthermer, who now lies mortally ill, dying of some malignant disease. A weak old man who has confided in you about what happened years ago. How his beloved Princess Joanna, daughter of the old king, sister of the present one, fell in love with him and conceived, giving birth to a boy child whom the old king grievously wounded. The child survived and spent years in the Valley of Shadows, until he was captured at the bloody battle of the caves. He has been caged and held prisoner ever since. Yes? You look surprised, Mortimer, but I am right, am I not?' The marcher lord simply nodded. 'Good, now I will tell you something else. The Ravenmaster . . .' Corbett watched Mortimer visibly pale, 'the Ravenmaster has been dispatched to Holyrood to execute the prisoner kept here. As you know, he has the legal authority for this, because the prisoner claims to be the old king's true son and heir, and that—'

'Is treason,' Mortimer interjected. 'Even to say it once, to claim to be this kingdom's true prince, is a rejection of our sovereign lord, and thus high treason. The prisoner has convicted himself out of his own mouth.'

'Which is my conclusion also.' Corbett rose, took the crucifix off the far wall and returned to his chair. 'Mortimer, you must have heard the news about de Craon's galleymen advancing on Holyrood to escort their master back to his ships?'

'Yes, your Clerk of the Stables told me the same in the bailey below. Why do you mention this?'

'Time will tell, but in the meantime, it is important for me to distinguish my friend from my enemy. Indeed, it is quite simple. Are you with me or are you not? Will you do what I ask and obey the royal writ I carry? Yes or no? The choice is stark, clear, but yours to make. If yes, give me your oath on this cross. If no, get out of this chamber and take whatever comes. Well, my lord?'

Mortimer grasped the cross in both hands and gave his solemn oath, then kissed the figure of the crucified Christ and handed it back.

'Me and mine,' he whispered, 'are at your disposal. So what now?'

'As a reward, a token of my gratitude, you shall see the prisoner and tell your kinsman that he is still alive and well protected.'

Mortimer nodded his agreement and got to his feet. 'How did you know?' he demanded.

'I didn't.' Corbett smiled. 'I simply guessed. There's a likeness between your names, and you and Lord Ralph are both marcher lords. I also received information from Mistletoe, a clerk of the Secret Chancery whom you will undoubtedly soon meet, that Lord Ralph is so ill he has been moved to the abbey of Wigmore, which lies at the heart of your estates. My lord, time is passing. Let us keep to the business in hand.'

Corbett took Mortimer and Ranulf down along the passageway beneath Falcon Tower, now closely guarded by Ap Ythel's bowmen. He paused to give Ap Ythel instructions to steal or borrow a brown robe like those worn by members of the community. The captain of archers was also to discreetly order the buttery to prepare food and drink for two people who were about to go on a long journey. He was to put all this, together with a knife, an arbalest and a short stabbing sword, into a leather pannier and bring it to the prisoner's cell.

He must also ensure that the battered sledge Matilda Beaumont had hauled close to Osprey Tower remain here.

As Ap Ythel hurried away, Corbett led Ranulf and Mortimer to the prisoner's cell, where Fitzroy and Matilda were deep in conversation. The door was unlocked, and the clerk entered, introducing Mortimer as his friend and henchman; he had insisted that the marcher lord not tell the prisoner the full truth, as it was neither the time nor the place to reopen the past. Mortimer kept his promise, clasping Fitzroy's hand and assuring him of his good will.

'Why all this?' Matilda demanded, hurrying forward. 'Sir Hugh, what do you intend?'

'That you both leave now. Edmund Fitzroy, your days as a prisoner are over. If you stay here, you will be executed.' Corbett paused, deeply sorry at the shock and consternation he had caused both the prisoner and Matilda. 'I must tell the truth,' he insisted. 'I will not lie or underestimate the danger you face. The Ravenmaster is on his way here. He has the authority to execute you. You claim to be the old king's son, and therefore implicitly assert that our present monarch has no right to wield the authority he does.'

'But Sir Hugh, you know—'

'Hush, Matilda. It's too late now to change the verses of the hymn; it has already been sung and there are those utterly determined that it will not be sung again. You must go. You must leave now.'

'Where shall we flee?'

'I would advise you to go back into the Valley of Shadows and hide there as deep as you can. Wait for this storm to pass, then plan again.'

Matilda stared hard at the clerk. 'It is as bad as this?' she asked.

'Worse, mistress. Death, sudden death, brutal and sharp, is only a brief horse ride away.'

Fitzroy made to object, but Matilda grasped his hand, whispering heatedly that the danger facing them was grievous and present.

'You'd best go now,' Corbett declared. 'My lord Mortimer will escort you to a postern gate. My captain of archers will supply you with a robe and ensure you have all the necessities for your journey.' He took from his belt wallet a pouch of coins he'd filled before leaving his chamber and thrust it into Matilda's hands. 'Go,' he urged quietly, 'go now.'

Corbett left the cells. Mortimer and Ranulf would take care of Matilda and Fitzroy, with Ap Ythel trailing behind to protect their backs. As he crossed the inner bailey, he sensed a subtle change. Chanson's report about the fast-approaching galleymen was now well known and having its effect. Corbett glimpsed Abbot Henry, no longer with his walking cane, directing ostlers and grooms, who were bringing horses into the bailey before Falcon Tower. Chests, coffers and caskets were being carried out. Carts were being prepared, whilst the abbey's hobelars were all harnessed and armed.

Corbett returned to his own chamber and waited. Devizes came up to complain that the entrance to the tunnel beneath Falcon Tower was still guarded and sealed by Ap Ythel's archers, who would allow no one access to the prisoner. Father Abbot now demanded this. Corbett, leaning against the half-open door, simply shrugged and smiled at the handsome master-at-arms, promising to look into the matter before he slammed the door shut.

Ranulf eventually rejoined his master to report that Matilda and the prisoner had slipped out of Falcon Tower, pulling the sledge to a postern gate, where Mortimer had ensured that the two were safely allowed through. Ranulf, standing on the parapet along the great curtain wall, had watched them disappear into the icy green vastness of the valley. He also reported how Chanson had stayed with Ap Ythel's archers, who continued to guard the passageway down to the prisoner's cell as if Fitzroy was still being held there. Mortimer, Ranulf added, was growing increasingly apprehensive about what was happening in the abbey. Rumours were circulating that Maltravers and his principle henchmen, tired of the constant dangers Holyrood faced, were seriously considering joining de Craon: they would ask for the envoy's protection on their journey to Tewkesbury.

'Of course, of course,' Corbett murmured. They would do, wouldn't they? Indeed, I am certain they will try and force us to do likewise.'

The tension in the abbey deepened. Corbett saw how matters were developing. Abbot Henry was becoming increasingly assertive. Devizes now had the abbey hobelars in full battle harness guarding the main gateway.

Corbett was quietly relieved that Matilda and the prisoner had slipped out just in time. Ranulf kept asking what was happening. He had approached a postern gate only to discover a close guard over it.

'Can't we force the issue?' he pleaded.

'For what purpose? To go out into the open countryside? And, if we did, what strength can we rely on? Ap Ythel and a few bowmen, as well as a small number of hobelars wearing the Mortimer livery?' Corbett grinned and patted his henchman on the shoulder. 'No, no, Ranulf, what is happening is how I thought events might play out. Oh, by the way, you took my message to Brother Dunstan at the forge? He can do what I ask?'

'Yes, he said he would.'

'Good, so let's wait on events.'

Later that day, the gate bell began to toll and the abbey community climbed the steps to the parapet walk above the gatehouse, leaning against the crenellations to stare out at the two columns of men marching towards Holyrood. The blue and silver livery of the French king and his personal escutcheon of three golden lilies were very clear to see. Ranulf quietly cursed. Corbett just narrowed his eyes and smiled as he glimpsed the black-garbed Ravenmaster amongst the small huddle of horsemen. Orders were issued, Devizes acting very much as though he was in charge. The portcullis was raised, the drawbridge lowered and the horsemen clattered across, followed by the two columns of marching men.

Corbett waited until the entire comitatus had entered the abbey, then he nudged Ranulf.

'The maypole is up,' he whispered. 'Its ribbons are fastened. Let's go down and join the dance.'

By the time they had reached the cobbled yard, the surprise and consternation had spread, Abbot Henry, de Craon and even Mortimer exclaiming at what was happening. Despite the blue and silver livery of the arrivals, it was now obvious that the battle column consisted of English soldiers under the command of the ever-smiling Mistletoe, who slid off his horse clapping gauntleted hands, bowing and scraping to everyone as he pushed through the throng towards Corbett.

'Sir Hugh, what do you think?'

'I couldn't have done better myself.'

'The Sheriff of Gloucestershire proved most amenable,' Mistletoe declared. 'A good friend of yours, Sir Hugh, Miles Stapleton. He ordered his commissioners of array to summon up the entire comitatus of the shire, along with a cohort of men-at-arms camped close to Berkeley. As for the French livery, de Craon's galleymen were only too willing to share it with us once I explained what a great honour was being bestowed.' His smile widened. 'Think of it, Sir Hugh, English soldiers donning French livery as a mark of respect to King Philip's most august envoy. I also made sure no French courier tried to slip out of Tewkesbury to spread the news.' His smile faded. 'A shrewd suggestion. The swiftest and easiest way to get into Holyrood. If we had displayed royal colours, matters may have taken more time. So,' he continued, 'let us now inform our lord abbot and Monsieur de Craon exactly what is happening here.'

'Sir Hugh!' The Ravenmaster led his horse through the press, escorted by two burly ruffians. He stopped and bowed. Corbett responded, clasping the man's black-gloved hands. '*Pax et bonum*, Sir Hugh. I have been dispatched by the king to carry out certain business here.'

'Your business will have to wait, sir. Trust me,' Corbett waved to where Abbot Henry, Devizes, Jude, Crispin and de Craon stood deep in conversation, their surprise and shock at what was happening clear to see, 'we have more pressing business.' He turned back to the Ravenmaster. 'I would be most grateful, sir, if you could join me as a most trusted retainer of the king, a man who I know enjoys our prince's favour. You are skilled and shrewd; your assistance would be deeply appreciated.'

The Ravenmaster, mollified by such flattery, bowed and agreed, declaring that he would place himself and his small escort at Corbett's disposal.

'Good, good.' Corbett raised a hand and summoned Ap Ythel, who was standing close by with four of his bowmen. The captain of archers was smiling slyly to himself as he pushed through the milling crowd.

'Sir Hugh, a great surprise!'

'The first of many.' Corbett grasped Ap Ythel by the shoulder. 'Deploy your men, Mistletoe's comitatus and Lord Mortimer's at every gate and door. No one is to move anything from anywhere. Bring this abbey firmly and securely under my grip. Make sure our new arrivals are given food, drink, warmth and rest. I also want you and Ranulf to set up a court in the nave of the abbey church, a special session of King's Bench under my commission of oyer and terminer. We will need a broad table with three chairs behind it and two more facing. At my orders, you will deploy your archers and other men-at-arms around the church, both within and without. Seek out Chanson; he will also help. Keep a close – and I mean very close – eye on Falcon Tower, above and beneath. You have all that?'

Ap Ythel, still smiling to himself, faithfully repeated in his soft sing-song voice what Corbett had asked.

'Good. My friend, you are smiling, but believe me,' the clerk whispered hoarsely, 'what I intend is grim and final. Use Chanson to keep in touch with me.' He patted Ap Ythel on the shoulder, bowed to the Ravenmaster and walked over to Maltravers and the rest. 'My Lord Abbot, I believe we should meet, and the sooner the better.' The abbot, glaring furiously, agreed, and Corbett invited Brothers Jude and Crispin, Mortimer, the Ravenmaster, Mistletoe and de Craon to attend as well. The French envoy was strangely silent, his usually ruddy face now white with either anger or fear at what was unfolding. Corbett also summoned Devizes, saying he could join his master.

They gathered in the council chamber. Corbett insisted on taking the throne-like chair at the top of the table, with Ranulf sitting on his left, the Clerk of the Green wax laying out the royal commission as he whispered messages from Brother Dunstan. Corbett nodded his thanks and asked Ranulf to serve goblets of mulled wine. Once this had been brought from the buttery and the cups laid out, he insisted that the door be closed. Ranulf ensured that two bowmen stood on guard outside, with another in the far corner of the chamber, bow strung and arrow notched.

'Well.' Corbett tapped the royal warrants before him. 'I am here to honour Monsieur de Craon.' The French envoy forced a smile. Corbett continued blithely. 'My colleague Master Mistletoe and I thought it would be a great privilege if you were escorted back to Tewkesbury by servants of the English Crown displaying the glorious livery of the French king.' He tried to keep the laughter out of his voice. 'Your galleymen have been told to relax and enjoy a well-earned rest. So keen were we to ensure that all this was a pleasant surprise, we allowed no courier to leave Tewkesbury to spoil the pageant now unfolding around us. However, since we first organised this celebration, certain – how can I put it? Certain anomalies have surfaced.'

'Such as?' de Craon spluttered.

'Oh, we shall come to that by and by, but in the meantime, more pressing business demands my attention.' Corbett abruptly rose to his feet and pointed at the abbot. 'Henry Maltravers, former Knight of the Swan, self-styled Abbot of Holyrood, I indict thee of high treason, murder and theft.' He ignored the cries and exclamations as he turned slightly and pointed at Maltravers' master-at-arms. 'John Devizes, self-styled master-at-arms to the said Maltravers, I do indict thee of high treason, murder and theft. Both of you will be immediately taken into custody and brought before King's Bench under a special commission of oyer and terminer, tomorrow morning at first light, in the nave of the abbey church. The justiciars who will hear the indictment will be myself, Lord Roger Mortimer and Ralph of Ancaster, popularly known as the Ravenmaster. I hold the right to convene such a court; to listen, judge and dispense justice. For the moment, I am finished. Take the prisoners away.'

Corbett's proclamation caused deep consternation. Abbot Henry banged the table. Devizes made to draw his dagger, but the men Ap Ythel had massed in the stairwell outside pushed into the chamber, and Ranulf, who'd hurried around the room, struck the master-at-arms a stinging blow so that he staggered back, dropping the blade. The tumult lasted a little longer until the two prisoners were held fast and hustled out of the room. Jude and Crispin continued their pleas that the pair must be innocent. Corbett refused to listen. He ordered that the chambers and the possessions of both men be rigorously searched, and shouted at de Craon to keep to his quarters or he would answer for it.

He then made a swift survey of Holyrood. Satisfied that the combined cohorts of Ap Ythel, Mortimer and Mistletoe had now secured the abbey, its defences, doors and stores, he returned to his chamber. He refused to meet a delegation from the community, led by the prior, pleading for their abbot. Instead, he concentrated on his bill of indictment against Maltravers and Devizes. He revised it again and again. As he did so, he carefully reflected on what he had written, and the more he did, the more certain he became of one great weakness in his opponents. He quietly vowed that he would exploit this in the coming confrontation with the accused.

Early next morning, after he had washed, shaved and changed into fresh clothing, Corbett met the others in the refectory to break his fast. He had decreed that a strong cohort of men-at-arms both within and without the abbey church would keep the peace. He shook his head at Mortimer's warning that rumours about what was happening in Holyrood must have seeped out into the valley. 'Even if they have,' he declared, 'the fire arrows and the threats are nothing but empty mummery, no more dangerous than a burning log.'

Once they had finished in the refectory, Corbett and his companions moved to the abbey church. The area of the nave close to the sanctuary had been turned into a special court, with a huge table, which would serve as King's Bench, set up before the entrance to the rood screen. It was covered with a red baize cloth, and laid out across it were Corbett's war sword, a crucifix and a book of the Gospels, as well as writs and warrants, all sealed by the king, giving Corbett the authority to act as he saw fit in his role as the Crown's special justiciar. It was decided that Mistletoe would act as scribe. Ranulf would be clerk of the court, responsible for good order and harmony during the proceedings. De Craon, Jude, Crispin and others sat on benches to Corbett's right, almost hidden by the shadows of the transept. Men-at-arms guarded every entrance. Ap Ythel's bowmen stood very close, weapons at the ready.

The court sat shortly after first light. The abbey nave was now warmed by a line of braziers, whilst cresset torches and every available candle had been lit to dissipate the gloom as well as fend off the morning mist, which crept beneath doors and through shutters to drift ghost-like along the nave. Corbett took his seat, Mortimer and the Ravenmaster sitting self-importantly on either side. Ranulf proclaimed the court to be in session and declared that all who had business before it now be brought in. He rang a handbell. A door opened and Maltravers and Devizes, their hands tied before them, were escorted in by two bowmen, who made them sit on chairs facing the bench. Both prisoners struggled and began to protest. Ranulf shouted at them to be silent.

A high stool was placed close to the side of the table, where witnesses could sit and extend both hands towards the book of the Gospels and the crucifix when taking the oath. The thick beeswax candles standing in spigots on each of the table's four corners were lit. Ranulf again shook the handbell and shouted instructions at the guards. Brother Dunstan, assisted by three lay brothers, came out of the dark carrying a door taken off its hinges from one of the cells below Falcon Tower. This was cleverly positioned between two of the pillars along the north transept: a neat fit, so that its high metal grille could be clearly seen.

Corbett glanced swiftly at the two prisoners. Both had given up protesting their innocence and had lost their haughty outrage at being accused. Devizes remained iron-faced, but Maltravers was clearly agitated, and openly winced when Chanson and some ostlers brought in a man of straw fashioned in the stables. This was placed next to the cell door. The huge straw doll was flimsy, though its head was a thick ball of tightly inter-woven strands. Jude and Crispin looked openly mystified at proceedings, but de Craon sat with his lips tightly pursed. He grasped the arms of his chair as if he intended to rise and protest, but caught Corbett's glare and slumped back.

Ranulf called for silence, then slowly repeated the indictment Corbett had issued the previous day. He asked how the prisoners wished to plead. Both men replied with 'not guilty'. Maltravers then demanded to see the evidence for what he called 'a litany of heinous and false allegations'. Corbett replied that he was only too willing to provide it, as he would soon demonstrate.

Brother Dunstan was summoned and took the chair of testimony. He stretched across and touched both the crucifix and the book of the Gospels as he repeated after Ranulf, 'I have sworn a great oath and I will not repent of it. I shall tell the truth and only the truth or suffer the fires of hell.'

'Brother Dunstan,' Corbett demanded, 'you are the blacksmith in Holyrood?'

'I am.'

'And you are most skilled in all matters of the forge?'

'I hope so. I pride myself as such.'

'And you fashion weapons?'

'Of course.'

'Including arbalests?'

'Occasionally.'

'Could you show my fellow justiciars what I found in your forge, consigned with other items to the rubbish heap?'

Brother Dunstan opened the sack he'd brought in and placed between his sandalled feet. He took out an arbalest and handed this over for Mortimer and the Ravenmaster to inspect before passing it to Corbett.

'Brother Dunstan, what is so unique about this crossbow?'

'The groove is narrower than on an ordinary arbalest, which is usually broad because it has to take a bolt that is closely feathered at one end, hard and bristly, while the killing end consists of a point with five or six jagged barbs. Little wonder successive popes have decreed that all who use a crossbow are subject to excommunication from the Church.'

'Yes, quite!' Corbett picked up the weapon and handed it back to Dunstan. 'And you collected from Brother Crispin, as I asked, one of the nails used to kill a member of this community?'

'I did.'

Brother Crispin kept his head down but nodded in agreement.

'Brother,' Corbett demanded, 'you must reply.'

'It is the nail that killed poor Mark,' the infirmarian declared.

'And on my request, Brother Dunstan,' Corbett continued, 'you used this nail in the arbalest you now hold as you would a crossbow bolt?'

'Yes, and it worked.'

'You have it ready now?'

'Yes, Sir Hugh.'

'So.' Corbett pointed to the straw man. 'Show the court.'

Dunstan lumbered to his feet. He opened his wallet, took out the nail and slid it into the narrow groove on the arbalest, its point jutting out and its broader base resting against the cord, which was now winched back so the weapon was primed.

'Continue.'

'Yes, Sir Hugh.' The blacksmith walked slowly towards the straw man. He took aim, positioning the crossbow carefully, and then pulled the lever. A sharp click and the nail hurtled forward, piercing the centre of the straw man's tightly woven head.

'That,' Corbett declared, 'is how the murders were committed! A specially crafted hand-held arbalest fashioned to deliver a long, sharp nail with great force at close quarters.'

'And what has this to do with me?' Maltravers shouted. He gestured with his bound hands. 'Arbalest, nails, grooves, so what?'

'Brother Dunstan,' Corbett said, 'I found that

crossbow in the rubbish heap of your forge. Did you make it?'

'No, but,' Dunstan turned to point at Maltravers, 'you came to my forge some weeks ago. You worked on fashioning something. After you left, I found scraps, pieces and other items rejected by you; that crossbow, unfinished, was one of them. Sir Hugh asked me to complete it, and I did.'

'That is not true!' Maltravers yelled.

'Oh, but it is. Ranulf, show them what you found in our abbot's chamber.' Corbett gestured at the Clerk of the Green Wax, seated at the far end of the table. Ranulf rose, walked into the transept and brought out a sack from which he drew another arbalest, similar to the one Dunstan had used, as well as a small quiver pot crammed with flat-bottomed spiked nails. Corbett asked Dunstan to inspect these and then to prime the second arbalest. The blacksmith sent another nail whirring through the air to smash into the straw man's head. The silence in the nave was now palpable. Jude and Crispin were distinctly uncomfortable, Mortimer and the Ravenmaster clearly absorbed, whilst Mistletoe kept scrawling swiftly, though now and again he would pause to shake his head.

'That arbalest, those nails were found in your chamber, Father Abbot.'

'I know nothing of this,' Maltravers stammered. 'Sir Hugh . . .' He turned and glared at Devizes, who sat as if carved out of stone, staring fixedly before him. Corbett felt a quiet stab of pleasure. He was correct.

There was a grievous weakness in the chain that bound his opponents, and he was determined to exploit it.

'You were saying?' Mortimer demanded.

'Of course I know nothing about this,' Maltravers repeated. 'I can produce witnesses who will describe how an assailant, armed with a spike and mallet, entered my chamber and tried to kill me.'

'Nonsense,' Corbett riposted. 'A masque, a mummer's ploy arranged by you and your henchman. You used one of the assassins hidden away in those secret tunnels and galleries. He was your pretended assailant, lowering over you then fleeing from your room, knocking aside other members of the community including Devizes. A miracle play for all to see! You were never in any danger. Devizes managed it all.' He paused. 'Of course we could ask how such an attack could take place, given Devizes' constant protection of you. In the end, it was easy to arrange. The same is true of the poisoning, a fable to present you as a victim being stalked by an assassin, the injured party rather than the perpetrator.

'What is significant,' Corbett continued remorselessly, 'is the identical language you and Devizes used when describing the murderous attacks on other members of your community. Brother Crispin?' Corbett gestured at the infirmarian. 'How did you describe the way those nails pierced the victims' foreheads?'

'Oh,' Crispin spread his hands, 'the same as everybody else, that they were driven into the murdered man's skull.'

'Brother Jude?' Corbett asked. 'Lord Mortimer, wouldn't you agree?'

'Yes,' they chorused. 'And,' Mortimer added, 'that is exactly how you, Sir Hugh, described the killings. And that was the mystery. How could a nail be driven in at close quarters, killing a former warrior with no sign of a struggle or any evidence of resistance?'

'Yet,' Corbett accused, 'you, Devizes, and you, Maltravers, both talked of nails being loosed at their victims, which is how you would describe a crossbow bolt being delivered.' He paused. 'Don't you remember, Maltravers? You used the word when we first met. Devizes did the same after the pretended attack upon you.'

'Words, clerk, clever tricks,' Devizes snarled, half rising from his chair, the archer standing behind him forcing him back down. 'How on earth,' he demanded, 'could we kill those . . .' He stumbled over his words, and Corbett wondered what he was going to say, but Devizes, licking his lips, eyes blinking, abruptly paused, rocking backwards and forwards in the chair. 'How could we kill those comrades?' he blurted out.

'Oh, very easily. Brother Anselm was your first victim. He answered the door to his chamber, not expecting any danger, even more so when he saw you, or his father abbot, or perhaps even both. He stood there almost unaware of the crossbow rising, so quick, so easy, and the nail was released. It was the same with Brother Richard. He opened a door to go down the steps of one of the towers. He met a comrade. He sensed no danger yet in a matter of a few breaths he was slain, a nail loosed direct into his forehead, a killing blow. Now as for the other murders . . .'

Corbett paused, sifting amongst the papers before him. He knew the path he was about to follow, fully determined to break the murderous pair before him.

'Oh yes, the other murders, hideous killings.' He leant his elbows on the table. 'I will finish describing the dreadful slayings you are responsible for, and only then will I give the reasons behind them. So we now come to the murder of Lord Mortimer's man as he rested in the abbey guest house. This unfortunate posed as a wandering beggar. In truth he had come to Holyrood to meet Lord Mortimer and inform him about what was happening in the valley.'

'He collapsed and died!' Devizes shouted. 'Brother Crispin dressed the corpse; he found no . . .' He fell silent, shoulders sagging.

'Yes, yes.' The infirmarian jumped to his feet. 'You came down to the corpse chamber, you were most curious about that old man and how he died.'

'You knew full well, didn't you, Devizes?' Corbett mocked. 'You keep a strict eye on Holyrood. You scrutinise all visitors, including that old man who seemed to be so interested in Lord Mortimer's imminent arrival. You suspected he was Mortimer's spy bringing crucial information out of the Valley of Shadows. Did you learn that directly from him, or was it the inquisitive Brother Norbert? Whatever, you certainly did not want Lord Mortimer to be appraised about what was happening around Holyrood.' He held up a sheet of parchment. 'We have thoroughly searched all your belongings and we found a small coffer containing certain powders and potions. I am sure they are poisonous. You gave that old man a blackjack of mulled ale, laced with some venomous concoction.'

'I did not.'

'Master Devizes, you were seen by no less a person than the abbey kitchener, Brother Mark. He noticed the blackjack prepared in his kitchen, which some servitor was to take to the beggar man waiting in the guest house. Brother Mark wondered why someone else had taken that tankard to the visitor and not returned it. He was referring to you, Devizes. He was puzzled about why the all-important master-at-arms should bother himself with a beggarly visitor. He mentioned the matter in Raphael's hearing when the sacristan brought candles to the kitchen that evening. You were quick, my Lord Abbot, to cast doubt on Raphael, saying he was the only senior brother who did not attend compline at the very time Mark was murdered. You were implying that perhaps he might be responsible for the kitchener's death, especially as he had disappeared by then.'

'I hear what you say, Corbett, but Master Devizes was with me in church at the time our kitchener was killed.'

'Murdered,' Corbett retorted. 'Brother Mark was murdered.'

'How could Devizes be responsible when he was in church with me?'

'No, he wasn't!'

Corbett glanced in surprise at Brother Jude.

'He wasn't,' the prior repeated. 'I remember that hideous night well. I was nervous, agitated by the horrid events occurring in Holyrood. I was late for compline that evening because of you.' He pointed at de Craon. 'You had just arrived, loudly demanding to see Abbot Henry. I went into the church, but of course, apart from the candles, the sanctuary was shadow-filled, so I wasn't seen. I considered approaching you in your stall, Lord Abbot, then thought I would try and catch the eye of Master Devizes. However, I could not see him, so I decided otherwise. Only now,' he cleared his throat, 'here this morning, do I remember it.'

'You killed that beggar man, Devizes,' Corbett declared. 'You murdered him to silence his tongue. I suspect you returned to the kitchen and Brother Mark greeted you with an innocent enough question. Why had the abbot's important master-at-arms bothered to take a tankard of ale to a beggar man in the guest house? He would have been intrigued by such an occurrence. He must have asked you where the tankard was. Brother Mark was most scrupulous about the contents of his kitchen.'

Corbett heard a murmur of agreement from Crispin and Jude. Devizes turned and threw them a venomous glance.

'After consultation with your master,' Corbett continued, 'you hastened back through the abbey. The kitchener's clacking tongue had to be silenced. Most of the community were in the choir, singing compline. You crept into the kitchen yard. You knew Brother Mark would come out. When he did, you emerged from the dark like the midnight thing you are, raised that specially fashioned arbalest and released its clasp, loosing a spiked nail straight into his forehead.'

Corbett stared down at the sheets of parchment in front of him. When he glanced up again, he felt a glow of pleasure. Devizes had moved slightly away from his master, turning in the chair as if he wished to distance himself as much as possible. The clerk was desperate to break this malicious pair. He had swiftly read a scribbled note from the Ravenmaster: deft strokes of the pen that described Corbett's indictment as logical and plausible though still lacking that vital evidence that could send a man to the gallows.

'As for the other murders,' he sat back in his chair, pointing at Devizes, 'you know the customs and traditions of the Welsh tribes, especially those bitterly opposed to English rule. You must also be aware of the rituals of covens such as the Black Chesters. These groups have two things in common. First, an implacable hostility to the English Crown. Yes, Monsieur de Craon?' Corbett smiled thinly at the French envoy. 'Am I boring you? Rest assured I will come to you by and by.' He returned to the indictment. 'Second, both these groups believe in immolation. Those who have fought in Wales know all about this, don't they, Ap Ythel?'

'Yes,' the captain of archers replied, coming forward as Corbett beckoned him. He sat in the testimony chair, hands outstretched to touch the cross and the book of the Gospels. 'On my oath,' he declared, 'I know all about immolation, as do my comrades. It is the act of self-sacrifice a warrior makes for the common good of his tribe. He will lay down his life for the many.'

'When we took those two prisoners during the battle in the Valley of Shadows,' Corbett continued, after thanking Ap Ythel, 'they were placed in the cells beneath Falcon Tower. Now Norbert, that drunken old lay brother, heard the approach of the assassin – you, Master Devizes. Cowled and masked, you crept to the cell door and beckoned the two prisoners close. You heatedly urged both to immolate themselves: to sacrifice their lives for the tribe, the cause, or whatever bound those two men together in their struggle against the English and the abbey of Holyrood in particular. Indeed, they had no choice. They must have known they would be interrogated, tortured, condemned to a gruesome death, for they had fought against the English king's own special envoy to these parts. I rode into the Valley of Shadows with the royal standard unfolded; all opposition to that is high treason. A man convicted of such rebellion could be hanged, drawn and quartered. You, Devizes, offered those prisoners the warrior's way out, an honourable death that would not give their captors any satisfaction. You then carried out the executions, first one and then the other. Death would have been swift.

'Brother Dunstan,' Corbett snapped his fingers at the

blacksmith, still standing in the darkened transept, 'bring the arbalest, show us how nails can be loosed through the grille in that door.'

Dunstan approached. He brought up the arbalest, placing a nail in the groove, pushing it tight, as he winched back the cord. He rammed the crossbow hard against the grille of the cell door brought up earlier, positioning it so the nail would clear the small iron bars either side. He released the catch, and the nail whirled out to smash against the wall beyond.

'See,' Corbett proclaimed, 'how swiftly it can be done. At the same time, you posed a great mystery. How could two able-bodied men, warriors, be killed in a secure, sealed chamber, the door held fast, with no sign of resistance or the slightest indication of a struggle? Well?' He clapped his hands. 'Now you have it.'

'Very clever,' Maltravers snapped, 'but who is being charged here? Me, Devizes or both of us?'

Corbett stared long and hard at the sheets before him. He dared not glance up. He could not hide the pleasure, the sheer joy at Maltravers' question. The separation was about to begin.

'Both of you,' he said at last, still keeping his head down. 'And I shall prove that.' He paused for effect. 'At least against one of you. However, at this moment in time, I truly believe Devizes was the dagger, and you, my Lord Abbot, the hand that held it.'

He glanced up. Maltravers was leaning forward, hands on his knees; now and again he moved his head as if he wanted to study Devizes sitting beside him. 'Oh, please God,' Corbett prayed silently, 'help me to divide and to vanquish.'

He paused, as if listening to the silence that stretched along that long, dark nave. When he spoke again, his voice was quiet.

'The act of immolation was the key to another killing. You remember the third prisoner we took during that frenetic fight in the snow just beyond the main gate? We were about to interrogate him. We threatened him with torture. Apparently terrified, he agreed to confess but then began to shout how he was prepared to immolate himself. At the time, Ap Ythel was intrigued by this but did not realise what the prisoner truly meant. Our captured rebel certainly did. He knew that his leader, his ally who sheltered in Holyrood, would undoubtedly be close enough to hear him, and would carry out the act for him.

'You, Maltravers, and your accomplice prepared for this. We took that prisoner from the cells at his own insistence. He acted as if he wished to put as much distance as possible between himself and the place where he'd been threatened. He was moved, made to walk across the bailey, and in doing so, he made his own immolation all the easier. You and your familiar are undoubtedly skilled bowmen. You visited the cells where we first lodged that prisoner. You could have hidden in one of those secret tunnels and passageways that run like a maze beneath Holyrood. You would have learnt everything you needed to. As for the actual killing, one of you positioned yourself near a window or in some dark recess to loose the deadly shaft. There again, it might have been one of those secret, silent assassins you allowed into Holyrood to lurk and prowl along its hidden passageways and galleries: a matter I shall return to, I assure you.'

'Where?' Maltravers shouted, half rising, only to be pushed back by his guard. 'Where is the proof for all this? I am a Knight of the Swan, a close confidant of the old king, a cherished courtier of his son. I am a cleric—'

'You are not,' Corbett retorted. 'You assumed the garb of the Benedictine order. You follow its rule but you are not, nor have you ever been, a sworn cleric. You are what you are, an old soldier turned bitter and greedy. A man who has grown tired of his life here. A killer who will remove anyone who obstructs the path he wants to follow.'

'Proof! Evidence!' Maltravers yelled back. 'Or will we come to that by and by, which, in my view, will be never?'

'I have the casket, Maltravers. I have the casket, the dagger and the diagrams describing those secret tunnels beneath the abbey.'

'You can't have . . .' Maltravers fell silent as he realised what he'd said.

Corbett's declaration and Maltravers' response stilled all noise along the nave. The disgraced abbot sat as if poleaxed, and for the first time, Devizes looked deeply anxious and alarmed.

'I have the casket and the plans, Maltravers, and yes,

I will come to that by and by. Everything in its due order. So let us return to the murders, and your next victim. Brother Norbert, poor man, a toper deep in his cups, a bore whom people avoided. Nevertheless, he was sharp enough. He had a conversation with that beggar man who wanted to meet Lord Mortimer. He also glimpsed at least one of our enemies being allowed into Holyrood. As regards the latter, I suspect, Master Devizes, that he informed you about it.' Corbett composed himself for the lie he was about to tell. 'He certainly told me what he had seen, and how he had spoken to you, the abbot's master-at-arms.'

'That drunken old fool couldn't have . . .' Devizes' voice trailed away.

'Oh, he certainly did, so why didn't you inform anyone else?'

Devizes, slumped in his chair, just shook his head.

'Norbert was a gossip,' Corbett continued. 'He talked to Raphael and God knows who else, which is why you decided to silence his clacking tongue forever. He had seen things near a postern gate he shouldn't have. He gabbled about mysterious lights, individuals appearing where they shouldn't be. He was referring to the cohort of assassins you allowed into that secret hidden maze beneath Holyrood. Above all, he had been in a cell directly opposite the one holding those prisoners taken in the Valley of Shadows. Deep in his cups, he had overheard a conversation about what he thought was emulation but of course was really immolation, the act of self-sacrifice on behalf of the entire tribe.'

Corbett shrugged. 'Norbert peered through the grille of his prison door. He glimpsed something that looked like a hammer but was actually the crosspiece of an arbalest.' He glanced at his two fellow justiciars and took heart from their hard, set faces. They were hunters, and he believed they were committed to pursuing a powerful and dangerous quarry, not just empty, flitting shadows. He gestured at the accused. 'You slipped down to those cells. So easy for you, Devizes.' He decided to concentrate on the handsome young man whose face was so contorted in hate. 'After all, you are master-at-arms here. You enjoy the full authority of your abbot to come and go as you please, and of course, you had access to that sprawling secret maze beneath the abbey. You could disappear and re-emerge at will and no one would be any the wiser. Along those galleries weapons and stores were piled, and as I shall demonstrate, your comrades lurked there waiting for the signal to emerge.

'Anyway, to return to Norbert, he would have been an easy victim, coaxed to draw close to the cell door under some pretext or other. He pressed his head against the grille to peer out, and so met his death.'

Corbett pushed back his chair. 'I have said enough for the moment,' he declared. 'Captain Ap Ythel, offer the prisoners food and drink.' He pointed to the serving board Ranulf had set up in the transept. 'There is sustenance: wine, ale, cooked meats and whatever the buttery can provide. During this respite I would be grateful if neither I nor my fellow justiciars are approached.' He rose, clasped on his sword belt and swung his cloak about him. Noticing a flurry of movement out of the corner of his eye, he turned to confront de Craon.

'I . . . I . . .' the envoy stammered.

Corbett's hand fell to the hilt of his dagger. 'Keep away, sir, or I'll hang you from the battlements and take the consequences. I know that you are deeply involved in this mischief.'

De Craon backed off, fingers fluttering. Corbett walked around him and down the nave, Ranulf trailing behind. They passed the guard Mistletoe had posted. Corbett raised a hand in salutation and walked out through a postern door to stand on the main steps of the abbey church.

'Sir Hugh,' Ranulf whispered, 'we do not have the casket or any of those documents.'

'I know,' Corbett murmured, 'but Maltravers betrayed himself.' He turned to face Ranulf. 'You know about the game of five peas?'

'Of course. You have five cups. One of them hides a pea. You overturn them, move them about. You win if you choose the correct cup.'

'Very well. So if you turn over four cups and find no pea, where do you think it is?'

'Under the fifth, of course.'

'And if it's not there, where?'

'The cheating wretch who organised the game must have it.'

'Precisely. We have searched everywhere and not found anything even resembling the casket, so I can guess where it must be. Take two of Ap Ythel's archers and pull the abbot's chamber to pieces. This abbey is full of secret caches and hidden cubicles. I wager you'll find something cleverly hidden away. It's logical. Maltravers would have kept both items hidden until the last moment before leaving here.'

Corbett went back inside and the court reassembled, slightly delayed by Maltravers demanding to be taken to the nearest garderobe. He returned, hands rebound, and immediately began to protest at the legality of what was happening, demanding to be released. Mortimer ordered him to be quiet and Corbett resumed his indictment.

'What,' he declared, 'will be asked by those we answer to? What is the *fons et origo*, the root of all this evil? In truth, one strand is our previous king, God rest him and God bless his memory. We all know about the ferocious battle of the caves at the far end of the Valley of Shadows. During that battle a coven of warlocks together with a host of Welsh rebels were destroyed. Prisoners were taken, many of them cruelly hanged. Some escaped, retreating into the silent vastness of the forests that cover the valley. A certain mysterious young man was also taken prisoner during the struggle. An individual who, according to gossip and rumour, bore an uncanny resemblance to our late king. Indeed, it was the presence of this mysterious individual in the Valley of Shadows that led to the bloody confrontation at the caves.

'Now after the battle, this young man was not executed but was handed over to the old king's personal comitatus, the Knights of the Swan. They were ordered to keep him secure in one gilded cage after another until the old king died. Once this happened, they withdrew from court life to adopt the rule, garb and horarium of the Benedictine order. In doing so, they also had to select an appropriate site for their community. They were encouraged to choose this place. Brothers Anselm and Richard, men skilled in masonry, were entrusted with building the abbey fortress. An easy enough task with wood and quarry stone being so close and plentiful: they had at their disposal whatever resources they needed as well as the full support of the Crown. Holyrood was swiftly built, constructed over previous dwellings, perhaps an ancient fortress or shrine: a veritable maze of underground tunnels, corridors and paths that Anselm and Richard kept secret to themselves. Once it was finished, the community moved in, developing and enriching the place even further. They also brought with them that mysterious prisoner. Now at first,' Corbett spread his hands, 'Holyrood flourished, but a serpent had entered this Eden.'

'Devizes! Devizes!' the prior shouted. 'John Devizes, I always thought, I suspected something was wrong.'

'Did you?' Devizes yelled back, face contorted in anger. 'And what about you, the Knights of the Swan, soaked in the blood of innocents? I remember you at the battle of the caves: your sword scarlet from tip to hilt, kicking aside the corpses of my loved ones. I saw you and the others hacking and hewing, shattering bone, splitting flesh. I remember the bodies falling, smashing

against the cliff side to be pierced on the rocks below.
And that wasn't enough. You fastened ropes round the
necks of men, women and children, tossing one end
over a branch. They were hoisted to kick, struggle and
choke to death. You group of bastards, you . . .'

Maltravers tried to restrain him, whispering heatedly,
but Devizes just turned away.

'You took a hostage after the battle of the caves,
didn't you, Maltravers?' Corbett declared. 'Remember?
In a fit of mercy, our former royal master allowed each
of you to choose one of the prisoners. You chose John
Devizes.'

'Gareth Aplandal!' Devizes shouted. 'My true name
is Gareth Aplandal.'

'Of course it is,' Corbett replied, keeping his face
impassive, though he secretly rejoiced at what was
happening. 'However, before this court you are John
Devizes, accused of hideous crimes. You were taken into
Maltravers' household, but in a matter of years the
servant became the master. I cannot comment on other
members of this community, but Henry Maltravers has
no love for women. However, his love for you was
greater than that of David for Jonathan as described
in the Book of Kings. You became lovers. You shared
the same bed. You indulged in the same sexual practices.'

Corbett's declaration provoked nothing but a deep,
stony silence from the accused and the others who sat
watching and listening. The love he was describing, of
one man for another, was common enough at court but
very rarely discussed or referred to. The Church strictly

proscribed it, whilst the Crown had no choice but to enforce dire penalties on those convicted of such practices.

Mortimer's harsh voice shattered the silence. 'You claim they are lovers?'

'Oh yes, their closeness is a matter of fact. Prior Jude, Brother Crispin? Their very closeness,' Corbett emphasised.

'Yes, yes,' both men replied. 'But,' Jude held up a hand, 'it is not for us to judge.'

'Of course not,' Corbett snapped. 'That is for me. Their closeness is one thing. What I describe is another. Maltravers, I was in your chamber once. I noticed your very comfortable four-poster bed. You made a mistake that day. The curtains on the bed had been pulled back. I noticed that the coverlet on both sides had been disturbed, both bolsters had been used. Two people had slept in that bed.'

'It's not uncommon,' Maltravers protested, 'for a squire or page to share the same bed as his master. An innocent practice devoid of any sin.'

His reply provoked a loud, sneering laugh from Mortimer and a wry smile from the stony-faced Ravenmaster.

'Sharing a blanket on the edge of a battlefield or on duty in some freezing castle is one thing,' the marcher lord scoffed, 'but a luxurious four-poster bed in a warm, scented chamber is another. You do not deny it, Maltravers, nor does your familiar Devizes. Why? Why should he sleep with you? Is there not a cot bed in your chamber, Father Abbot?' Mortimer's voice was heavy with sarcasm. 'And doesn't Devizes have his own quarters, his own bed?'

'You were, and are, lovers,' Corbett declared, quietly wondering how Ranulf was faring in his search of Maltravers' chamber. 'And so we turn to another powerful strand in this murderous masque. Henry Maltravers, you were a leading knight of the old king's court. You revelled in all the chivalry and pageantry of Westminster and Kings Langley. You sat high in the councils of the king. You rode next to him in battle. You were a lord of the soil before whom everyone scraped and bowed. You dressed in the finest linen. You drank the richest wine and ate the most delicious food. True, you fought on stinking battlefields, in the dark woods of Wales and along the windswept glens of Scotland, but your rewards were very great. Indeed, you were a king in everything but name. You could go where you wanted, do what you liked. You waxed arrogant and proud.

'However, you were committed to the vision of the Knights of the Swan and their vow to leave public life once the old king died. So when you had to embrace another life, one most suitable for your comrades, men such as Crispin and Jude, you soon grew tired of it. True, you were the abbot of Holyrood, the official keeper of the king's great relic, the dagger in its priceless casket, and responsible for the Crown's most important prisoner: that young man masked and confined in the vaults beneath Falcon Tower. But that wasn't enough. You'd tasted the wine of power and thirsted for it again. More importantly, John Devizes, as we shall call him, captured your heart, your mind, your soul and above all your body. I suspect,' Corbett continued, 'you became infatuated with him, that very handsome young man. You took great pride in raising him, educating him in the skills of battle and the use of weaponry. A man to become your bodyguard by day and night.'

He paused as the postern door at the far end of the transept opened and Ranulf strode noisily up the church, beckoning to Corbett with one hand whilst holding a leather sack in the other. Corbett waved him on through the rood screen and then declared that the court would adjourn for a short while.

Once in the sanctuary, the whispers of those gathered in the nave beyond echoing eerily, Ranulf crouched down. He undid the neck of the leather sack and took out a thin folio of vellum sheets pressed between leaves of stiffened parchment. He put this on the floor, then drew out the precious casket with its keys. Corbett hurriedly tried one and then the others, opening the casket and staring at the assassin's dagger lying within. '*Hoc habeo*,' he whispered. 'I have it.' He patted Ranulf on the shoulder. 'You are God's own true good clerk.'

Ranulf glanced away in embarrassment.

'Where did you find it?' Corbett asked.

'As you said, in Maltravers' chamber. There's part of a wall, what looks like an ordinary slab of stone, no different from the rest, deep in a shadowy corner, with a table pressed against it. In reality it is a cleverly dressed square of wood, carved, coated and depicted to look like grey stone. We discovered this by tapping every bloody inch of that wall until we discovered what it concealed.' Ranulf got to his feet. 'We found the sack.'

Murmuring his thanks, Corbett picked up the folio and took it across the sanctuary to catch a sliver of light. He leafed through the pages, studying the intricately drawn plans, which showed in bright red ink the maze of corridors, paths, passages and galleries running beneath Holyrood. Lines of black ink ran parallel to each of these, twisting and turning to indicate the galleries, steps and stairwells of the abbey above. He noticed how an 'S' painted in white demonstrated where a secret opening could be found. Often this symbol had a finely etched note beside it, such as 'paving to the right of devil's door' or 'stone before the centre of the rood screen'. He could imagine how Anselm and Richard had recorded all this as they plotted the intricate map, taking great pride in what they were doing. Both men had kept what they had found a secret, even from their abbot and his familiar. In the end, this had proved to be a hideous mistake, and the two masons had paid for it with their lives.

Corbett was tempted to adjourn the court and study the folio in greater detail, but the murmur of voices from the nave was growing louder. The hours were passing and he wished to proceed as swiftly as possible. Ordering Ranulf to keep the sack and its contents safe and, for the moment, secret, he returned to the court and resumed proceedings.

'You,' he pointed at Maltravers, 'became bored of your life here, frustrated and angry. You wanted to be away, safe and comfortable with your young lover. In a word, you had grown tired of all the nonsense surrounding the Knights of the Swan and the old king, and had had enough of being lord of a lonely, bleak abbey fortress along the wilds of the Welsh March. You wanted to return to a life of luxury, but how?' He shrugged. 'You missed what you once had, but you had responsibilities here. And where could you go? Oh yes,' he raised his voice and glared at de Craon, 'this Eden had more than one serpent.'

'Be careful, Corbett, I am an accredited envoy.'

'Oh shut up,' Corbett retorted. 'You are now before the Crown of England's court of King's Bench, accused of meddling in matters no accredited envoy has any business with, so no more of your nonsense, your posturing, your rank hypocrisy.' He sifted amongst the sheets of vellum. 'To return to this precious pair, these assassins, murderers of their own brethren. You certainly prove the dictum that man can become wolf to man, for that is what you two are: slaughterers, killers to the bone. You, Maltravers, plotted how you could still live in the luxury you were accustomed to if you gave up this abbey and all it held. You were already walking down a path leading into a deep spiritual darkness. Devizes became your lover between the sheets. He held you close as he turned your soul and twisted your mind.

I do not know if he loves you, but I am sure he hates what you and this abbey represent.'

Corbett rose and came around the court bench to confront Maltravers. 'Do you think,' he leant down, 'do you really think that he has forgotten or forgiven the battle of the caves? The hideous massacre of his family and loved ones? He may have been a boy, but a child can hate as much as he can love, and that is passionately. Isn't that correct?' He turned to Devizes. 'You watched your loved ones die. Did you see them hanged like hunks of meat from the trees? Did you?' he taunted. 'Do you remember that? Were you there as they gasped out their last breath, bodies twitching, legs kicking, their faces turning purple? Is that what made you the killer you now are? Come, come tell me.'

Devizes, his features mottled with anger, abruptly brought his head back and spat into Corbett's face. The bowman standing behind him punched the master-at-arms, and would have done so again, but Corbett raised a hand.

'I have my answer,' he murmured, and taking the napkin Ranulf brought, he wiped the spit from his face and walked back to his chair. 'Devizes never forgot the massacre, but others did. The seasons passed and the Knights of the Swan prepared. I am sure the location of Holyrood was chosen by the king, because he wanted an English presence close to that sombre valley. Anselm and Richard would have been delighted at such a site, and I am sure that you, Lord Abbot, and the handsome young man who pleases you so much heartily concurred.'

'We all agreed to this place,' Brother Jude intervened. 'But from the very start, Devizes was close to Maltravers, forever whispering into his ear.'

'True, true.' Crispin was staring at Maltravers with an expression of compassionate desperation, as if he wished to help his former master but realised he couldn't. 'This venture was begun eleven years ago,' he continued, 'and finished about seven years later. The old king died and we assembled here. However, from the very start, Devizes was so close to our abbot we called him his shadow. We thought it innocent enough, believing that Maltravers may have seen him as his son; he was certainly his constant companion.'

'Think of a web being woven,' Corbett declared, 'or the twisting of cords into a rope.' He emphasised the point with his fingers. 'The location of this abbey fortress, its bleakness, standing so close to the Valley of Shadows. The survivors of the massacre sheltering there, full of hatred for the English and certainly for Holyrood. Maltravers growing tired of it all, absorbed, infatuated with his young lover, who in turn dreams dire dreams of revenge against the abbey and all it symbolises.'

He rose and came round the table to stand over de Craon, who glared sullenly back. 'And so at long last, monsieur, we come to you. You see,' Corbett bent down, staring into the envoy's hooded eyes, 'we all know that the Benedictine order originated in France and has the French king as its protector. However, this ancient and sacred privilege covers all offshoots of that great order, including the community at Holyrood. Indeed, in the charter of foundation of this abbey, a copy of which is kept in its library, both the king of England and the king of France are styled as protectors to whom the abbot has the inalienable right to appeal for help, sustenance and defence. It is a right enshrined in the order, confirmed by kings and declared sacrosanct by popes. The present Holy Father, the Frenchman Bertrand de Got, Clement V, living in exile, the guest of your august master, has confirmed this.' He returned to his chair. 'In truth, Maltravers, you plotted to create a *casus belli*, a case for war, a pretext to appeal to the king of France.'

'Why?' de Craon demanded. 'What good—'

'Not for the English Crown, I agree,' Corbett interrupted. 'But your friend and ally Maltravers, well known as an envoy to the French court, was to spin a web and so provoke a veritable storm. You, my not-so-saintly Lord Abbot, entertained de Craon at Holyrood last Easter. By then, the murderous mischief you were brewing was coming to the boil. First Devizes would secretly negotiate with the valley dwellers: the survivors of the tribe who had sheltered there after the massacre as well as those in alliance with the Black Chesters. The word would go out to other wolfsheads, outlaws and rebels that a profit was to be made in the Valley of Shadows. An opportunity to wreak terrible revenge by plundering and destroying an English stronghold, a fitting response to Edward of England. Naturally, the French Crown would be only too willing to assist such mischief. No, no, de Craon, save your protests of outraged innocence. More importantly, Devizes made it known that the rebels in the valley had support from within Holyrood. Someone who would encourage them and sustain them with money and weapons, and give them the means to take the abbey fortress that could otherwise easily withstand any attack from outside. This someone, this leader, was called Paracelsus, in this case one name for two souls united in the most devious plot.'

Corbett paused. 'And so we come to how this murderous scheme was brewed.'

The Ravenmaster spoke up, raising his hand slightly. 'Surely what was happening in the valley would have reached the ears of the community here. Crispin and Jude are veteran warriors.'

'You must remember,' Crispin called out, 'that although we were highly suspicious of the valley and knew that the people who lurked there did not like us, we also concluded that they could do little about it.'

'Very true,' Corbett agreed. 'And think, sir.' He smiled at the Ravenmaster. 'People did get to know. People did try to inform the community.'

'That's correct,' Mortimer said. 'I had my own spy, that beggar man whom you, sir' – he pointed at Devizes – 'poisoned. He was bringing me information about what he'd learnt.'

'We have established that.' Corbett spoke up. 'Nor must we forget that Devizes was master-at-arms at Holyrood. Correct me if I am wrong, but wasn't he the person responsible for leading patrols into the valley?' A murmur of agreement answered his question, Crispin and Jude nodding their heads.

'Nor must we forget that hunting party,' added the prior.

'Oh no,' Corbett replied. 'That hunting party was slaughtered because of what they may have seen, something dark and malevolent forming in the valley, a real threat to Holyrood. Of course their destruction was also part of the fires of terror being stoked and fanned in and around this abbey.'

'You can prove all this?' Maltravers stirred, lifting his bound hands.

'I have the casket containing the dagger,' Corbett retorted. 'I also have the folio, the map of that secret maze. Both these you hid in your chamber. You were going to leave them there until just before you left with de Craon. Yes?'

Maltravers kept his head down and did not meet Corbett's gaze.

'So we shall start with that folio. Somehow you discovered that Anselm and Richard knew about the maze and kept its whereabouts in a secret document. They had to be removed. You coldly plotted their murders for four reasons. First, to silence them. Second, to steal that secret. Third, it gave de Craon a pretext to bustle in here all concerned about the brutal murder of a kinsman, albeit a very distant one, of his royal master. Of course he also brought a repeat invitation for you to attend the lavish royal pageant being planned for next year in Paris. It was all a sham. You plotted to be in Paris long before then.'

'And the fourth reason?' Mortimer demanded.

'Oh, to bring you here, my lord, not that you needed much encouragement.' Corbett glanced meaningfully at the marcher lord. 'You came as the king's justiciar, yes?' Mortimer nodded. 'But Maltravers also invited you,' Corbett smiled, 'as he did me. He wrote to both the king and the Secret Chancery about the hideous murders committed here and his sense of growing danger following an attempt on his life. Naturally, because of Holyrood's reputation, the treasures it held and the special prisoner it housed, my presence here as Keeper of the Secret Seal was also urgently needed. In fact, both you and I were enticed here to act as witnesses.'

'To what?' the Ravenmaster demanded.

'To what I am going to describe. Now, Anselm and Richard were murdered in the way I have explained earlier. On the night we arrived, Brother Mark was killed because of what he had seen, whilst the beggar man had been poisoned to silence him. Oh, it was all a great mystery! Maltravers claiming he too had been poisoned, his life threatened. Fire arrows seared the night sky. One of Holyrood's sentries was killed on the parapet. All ominous echoes of the old king's war in Wales. Of course the firebrands and the murder of that poor sentry were simply distractions, as well as a way of keeping our watchmen away from the walls. You, de Craon, arrived, but I suspect that a sumpter pony from your retinue turned off in the darkness to carry sustenance and weapons to our enemies in the Valley of Shadows.'

'Nonsense!'

'Nonsense, monsieur?' Corbett retorted. 'Brother Dunstan has a pile of weapons seized from those we killed in the passageways below. Most of these came from the royal foundry at Dijon.' Corbett gestured at Dunstan, who still stood watching from the darkness of the transept. 'Our Brother Dunstan is an expert on all kinds of weaponry.'

'Weapons from Dijon are used by many mercenaries.'

'Hired by you!'

De Craon just shook his head and glanced away.

'To return to my indictment. The murderous masque so cleverly plotted and planned hurtled on. There was no respite. We were hardly here when we were dispatched into the valley, at your insistence, Maltravers. We were to seek out the hunting party. We discovered that they had been slaughtered. We in turn were attacked and suffered casualties. God knows what you really intended, but such mayhem simply provided further grist to your mill. We took prisoners, who were later murdered. We then we suffered mysterious attacks from within. Somehow a hostile force had managed to get into Holyrood and stalk its community like a pack of wolves would a flock of sheep. But why?' Corbett rapped the table top with his fist. 'Why?' he repeated.

'And there's more,' Mortimer declared.

'Yes, my lord,' Corbett agreed. 'There is certainly

more. The precious casket, the sacred relic of our former king. I think it's time we saw these.'

He turned and nodded to Ranulf, who brought the sack from the transept, opened it and drew out the folio, followed by the casket, which provoked exclamations and cries of surprise. Maltravers just sat, mouth slightly gaping, whilst Devizes closed his eyes, lips moving soundlessly as if he was quietly praying.

'You stole this casket and the folio,' Corbett accused. 'You concealed them in that secret cabinet in the wall of your chamber, Maltravers, all ready for your abrupt departure. You wanted to make it look as if Raphael had stolen the casket, which is why you abducted him as well as my comrade Ranulf.'

'But why?' The Ravenmaster spoke up.

'I will answer that. I have touched upon it before. But we now come to the very root of all this evil. You, Maltravers, with your accomplice, entered into a secret pact with de Craon.' Corbett glanced at the envoy, then tapped the hilt of his sword, lying close to him on the table. 'Good,' he breathed, 'no more stupid protests. You intended to flee to France with that casket, taking with you Holyrood's mysterious prisoner. You would leave this abbey fortress as if it were some abandoned ruin, its community of former Knights of the Swan in total and utter disarray. Holyrood would be depicted as a place of pressing danger, offering no defence despite the best efforts of the English Crown. You would invoke your charter of foundation, the rule of St Benedict and appeal to the king of France. I can only imagine the glee of King Philip and his council, whatever they might say in public.

'The old king's precious relic, in its priceless casket, would be given place of honour in the royal chapel at Saint-Denis. And of course, think of the mischief that could be stirred by possessing a prisoner who looks so much like the old king. The gossip and chatter that would sweep the courts of Europe! The cries and exclamations! The suggestions and the comments! More importantly, certain questions would be loudly and publicly aired to embarrass the English Crown further. Such as: is our present king the true monarch and rightful heir of his father? Reflect on the mockery, the hypocritical cant, the false concern, the treachery and intrigue that would spill from the cauldron of devilry tended so lovingly in the chambers of the Secret Chancery at the Louvre.'

'But surely,' the Ravenmaster protested, 'the English Crown would have Maltravers and Devizes, as well as the prisoner – whom I must see – proclaimed as criminals, traitors and thieves.'

'No, no,' Corbett shook his head, 'and this is the hideous paradox, the subtle contradiction in all of this. Maltravers would claim that he and Holyrood had come under brutal attack from within and without – its abbot almost murdered, some of its leading officers slaughtered, and a precious relic stolen by a prominent member of the community – and what could he do about it? He had appealed to the English Crown, but this profited nothing. Not even the presence of Sir Hugh Corbett,

Keeper of the Secret Seal, and Lord Mortimer, the king's justiciar, could deter the perpetrators. You and I, my lord, were to be Maltravers' witness to the chaos and turbulence that swept this abbey. We could do nothing to prevent it. Even our beloved comrade Ranulf-atte-Newgate, senior Clerk of the Chancery of the Green Wax, was abducted and was to have been murdered. If we could not protect him, what sustenance could we provide anyone else?'

'You talk of defence, protection,' Mortimer queried, 'but to return to those assassins who prowled Holyrood . . .'

'What about them?'

'Sir Hugh, it's the depth of winter; everyone was swathed, cloaked and hooded against the cold. How could those bowmen distinguish friend from foe in the bailey below?'

'Ah yes.' Corbett tapped the sheet of vellum before him. 'On reflection,' he continued, 'I noticed that when it comes to dress, de Craon, Maltravers and Devizes always wear something red. That is your colour, isn't it, de Craon?' The envoy just stared back. Corbett pointed at the master-at-arms. 'You, Devizes, with your so-called holy hood, whilst your master wore a pectoral cross on a red ribbon – yet you know all this, don't you, de Craon?'

The French envoy simply shrugged and glanced away.

'I suspect our assailants,' Corbett continued, 'were under strict instructions not to harm anyone wearing red.' He paused. 'Strange, Norbert in his rantings about demons entering Holyrood mentioned he'd glimpsed the Angel of Death tinged with red. I suspect he was referring to you, Devizes.'

Mortimer pulled at the collar of his own blood-coloured jerkin. 'And if you wore red by chance, then you were truly fortunate.'

'As long as someone was killed,' Corbett agreed, 'it did not really matter. The terror deepened.'

'All very well,' the Ravenmaster interjected, 'but this casket – surely the English Crown would demand the return of such a precious relic?'

'Oh I am sure it would, but there again,' Corbett shrugged, 'Maltravers is its official keeper, whilst the casket was once housed in the Temple at Paris, and . . .'

'Since the dissolution of the Templar order,' the Ravenmaster smiled, 'everything once owned by them is forfeit to King Philip. Moreover, as has been noted, Pope Clement V is firmly in the French king's power. He would uphold such a claim.'

'But the blame for the theft of the casket was placed on poor Raphael. How would Maltravers account for having the casket if Raphael had stolen it?'

'My lord Mortimer, you have seen the maze of galleries beneath this abbey. Maltravers would concoct a lie, one amongst many. How his faithful master-at-arms searched the labyrinth and found where Raphael had hidden the casket. How, fearful of it being stolen again, he kept the discovery secret until he was safely in France. In the end, he would depict himself as the loyal abbot, the faithful keeper of the relics of Holyrood, who was poisoned, attacked and threatened. He first turned to the king of England for help, and when that failed, to Philip of France. In truth, he was tired and sick of Holyrood and all it stood for. He wanted a life of quiet opulent luxury with his young lover. Philip of France would provide that.'

Corbett steeled himself, maintaining his composure as he prepared the lure, the trap for this precious pair. 'Naturally,' he waved a hand, 'I may have it all wrong. I have accused both of you.' He stared hard at the prisoners. 'I admit, the evidence does point at two, yet one of you may have been an unwilling spectator, forced by circumstances to act as you did. Nevertheless . . .' He rose abruptly. 'Let us adjourn for a short while. Please do not approach or speak to the justiciars.'

Corbett walked into the transept and poured himself a stoup of ale. He turned and stared back. Others had risen to stretch and talk quietly amongst themselves. The prisoners' hands were freed and they were given tankards of ale. Maltravers apparently demanded to relieve himself again and was escorted under close guard to the nearest garderobe. Corbett watched him return. Maltravers blatantly ignored Devizes, who responded in kind. The clerk closed his eyes in pleasure, quietly rejoicing at the gulf opening up between the accused.

He reconvened the court and for a while sat staring silently at the accused. He then asked Mortimer and the Ravenmaster if they had any questions. Both men shook their heads. Corbett was pleased; he could tell from their faces that his fellow judges supported the indictment. He pointed at the prisoners.

'Do you have anything to say in reply to these accusations?'

Devizes spoke up. 'I do not answer to you or this court.'

Corbett stared down at the sheets of vellum on the desk before him. He quietly prayed for help with what might come next. He believed the indictment was true and correct, certainly worthy of a most detailed and clear refutation. Nevertheless, Maltravers was trapped, and there was only one possible way out of the murderous tangle he had immersed himself in. Devizes had shown his true colours. He had refused to plead or to answer, which in law was an admission of guilt.

'Maltravers,' Mortimer snapped. 'We wait.'

'I plead with the court,' Maltravers stammered. He paused and drew a deep breath. 'It may well look as though I was involved in these nefarious crimes, but I plead my innocence. True, I did fashion an arbalest, but it was a gift for Devizes. I did not know about the secret compartment in my chamber or the maze of galleries beneath this abbey. I was in church when Brother Mark was killed. Raphael was my friend, as were Anselm and Richard. Unlike my master-at-arms, I have no ties with those who dwell in the Valley of Shadows. He, however, often rode out there. After all, he is responsible for protecting us. He too is skilled in the arbalest. He—'

'Liar! Liar, abuser and coward!' Devizes sprang to his feet, knocking the chair over.

'Leave him!' Corbett shouted at the bowman who'd immediately seized the prisoner. 'Leave him, cut his bonds.'

'In God's name!' Mortimer exclaimed.

'Cut the rope binding his wrists,' Corbett repeated. 'Ap Ythel, notch your bow, but only loose if you have to.'

Ranulf came hurrying over and, ignoring the protocol, heatedly whispered his objections.

'Hush now,' Corbett soothed. 'But arm yourself.'

The guard sawed at the thick cord binding Devizes' wrists, and the prisoner shook these free. He glanced over his shoulder at Ap Ythel, then smiled to himself.

'I confess.' He took a step closer to the bench. 'All you have said is the truth. I have no regrets, none whatsoever, for my part in all that has happened. The Crown of England destroyed my world and all I truly loved, as they loved me. As a young boy, I saw them being cut down or hanged like outlaws from the trees deep in our valley. As for you, Maltravers,' Devizes didn't even bother to turn, 'I have nothing but contempt and disgust for you. I did not and never have loved you. I saw you for what you and the rest are. Forget the Knights of the Swan, or even men cloaked in the garb of St Benedict. You are killers to the very marrow of your being, and worthy of death.' He gestured contemptuously with his head. 'Henry Maltravers is as guilty as I, even more so. Yet rest assured, I feel no guilt, not now, not ever. I will not die like some felon, but as a warrior, dedicated to immolation.'

He abruptly lunged towards the bench, hand going out for Corbett's sword. He almost had it when Ap Ythel's arrow thudded into his back. As he turned, shouting defiance, a second shaft took him deep in the chest. He staggered forward, blood gushing from nose and mouth, hands extended as if he wished to embrace Ranulf, who, gripping his war sword, thrust its blade once, twice, deep into the master-at-arms' exposed neck and then withdrew it. Devizes, saturated in his own blood, collapsed to the floor.

Corbett stilled the ensuing consternation. 'You have heard the accused,' he proclaimed, 'the confession of a dying man, and it must be accepted as that. Now, as for the charges laid against Henry Maltravers, abbot of Holyrood and former Knight of the Swan, Lord Mortimer, how say you?'

'Guilty.'

'Ralph of Ancaster, how say you?'

'Guilty.'

Corbett rose and spread his hands to encompass all those who had watched the proceedings.

'How say you all?'

'Guilty,' came the reply.

Maltravers suddenly asserted himself, as if breaking free from a dream. He glared at Corbett, then over his shoulder at Crispin and Jude. 'Swans,' he declared, 'slide serenely into the dark.'

'The prisoner will face me,' demanded Corbett. One of the bowmen seized Maltravers by the head, forcing him to look at the clerk. 'You have been found guilty on all counts,' Corbett declared. 'You are worthy of punishment. Sentence is to be carried out after first light tomorrow. There will be no stay of execution, no respite, no pardon, no appeal. I have the authority to pronounce this on behalf of the king and his council. Take the prisoner away.'

PART FIVE

You are not my brother but wrongly and wickedly claim the kingdom for yourself.

The Lanercost Chronicle

Corbett spent what was left of that day preparing to leave. He gathered the entire community in the chapter house and informed them of what had happened. He said that heinous crimes had been committed so justice had been carried out and punishment imposed. The abbey church would need cleansing and re-consecration. Devizes' corpse would be publicly gibbeted, whilst the execution of Maltravers would take place early next morning. Prior Jude would take over the leadership of Holyrood till the king's wishes in the matter were known.

The community, shocked and fearful, could only stand and listen to what was said. Afterwards they silently filed out across the bailey back to their respective duties, which, Corbett insisted, must continue.

An hour later, he met Ranulf, Mistletoe, Mortimer and the Ravenmaster in his chamber. The latter had already visited the cells beneath Falcon Tower and found no prisoner, and he now demanded an explanation. Corbett just sat and held the Ravenmaster's eerie gaze. He then shrugged and declared that the prisoner must have escaped during the chaos and confusion that had swept Holyrood. The king's executioner pulled a face and wondered if he might still be hiding in the maze of galleries below. Corbett shook his head in disbelief, but offered a guide to lead the way through the labyrinth. The Ravenmaster hastily refused and, pointing at Mortimer, declared that the prisoner, wherever he might be, was now the business of the king's justiciar in these parts. Corbett smiled his thanks and they passed on to other business.

They all agreed that the casket would remain with Corbett, and that de Craon and his retinue would be given an escort back to Tewkesbury and on to the waiting barges. Mistletoe gleefully repeated how the Sheriff of Gloucester had ordered the French galleys to remain at their moorings, their crews being given comfortable lodgings at riverside taverns as they could not journey anywhere else. Mortimer then raised the question of Maltravers' punishment. The marcher lord argued that the convicted man should suffer the full rigour of the law for treason, being hanged, drawn and quartered. Corbett demurred, saying such a penalty was too gruesome. Mortimer claimed the rebels in the Valley of Shadows should be given a harsh, cruel lesson about royal justice. The argument continued, Corbett refusing to concede, and it was eventually agreed that Maltravers' execution would be slightly delayed, taking place at first light the day after tomorrow, and that he would suffer decapitation carried out by the Ravenmaster.

Devizes' corpse would be gibbeted on the battlements, and the entire punishment would be proclaimed throughout the abbey and elsewhere. Nor had Corbett forgotten de Craon, now confined to his chamber: the French envoy would be compelled to witness the execution of his former ally.

Just before noon the following day, Mortimer and a formidable retinue of foot soldiers and cavalry, along with two trumpeters, rode out of Holyrood. The cavalcade clattered across the drawbridge, making its way carefully across the slushy ground towards the Valley of Shadows. Corbett, standing cloaked and cowled on the parapet above the gatehouse, watched them go. At the mouth of the valley, Mortimer paused, and the trumpeters blew three shrill blasts. Then the marcher lord stood high in his stirrups to proclaim how Maltravers, who had styled himself as Paracelsus, would be executed in full view of the valley: his accomplice Devizes had already suffered death and his corpse would be gibbeted for all to see. Punishment would be carried out at first light the following day.

Corbett clearly heard the trumpet blast, but Mortimer was too distant for him to make out the proclamation. He knew, however, what had been agreed, and he was certain that those who lurked in the trees clustered so close to the valley mouth would understand the marcher lord's words, proclaimed in English and repeated in Welsh. To ensure that this was the case, Mortimer thrust a long pike into the soft ground and securely pinned to it a proclamation clearly repeating what he had said.

Once Mortimer had returned, Devizes' bloodied corpse was taken up to the parapet walk above the gatehouse. A rope was tied around the dead man's neck and his corpse was tossed over to dangle and swing eerily in the strengthening wind. At the same time, Brother Dunstan, under the Ravenmaster's supervision, built a makeshift execution platform that jutted well above the battlements for all to see: a black-timbered framework, stark and clear, with steps leading up to the execution block, a large basket standing beside it.

Corbett rested in his chamber that evening, revising his indictment against Maltravers. He wanted to make sure all was correct, for when he returned to Westminster, both king and council would demand a detailed account of what had happened at Holyrood. He still felt tense. There was unfinished business to attend to. In his agitation, he went and stretched out on the cot bed, staring up into the dark, wondering how Maeve and his two children were faring.

He had left strict instructions with the Sheriff of Essex that Leighton Manor be brought under keen scrutiny and close guard. He was still apprehensive about the Black Chesters. He was sure he had inflicted a grievous wound, a deadly blow to that coven of wickedness along the Scottish border and on the Welsh March. The Black Chesters would soon realise, if they had not done so already, that the mischief planned in and around Holyrood had been brought to nothing. They would not waste time, energy or precious resources on a battlefield where they had been comprehensively routed. They would withdraw, slink into the darkness and wait for another day to wreak their devilry. They would, like the malignant monsters they were, prowl through the murk, ever vigilant, ever watchful for fresh opportunities.

Corbett prayed that his family would remain safe. A cohort of Tower archers, garbed in green and brown, was camped discreetly in the orchards and woods around Leighton. They had their orders, whilst the great war dogs Corbett had trained were sure protection against any intruder. The Keeper of the Secret Seal murmured a prayer to the Virgin, a simple Ave.

His eyes were growing heavy when there was a knock on the door. He swung himself off the side of the bed and grasped the hilt of his sword lying across a stool. He rose and demanded who it was, though he half suspected the messenger and the message he carried.

'Sir Hugh, it's Ranulf. We have been approached. We have been asked . . .' Corbett unbolted the door and Ranulf, shaking the raindrops from his cloak, slipped into the chamber. 'Master,' he grinned, 'you should tell fortunes. Brother Crispin, our noble infirmarian, has asked to see his former lord abbot one last time. He has brought a jug of claret and two goblets to share this final joy with the prisoner.'

'I am sure he has, but he is not being admitted?'

'Oh no, Ap Ythel and his bowmen guard that cell as if it contained the Holy Grail.'

'Then let us join them.'

The passageway beneath Falcon Tower was under strict guard. Every available torch and lanternhorn flared. Hobelars patrolled the entrance, whilst Ap Ythel's archers, arrows notched, controlled the long, cold tunnel that cut past the cells. Maltravers had been lodged in the same dungeon as Brother Norbert. Ap Ythel stood on guard outside, talking quietly to Crispin, who almost dropped the tray he was carrying when Corbett, as silent as a ghost, came up and tapped him on the shoulder.

'No, no.' The clerk smiled, taking the tray from the infirmarian. 'Let me carry this. Ap Ythel, open the cell. Ranulf, stay with me.'

The door was unlocked. Ap Ythel brought three stools so they could sit facing Maltravers, who slouched on the palliasse against the far wall. The former abbot looked a broken man: his unshaven face was pallid, eyes fearful, lips constantly twitching. He stared mournfully at Crispin, then thrust his hands forward in a rattle of chains, as if desperate to grab the jug of wine from the tray Corbett had placed on the ground.

Corbett picked up the jug and filled a goblet to the brim. He did not hand this to Maltravers, however, but thrust it under Crispin's nose. The infirmarian stared back all fearful, eyes questioning.

'What is this?' he exclaimed. 'Sir Hugh, the wine is not for me.'

'Drink, Brother Crispin, go on,' Corbett urged. 'Take this cup and drink every drop. Or shall I?' He withdrew the goblet. 'No, of course I won't. It's a poisoned chalice, isn't it? Rich Bordeaux laced with a deadly poison that would give your former abbot, your comrade of yester-year, swift and relatively painless passage from this vale of tears. No ceremony, no public disgrace or cruel execution. Nothing but an easy step into eternal night. One last favour.'

He glimpsed it then, a sudden cunning shift in Crispin's deep-set eyes. You're acting, he thought, this is a cat's paw, a sham to hide something else.

'Sir Hugh,' the infirmarian stammered, 'I'm sorry, I was taken aback. I did not know what you intended. The wine is not poisoned, I assure you.' He grasped the offered goblet, lifted it in toast and took a deep gulp. Corbett glanced quickly at Maltravers, who still sat like some dream-walker. Crispin returned the goblet. Corbett put it down on the tray and pushed it closer to the condemned man.

'Drink,' he urged. 'Prepare yourself. As for you,' he turned back to Crispin, 'keep your hands out of your robes. Ranulf, take our infirmarian from the cell. You and Ap Ythel must search him.'

Crispin rose abruptly to his feet, one hand going to the side folds of his robe. Ranulf, shouting for Ap Ythel, seized the infirmarian, holding him close until the captain of archers burst into the cell to assist. Crispin, still struggling, was dragged out into the passageway. Corbett stared at Maltravers, but he seemed more inter-ested in the wine than anything else. Corbett gestured at the jug.

'Drink it all,' he whispered, and left, following the

others across the passageway into a cell, its door flung open.

Crispin had been stripped of his cloak, robes and breeches. He looked a pathetic sight in his linen undershirt and loincloth. He had already been roughly searched, loudly complaining at the insult and abuse he had received. Corbett ignored him, watching Ranulf and Ap Ythel go through the infirmarian's wallet and belt pouch.

'I have it.' Ranulf drew from an inside pocket a small phial, the glass a dark brown, its stopper firmly thrust in and covered with a seal. He handed this to Corbett, who broke the wax. He removed the stopper and flinched at the nasty odour.

'Poison,' he murmured. 'Probably some herb.' He pushed the stopper back and threw the phial into the jakes pot, then stared at the now fearful Crispin. 'Ranulf, dress this man and bring him to my chamber.'

Crispin was still shaking when Ranulf thrust him into a chair before going to sit on Corbett's right. The chamber was warm and well lit. Corbett had moved the candle spigots so he could closely study this most devious of men.

'Brother Crispin, apothecary, leech and herbalist. You probably know more about physic and the treatment of bodily humours than any London doctor.' Crispin stared bleakly back. 'So tell me,' Corbett continued, 'why didn't you deduce that the beggar man, Mortimer's spy from the Valley of Shadows, had been poisoned? I glimpsed his corpse. I saw the discoloration of his skin, both face and belly. The slight froth between his lips. At the time I did not even consider poison; after all, sudden death takes many forms. And why didn't you mention Devizes' curiosity about the corpse? I mean, the mighty master-at-arms so interested in the pathetic remains of some wandering beggar?'

Crispin remained silent, wary of speaking, of making a mistake, of being drawn deeper into the indictment presented against him.

'Father Abbot,' Corbett continued, 'claimed to have been poisoned. You examined him, yes? What poison had been used? What symptoms did he show? Did you investigate? Did you ask how he was poisoned? You just agreed with him, didn't you? Which is why you cannot answer my litany of questions. You cannot tell the truth, so I shall do it for you.'

He leant forward in his chair. 'You knew, didn't you? You suspected something was very wrong with your abbot. He was *faux et semblant*, false and dissimulating. Now a patient can create fictitious symptoms, but not sustain such a show over an extended period of time, especially when someone as skilled as yourself is carrying out the diagnosis. You reached the conclusion, which I did more slowly, that Henry Maltravers was sick, but not due to any poison. He was simply tired of his life here. You are an acute observer of human foibles, Crispin. You would, like I eventually did, wonder what path your abbot was taking. Why was he pretending so determinedly? Did he want to leave? If so, how? And where would he go? You asked yourself those questions, and like me, you began to wonder about the answers. Sharp of eye and keen of wit, you must also have deduced the true nature of the relationship between Maltravers and Devizes. You had access to their bedchamber. You too must have noticed the disarray of the coverlets and bolsters. Did you wonder how a man so visibly sick and weak still had the energy for bed sport? Did you hint at this knowledge?' Corbett paused. 'Oh, nothing direct, just an unspoken understanding with the abbot that where he intended to go, you would be included? A logical conclusion. After all, a man such as Maltravers wanted only the good things of this life: comfort, luxury along with his young lover.'

'And the beggar man?' Ranulf asked.

'Oh yes.' Corbett tapped the table. 'I suspect you soon discovered that he had been poisoned. You reported the same to your lord abbot. He in his wisdom asked you to keep the matter confidential. An incident of little significance. Holyrood had enough troubles without investigating the death of a wandering beggar.' The clerk pulled a face. 'I may have it wrong, but that is the general thrust of my argument. To be succinct, Brother Crispin, you knew the abbot hadn't been poisoned. You concluded that this was significant. After all, why should he pretend? You also realised that the beggar man had been poisoned but made little of it. You knew all about Maltravers' relationship with Devizes. You must also have suspected that the master-at-arms knew his lover had not been poisoned. You must have asked yourself: what did those two intend? Now such information would have been vital to me. It would also have saved a great deal of anguish and bloodshed. You remained silent. You may believe that you did nothing wrong. Believe me, you did nothing right.' He spread his hands. 'I will give you your life. I will let you walk away from this, but you must tell me the truth.'

Crispin put his face in his hands and for a while quietly sobbed. Corbett leant over and took the infirmarian's hands away, staring hard at a man who could have done so much to avert the hideous litany of killings.

'Well,' Ranulf demanded, 'the hours pass. Judgement awaits. My master has asked for the truth.'

'Of course I knew.' Crispin sighed deeply. 'I suspected Maltravers was dissembling and I wondered why. I knew of his relationship with Devizes. You are correct, Sir Hugh. I am a physician. I watch and I observe. It was apparent to me that Maltravers was tired of Holyrood, of the Knights of the Swan and our boring daily horarium. I recognised that he was infatuated with Devizes. I concluded that he wished to be gone. We spoke in parables to each other, but the meaning was very clear. An unspoken understanding was reached. In a word, Maltravers would look after me, take care of me whatever the future held.'

He drew a deep breath. 'I never knew, I never imagined what horrors would engulf us. The death of the beggar man should have been a warning. I was already deeply alarmed at the murders of Anselm and Richard. However, at the time, it didn't occur to me that they were so closely linked to Maltravers' devious plan.' He shrugged. 'I did examine the beggar man's corpse. I strongly suspected poison. I informed Maltravers and Devizes. They said that I only had suspicions, that it was vital not to deepen the atmosphere of distrust in Holyrood. That I should have the corpse swiftly buried and keep the matter confidential until Maltravers decreed otherwise.' He blew his cheeks out. 'When I was a boy,' he continued slowly, 'running in the long meadows outside Canterbury, I stumbled into a marsh. The more I struggled, the more trapped I became. So it was with this. I could only watch and weep at what was happening.'

'Maltravers knew that, didn't he?' Ranulf accused. 'That you were party to the suspicions Sir Hugh later developed into a damning indictment. At the end of the trial he was threatening you when he shouted about swans sliding serenely into the dark. He was demanding you bring poison for a swift, painless death, and so you did. You knew the wine would be tasted and found good. You secreted the poison on yourself, and when Maltravers was ready, he would administer it. The finger of suspicion might be pointed at you, but where was the proof? And in the end, who would really care? Maltravers was unmasked, disgraced and punished. You would argue that he must have kept a phial of poison hidden away. You would mention that Devizes had used such a noxious potion to silence the beggar man.' He clapped his hands in front of Crispin's face. 'And so we have it.'

Crispin just shook his head and looked at a point beyond Corbett. He blinked, swallowed hard and moved restlessly in the chair, clutching its arms as if he was in the grip of a deep fear. Corbett felt there was something very wrong but he could not put his finger on it; just a deep unease about this most cunning and devious man. He suspected the infirmarian was a skilled mummer, an actor donning and doffing various masks. Nevertheless, as yet he had no evidence, nothing to allege, accuse or indict, and so the die was cast.

'I promised you your life,' he declared brusquely, 'and I will keep my word. Collect your belongings and go. You are no longer a member of this community. You have forfeited your right to be a Knight of the Swan and your privileges as a former courtier. Be gone, for if I see you again after first light tomorrow, I shall arrest you as a felon.'

Crispin Hollister, former Knight of the Swan, once apothecary in the king of England's private chamber, leant against the crenellations on the top of Falcon Tower. He had waited and prepared in the hours following his confrontation with Corbett. He really could tarry no longer. Maltravers had demanded poison, but that was not to be, and perhaps it was for the best. He had to humour both his former abbot and that interfering royal clerk. Now it was time to leave.

He moved the lanternhorn so that it rested safely and securely on the stone ledge. He then raised and lowered the shutter, pausing to stare out through the darkness at the mouth of the Valley of Shadows. Still sweat-soaked after his interrogation by Corbett, he pulled both cowl and cloak closer about him, then returned to the lantern. He lifted the shutter a number of times, and smiled to himself in relief as an answering light flashed from the trees.

He picked up the lantern and hurried back to his chamber, where he collected a bulging leather pannier, leaving the room without a backward glance. He made his way down across the cobbled inner and outer baileys to a narrow postern door guarded by hobelars under the command of one of Ap Ythel's bowmen. He declared who he was, and the archer, already informed by his captain, unlocked the postern and ushered him out across the makeshift bridge, slamming the door firmly behind him.

Crispin allowed himself a wry smile. He had made mistakes, but so had Corbett, and this was one of them. He was free! He had escaped and was suitably prepared for his journey. Beneath the comfortable robe, he was garbed in the warmest woollen garments, and the boots he wore were of the finest Moroccan leather, whilst the pannier slung across his shoulder contained all the valuables he would need. He had also packed weapons: a thin Italian stiletto, and several small phials of the deadly poison he had distilled. He walked purposefully through the slush, pausing briefly to stare back at the looming mass of Holyrood, with its towers, roofs, cornices and battlemented walls.

'It's over, it's finished,' he whispered.

He stared around. He was confident he was not being followed. He could neither see, hear nor detect anything untoward. He looked up at the cloud-free sky; a full moon hung low, so the light was good and provided a clear view of the path leading into the valley. He trudged on, trying to ignore the eerie calls of the night and the sinister gliding shadows of the birds of prey. Memories flooded back as he recalled his life's journey to this very place and time.

His father, a prosperous London apothecary, had begun it all: he had taken his son to clandestine meetings of the coven in this ruined church or that derelict mansion on the desolate moorland north of the city wall. Crispin recalled the arrival of visitors, hooded and visored, at dead of night, long after the bells had fallen silent. His father had secretly supported the likes of de Montfort and other rebels against the English Crown. At the same time, he openly encouraged young Crispin to join the royal household as a page, a squire and then a full-belted knight.

From the very start, Crispin had been immersed in the beliefs and rituals of the Black Chesters. He had shared their vision of a kingdom without Crown or Church, free to act as they wished, including the worship of other gods. At the same time, he had acted the role of a loyal retainer of the Crown. Accordingly, there had been no clash, no confrontation. As Crispin had confessed to his dying father, he had slid into court life as smoothly as a knife into its sheath, though he had taken a blood oath that he would assist the coven whenever the opportunity presented itself.

He had kept his word. He had been in Outremer

with Prince Edward when the Old Man of the Mountain, leader of a sect of Islamic zealots, had sworn to dispatch his assassins against Edward's interference in a struggle that did not concern him. Crispin had learnt when the assassin would strike, and it was he who secretly advised his royal master to meet the sultan's envoy accompanied only by an interpreter. In the end, the attack had failed, the assassin killed and Edward saved by the loving ministrations of his wife. After that, Crispin had lain low and silent, acting as the king's most loyal henchman in both peace and war.

He paused at a mournful owl hoot from the fringe of trees he was now approaching. He stood listening for a while before slowly walking on. He had to get away. He was wary of Corbett, and wondered if his departure from Holyrood had been watched by one of Ap Ythel's keen-eyed archers. He stared around but could see nothing to alarm him, whilst he was determined not to hurry or give away the fact that he was fleeing for his life to the shelter of his coven. He realised that it would only be a matter of time before that interfering royal clerk continued his searches and so raised more questions about Holyrood's apothecary.

The valley he was now approaching had played such a vital part in his life. He had urged both the old king and the Knights of the Swan to choose this place for Holyrood, though that had not been difficult. Others of the brotherhood wanted the same, especially the masons Anselm and Richard, whilst the old king was only too pleased to have such a powerful presence on

the Welsh March. However, he had finally decreed that
Holyrood would be the place. The valley certainly had
its secrets. In his days at court, Crispin had heard
rumours about the rift between Edward and Joanna.
He had searched carefully for the reason behind the
violent quarrel between father and daughter. He'd also
learnt about that mysterious young man sheltering in
the valley and had passed such information onto the
Black Chesters. He had warned the coven about the
king's growing vigilance and his deepening interest in
their presence in the valley. Unfortunately, they did not
heed his advice and left it too late. No escape was
possible, so they decided to make a stand against the
encroaching royal army.

During the battle at Caerwent cliffs, Crispin had
secretly allowed some rebels to escape, among them the
twin boys he had saved, those master bowmen whom
Corbett had slain out in the snows. He moved the
pannier to sit more carefully over his shoulder. He felt
genuinely sorry for those who had died. Anselm,
Richard, Mark and poor Raphael, comrades who had
served in the shield wall alongside him for many a year.
The manner of Raphael's death particularly saddened
him, yet what could be done? Comradeship with the
Black Chesters was the most important thing. There
were tasks to be achieved, a vision to follow, and above
all, vengeance to be inflicted on those who opposed
them.

Crispin walked on. He was now in the entrance to
the valley, the trees dark and ice-covered, clustered close.

A sharp breeze stirred the frozen flakes and sent them all a-flutter. Eerie cries echoed loudly, then faded away. He took a deep breath. He was home! He was with his brothers, he was sure of it. He peered into the darkness and glimpsed lights glowing on either side of the path.

'Greetings, my brethren,' he called out. 'Greetings from Paracelsus, your leader.'

Dark shapes emerged from the trees. Six men, all cloaked and hooded, the clink of their weapons the only sound to break the silence.

'So you escaped, Paracelsus?' one of them demanded. 'We know what has happened. Mortimer's proclamation was clear and stark.'

'Enough of that.' Crispin beckoned them forward. 'My friends, let us clasp hands.'

They did so, Crispin patting each man on the shoulder to reassure them that all was well. They then led him off into the trees, following a narrow trackway that cut through the gorse and bushes, a secret path known only to those who had created and used it.

They walked silently until they reached a clearing. A derelict verderer's lodge stood in the centre of the glade; a stout, squat shed fashioned out of tree trunks with a moss-covered thatched roof, the door and shutters recently repaired. Inside, a fire in the centre of the room blazed fiercely, its smoke winding up through a large vent in the ceiling. Around it were leather-covered flock-filled sacks to serve as seats. Crispin made himself comfortable as his comrades hastily prepared a meal: strips of meat laid out over a grille placed above the fire. These were cooked to an even brown and served on wooden platters with a potage of stewed vegetables, some coarse bread and wine skins bought from a passing trader. For a while they ate and drank in silence. Crispin stared around; his comrades certainly looked as though they had spent days, even weeks, in this cold, hard valley. They were unwashed and unkempt, their clothes shabby, their hair, moustaches and beards uncut and straggling.

'We must leave here soon,' he declared, pointing at their weapons piled in a corner. 'It is too dangerous to stay. I no longer trust the valley. More importantly, our struggle has changed and we must turn our banners elsewhere.'

'Why?' one of his comrades demanded.

'Because I am your leader, Paracelsus,' Crispin retorted, throwing the remnants of his food onto the flames.

'So we have failed here?'

'No, no, far from it.' Crispin leant forward so the dancing fire illuminated his hawk-like face. 'Listen, my brothers, to what I say. You heard Mortimer's proclamation?'

'I thought he was one of us,' the Scotsman Dalrymple interrupted. 'The lord Mortimer,' he repeated, 'was supposed to be one of us.'

'And so he was, and so he is, and so he will be,' Crispin soothed.

'Even though we killed his men?'

'And they slaughtered ours. You know the letter and

the spirit of our bonds, the indentures we signed?' Crispin drew himself up. 'Each of us is to act as he thinks fit at a certain time and in a certain place. Mortimer's hour has not yet come, but it will. Only the future will tell. Now listen carefully. We may have seemingly lost in Holyrood, but that's not the truth. The abbey is now only a relic of what it was and what it should be. Corbett will return to London, Holyrood may well be abandoned . . .' He paused at the murmur of approval. 'And there's more. The Knights of the Swan have been dealt a grievous wound, disgraced and made to pay for the slaughter here in this valley. Oh yes,' he smiled thinly, 'think, my brothers. Most of the Knights of the Swan have been killed, executed for their crimes. They were former comrades of mine, but Anselm, Richard, Mark and Raphael have paid for their sins. Blood for blood, my brothers. All suffered a violent death, dispatched swiftly into the dark.'

'And Maltravers joins them tomorrow morning.' One of the group spoke up. 'A great loss, Paracelsus?'

'No, far from it. Maltravers' execution weakens the Knights of the Swan even further. He was never really one of us: he was just an old man who became slothful and lecherous, arrogant and greedy. He loved the luxuries of life. He was easy to twist; Devizes achieved that. After that, it was enough simply to watch the pageant unfold. And so it did.' Crispin proceeded to give a pithy description of recent events in Holyrood, now and again pausing to answer questions from his comrades.

'Holyrood will become a ruin and the Knights of the

Swan are depleted and disgraced,' Dalrymple murmured.
'Yet Corbett still survives. If it wasn't for him, we could
have wreaked more damage.'

'No, no, hush.' Crispin shook his head. 'Corbett can
wait. If we tried to destroy him, it would only be a
distraction, an obstacle. He has very powerful friends
at court and in the Church who would turn violently
on us. So first we must weaken them, then we can deal
with Corbett.'

'And the prisoner?'

'He has served his purpose. Let him wander the
kingdom: his story will only add to the growing clamour
against our present king. When the Crown weakens, so
will the Church. Chaos will reign and we can do what
we want.'

'But how? What path do we now follow, Paracelsus?'

'We must go to the heart of the old king's legacy.'
Crispin paused as he heard the screech of some animal,
followed by the chilling call of a night bird. 'We should
not delay here too long,' he murmured. 'But to answer
your question. We have a new battlefield. We must
prepare for that and get ready to reap a harvest that
has truly ripened over the last few months.'

'Gaveston?'

'Yes, my friend, the Gascon royal favourite. He too
may be of our persuasion.' Crispin laughed sharply. 'Or
at least his mother was, being burnt as a witch. We
should renew our friendship with Gaveston. We must
permeate his household, influence his retainers, advise
his henchmen that their master should stand his ground

and persuade the king to do likewise. Thomas of Lancaster and the others will respond in kind. Standards will be unfurled to the clatter of weapons and the kingdom will slip into civil war. So, you must depart from here and move close to the royal palaces such as Westminster, Beaumont, Kings Langley. Our brethren in Scotland will play their part. Bruce is fast encroaching on English strongholds; it is only a matter of time before they fall. Our comrades will give him every assistance in achieving this.'

'Does de Craon know of our existence, or does he think we are merely Welsh rebels fighting against the English Crown?'

'De Craon,' Crispin snorted, 'is a fool, pompous and arrogant. He completely underestimated Corbett. Anyway, what he thinks does not concern us. Remember, we are as bitterly opposed to Philip of France as we are to Edward of England – even more so. Philip has crushed the Templar order. Some of its members were our brothers. He too has to pay for his crimes. He may well be planning to glory in what he has done. However, he and his coterie are so arrogant they cannot see the filth in their own midden yard.'

'Which is?'

'Oh, my friend, a rich, ripening scandal, secret except to us. Did you know that all three of Philip's daughters-in-law are playing the two-backed beast with young knights of the French court? They meet long after sunset in the lonely, deserted Tour de Nesle, close to the Seine.'

'But not too deserted?'

'No, my friend. We have brought them all under close scrutiny.'

'Paracelsus?' Dalrymple's voice was thick with a Scottish burr. 'You talked of us leaving here, but what about you?'

'I am very wary of Corbett. I too underestimated him.' Crispin was determined to be honest. These men were members of his coven; deceit and subterfuge between them would not be tolerated. 'I described to you what happened in Holyrood, how Corbett let me go, but I could see from his eyes that he wasn't satisfied. I also made mistakes.'

'What mistakes?'

'Hush, my friend, not so harsh. You were sheltering here whilst I was being scrutinised. Now that Corbett is finished with Maltravers, Devizes and de Craon, he may well turn to me again. He knows I dressed the corpses of the dead. As I said, six of these were killed by Devizes with a nail loosed from a specially crafted arbalest. I demonstrated to Corbett how a nail could be driven into a man's skull using a mallet. He is going to wonder why I, a former knight, a soldier skilled in physic, did not reach the same conclusions he eventually did.'

'And why didn't you?'

'I did, but I kept my suspicions to myself. My task was only to watch, wait and secretly assist if I could. Neither Maltravers nor Devizes realised that I was one of your brethren. I had to maintain my mask. Easy enough. Maltravers was determined on creating chaos so as to escape, and I just watched.' Crispin paused. 'Corbett will also ruminate on Raphael's death, and again, on reflection, I made a mistake. Raphael was the sacristan, guardian of the precious casket. He would certainly not have allowed anyone to take it, and even if they had, they would have needed all the keys to free it from its chain and open it. The casket I saw during Maltravers' trial had certainly not been forced or damaged.'

'So Raphael must have taken it down?'

'Of course, but he was not going to flee with it. Accordingly, he must have released it on the orders of the only man who could demand it, namely Maltravers. Now on that same evening, Maltravers asked for a powerful potion. He complained that he could not sleep and his humours needed to be pacified. I prepared a draught for him. At the time, I wondered about the real reason for requesting it, and now I know.'

'Raphael?'

'Yes. I liked Raphael, I felt sorry for him, but Maltravers had decided on his death. I strongly suspect that my sleeping potion was mixed with a cup of the richest Bordeaux. Raphael, pleased to be given such recognition by his abbot, would have drained it to its very dregs. Maltravers seized the casket, whilst Devizes, at the dead of night and assisted by those he'd brought into Holyrood, took care of Raphael along those secret, hidden galleries.'

'Did you know of this?'

'Not really; just a suspicion.' Crispin sighed. 'The

potion I distilled was powerful. Raphael would have been left as easy prey for the war hounds. Moreover, on that particular morning, Maltravers betrayed no sign of a poor night's sleep or the effects of any sleeping draught.' He shook his head. 'I entered the potion in the ledger kept in the infirmary. At the time, I did not regard it as significant. Now, though, it's only a matter of time before Corbett finds that ledger and discovers the entry, the last I ever made.'

'You could have destroyed it.'

'Brother, I had no time. I was being watched, whilst any attempt to erase the entry would only have deepened suspicion.' Crispin fell silent. He took a swig from the wine skin beside him and passed it on. 'What now?' he murmured, wiping his lips. 'Well, because of Corbett, I had best go deep into the valley. I will watch Maltravers lose his head, and then I will disappear. You will also leave?'

'Like you, tomorrow,' replied Dalrymple.

'Good.' Crispin rose to his feet, fanning his face with his hands. 'I will take a breath of night air.'

'I will come with you.'

Corbett watched from his hiding place as the two men left the makeshift lodge. They kept the door open, allowing the light from the fire and the lanternhorns to illuminate them against the dark, making them easy targets for Ap Ythel's archers concealed in the undergrowth. The bowmen loosed, and their shafts took the two men in the chest, belly and neck. Crispin and his companion collapsed, alerting their comrades inside, who rushed out straight into an arrow storm.

Only when death had silenced the last man did Corbett, Ranulf, Ap Ythel and their guide Brancepeth emerge from the darkness, the other bowmen slipping around them to bend over their victims, searching for weapons and valuables. Corbett knelt beside the stricken Crispin and watched the light fade from those cunning eyes.

'Sir Hugh?' Ranulf knelt beside him.

'I had my suspicions,' Corbett declared. 'Crispin seemed to be very eager to be gone. Before he left, I dispatched Brancepeth with a lantern to the mouth of the valley. Sure enough, our keen-eyed archer glimpsed him shuffling through the slush. Brancepeth also discovered others lurking deep in the treeline, waiting for our apothecary, whose ledger betrayed him: a bold, clear entry describing the sleeping draught he distilled. Ah well.' Corbett rose to his feet. 'Drag the corpses into the hunting lodge. On our return to Holyrood, ask Prior Jude to dispatch a burial party late tomorrow. Come, let us return. This business is not yet finished.'

The next morning, with daylight strengthening, Henry Maltravers, garbed in a white shift, hands bound before him, was taken from the cells beneath Falcon Tower. Four of Ap Ythel's bowmen escorted him across the bailey, past spectators including de Craon. He was made to climb the makeshift ladder onto the execution platform, where the Ravenmaster, garbed completely in black, except for a red leather face mask, was waiting, resting on the hilt of his two-edged razor-sharp war sword. Corbett, Ranulf, Mortimer and Mistletoe followed as justiciars and official witnesses.

Corbett walked to the edge of the execution platform. Leaning against one of the corner posts, he stared out at the mouth of the Valley of Shadows, that place of gloomy greenness that had witnessed so much penetrating pain and deep hurt. A place of slaughter, a haven of ghosts, a valley reeking of murder and the spilt blood of innocents. He wondered about Matilda Beaumont and Edmund Fitzroy. Were they still sheltering in the valley, hiding in some dwelling deep amongst the trees, or had they already left? Corbett felt he had done what he could. He had saved that young man from summary execution, but what about the future? As long as Matilda lived, Fitzroy would be safe, but once she died, he would be left to his own devices, just another beggar wandering the roads of the kingdom. He might be tempted to proclaim his true identity. If he was foolish enough to do so, he would become an object of ridicule and mockery. Worse, his existence might become known to some cruel, sharp-eared official who wished to portray himself as a loyal and assiduous servant of the Crown. Fitzroy would be arrested and, if he persisted in his claims, executed as an imposter who spoke contumaciously against the king. Whatever the real truth about his parentage, be it Edmund's own story or Matilda's explanation, his best chance of survival was to keep silent.

Corbett closed his eyes and murmured a prayer for the young man's safety. He heard a sound behind him and glanced over his shoulder. The old priest, Father Bernard, had clambered breathlessly onto the platform and immediately intoned the psalm for the dying. The smoke from the beacon fires lit along the parapet cleared. Corbett, staring across at the valley mouth, could make out small groups beginning to gather. They would peer through the strengthening light and see Devizes' dangling corpse before viewing this last act in the bloody pageant played out at Holyrood. He wondered if Beaumont and Fitzroy were there, or the survivors of that ferocious battle at the caves where Maltravers had washed his sword deep in the blood of their family and friends. In a sense, they were seeing justice and retribution; a strange sort, yet still a reckoning for the vicious slaughter some eleven years earlier. More importantly, at least for Corbett, did more Black Chesters still lurk there?

'We are ready,' Father Bernard declared. Corbett turned. Maltravers, eyes blindfolded, now knelt before the block. Two of the archers made him edge closer, pushing the condemned man's head down so the nape of his neck was clearly exposed, his chin firm against the edge of the block. The archers withdrew. It looked as if Maltravers was trying to move, but the Ravenmaster, silent and swift, was ready. He stepped softly to the side, balancing himself carefully, then brought back his great sword, a flash of steel that hissed through the air, severing Maltravers' head in one sheer cut. The head bounced away as the torso, blood spurting, shuddered and trembled before collapsing onto its side.

The Ravenmaster picked up the head by its straggling hair and lifted it high so all could see. Corbett turned away.

'When spring comes,' Mortimer declared, coming up close beside him, 'I promise you, Sir Hugh, I'll take every one of my battle host, my war band, into that valley and sweep it clear.'

'I am sure you will,' Corbett murmured. 'Nevertheless, I doubt you'll find much, and when you leave, believe me, my lord Mortimer, the shadows will return.'

AUTHOR'S NOTE

Edward I was a great and terrible king. He was an outstanding warrior and a most able general, but he was also arrogant and subject to fits of violent temper. True, *Death's Dark Valley* is a work of fiction, but it faithfully recreates the character and moods of both Edward I and his son Edward II.

Edward I did fight in Outremer. He was attacked by an assassin, whom he killed, whilst the story of his beloved wife Eleanor sucking the poison from the wound he received is fairly well documented. Edward reckoned his survival was due to a direct act of God, and he kept the assassin's dagger as a sacred relic in his treasury in the crypt of Westminster Abbey. In 1305, a gang of burglars broke into the crypt and helped themselves to the Crown Jewels and other treasures, including the assassin's dagger. I cannot establish whether it was ever recovered.

Edward I's hot temper was legendary. He was given to throwing himself on the floor, screaming and cursing, beating and kicking anyone who was imprudent enough to get too close. He did attack his own daughter, Joanna, when she announced that she had secretly married Ralph Monthermer. According to the wardrobe accounts, he snatched the crown from her head and threw it into a fire, where it was rescued only by the intervention of a rather courageous servant. The king eventually relented and accepted Joanna's marriage to the love of her life.

Edward's son and heir was also the object of his father's violent temper. The prince was foolish enough to ask if certain territories could be handed over to his Gascon favourite, Peter Gaveston, and the king truly lost his temper, physically attacking the young man and calling him the son of a whore. Indeed, he seized his son's head so violently, he plucked out his hair. The prince was then banished from the king's presence for a considerable period of time, whilst Gaveston was sent into exile – the first of many!

Reports about Edward II not being his father's true son and heir did surface during Edward II's reign. In 1316, a clerk named Thomas de Tynwelle was accused of proclaiming this rumour publicly in an Oxford park. However, much more serious was the emergence of John Deydras, also known as John of Powderham, who appeared outside Beaumont Palace near Oxford and loudly proclaimed that he was the true heir of the realm, son of the illustrious King Edward, and that the latter's successor, who now occupied the throne, was not of the blood royal and had no right to rule.

Apparently John was tall and fair, with more than a passing resemblance to Edward II, although he was missing an ear. He claimed that when he was a baby, he had been attacked by a pig, and his nurse, terrified of the old king, had substituted a peasant's son in his place. He pointed out that the present king's absorption with rustic pursuits strengthened his claim. Deydras was eventually arrested and brought before Edward II at Northampton. At first the king welcomed him with sarcasm, greeting him with the phrase 'Welcome, my brother.' Deydras, however, insisted on his claim and was put on trial for sedition and treason. We do not know whether he was tortured, but eventually he confessed that he was an imposter and that he had proclaimed his story at the instigation of the devil, who had appeared to him in the form of a cat. His defence did not save him from execution. He was hanged on the gallows in Carfax in Oxford, his cat suffering a similar fate.

After 1311, Edward II seems to have sunk into a living nightmare. He must have felt haunted and hunted by forces beyond his control. In 1312, the barons, led by Thomas of Lancaster, seized Gaveston and cut off his head on Blacklow Hill in Warwickshire. Edward had the head sewn back on the corpse, which he embalmed and refused to bury until ordered to do so by the Church. In 1313, he joined Philip of France in a glorious pageant staged in Paris. It was during these celebrations that the Tour de Nesle scandal broke. Philip's three sons were left without wives. (They all later remarried, but not one of them begot a male heir, leaving the crown of France open to claims from their sister's son, Edward III of England.)

The following year, Edward II decided to settle the question of Bruce once and for all. He led a magnificent array into Scotland, only to be comprehensively defeated at the Battle of Bannockburn. There was no let-up in his troubles. In 1321, the barons, including Roger Mortimer of Wigmore, rose in revolt. Mortimer was captured and placed in the Tower. Ever resourceful, with a secret coven of supporters in London, he escaped that grim fortress, one of the few prisoners ever to do so, and fled to France, where he met up with Edward II's disaffected queen, Isabella. They collected an army around them and invaded England. Edward was captured, deposed and imprisoned in Berkeley Castle, close to the Welsh March. In September 1327, he was murdered, probably on the express order of Mortimer. For the next three years Mortimer acted as master of the realm, until he was seized at Nottingham, tried and sentenced to death. He was the first man to be hanged at Tyburn.

I thoroughly relished weaving all these different strands into *Death's Dark Valley*. I am also grateful to my secretaries and typists, Mrs Linda Gerrish and Mrs Sally Parry, for preparing the manuscript for publication. I do hope you enjoyed this tale of medieval, yet not so merry, England!

PAUL DOHERTY

THE MASTER HISTORIAN HAS CAST HIS MAGICAL SPELL OVER ALL PERIODS OF HISTORY IN OVER 100 NOVELS

They are all now available in ebook, from his fabulous series

Hugh Corbett Medieval Mysteries
Sorrowful Mysteries of Brother Athelstan
Sir Roger Shallot Tudor Mysteries
Kathryn Swinbrooke Series
Nicholas Segalla Series
Mysteries of Alexander the Great
The Templar Mysteries
Matthew Jankyn Series
Canterbury Tales of Murder and Mystery
The Egyptian Mysteries
Mahu (The Akhenaten-Trilogy)
Mathilde of Westminster Series
Political Intrigue in Ancient Rome Series

to the standalones and trilogies that have made his name

The Death of a King	The Haunting
Prince Drakulya	The Soul Slayer
The Lord Count Drakulya	The Plague Laws
The Fate of Princes	The Love Knot
Dove Amongst the Hawks	Of Love and War
The Masked Man	The Loving Cup
The Rose Demon	The Last of Days

LIVE HISTORY
VISIT WWW.HEADLINE.CO.UK OR
WWW.PAULCDOHERTY.COM TO FIND OUT MORE

HEADLINE

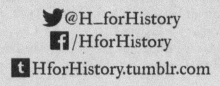